# Safe Haven: Doomsday

Christopher Artinian

CHRISTOPHER ARTINIAN

# DEDICATION

To Sally and Billy. They will never be forgotten.

CHRISTOPHER ARTINIAN

# ACKNOWLEDGEMENTS

I owe a huge debt to my wife, Tina. She is always there for me. She never lets me down, and I would be truly lost without her.

To the people across in the fan club — You guys rock! I will never get used to the loyalty and support you display. Thank you for everything you do.

A great big thanks to my pal, Christian Bentulan, for another awesome cover. Also many thanks to my editor, Ken – a great editor and a lovely chap to boot.

And last but by no means least, a very big thank you to you for purchasing this book.

# 1

The prime minister slammed his hand down hard on the desk. "I don't care what she said; I'm telling you now, if I see one more internal document using the word zombie, I'm going to have somebody's balls in a sling. We use the term Reanimated Corpses or Reanimates. Reanimated Corpses sounds scientific. It sounds like we might have some fucking idea of what the hell's going on. Zombies sounds like it's out of a bad nineteen seventies horror film. It spreads panic. That is the last thing we need now, don't you think? We are the government. We govern. We need to prove that we are in charge." He took the mug of coffee from his desk and walked to the window with the phone still pressed against his ear. He took a sip of the warm, black fluid and put the mug down on the windowsill, taking hold of the phone once again. "I swear you are testing my patience this morning. Look, I hired you because you're meant to be the best spin doctor in the business. Now start fucking spinning, you overpriced bag of hot air."

He took the phone away from his ear and pressed the red end call button before placing the receiver back in its cradle. He pressed the intercom button on the phone console. "Mel, get me the transport secretary."

"I'll put you straight through," came the voice through the speaker.

"No. Get him. Get him here, now."

"Yes, Prime Minister," came the response.

The prime minister turned back to the window. The small English garden looked so serene. How could the world around it be falling apart so quickly? He took another drink of coffee. In the last twenty-four hours, he'd only had forty-five minutes' sleep. When the reports had first filtered through, it seemed like it was all part of some elaborate social media hoax or the biggest fake news ever to hit. Due to sustained cyberattacks on communications and utility industries over the past several months, it did not raise any eyebrows when the internet and mobile services went down again, making domestic and international communication virtually impossible for anyone outside the military or government. Since coming to power three years ago, he had performed miracles. Investment in renewable energy, eco-housing, and sustainable farming and fishing had paid dividends, leaving counterparts on the starting blocks. Britain's name was synonymous with progression. Once again, they had become world leaders, and all of it was because of his leadership. Now, though, he was faced … his government was faced with the biggest challenge they or any government had ever encountered.

The intercom buzzed. "Mr Prime Minister, the transport secretary is here, sir."

"Already? Send him in," he replied.

An awkward-looking middle-aged man came through the door holding a few files with papers hanging out precariously. As he came to a stop in front of the sturdy antique desk, a wad of papers fell out of one of the files. The prime minister watched, unsurprised.

"How the hell did you get here so quickly?"

"I was already coming to see you when I got the

call," The transport secretary replied.

"You do understand what's happening, don't you, Richard?"

"Err … well … I think… Well, sir, I've seen…"

"Never mind," the PM replied. "Look, we are about to enter into a war. It won't be like any other. I'll need to surround myself with the best of the best if we have any chance of getting through this, and quite frankly, Richard, you're not even the best of the worst. In fact, if I hadn't had to guarantee you this position to get your uncle's support, I wouldn't have put you in charge of the stationery cupboard, never mind the Department of Transport. But with things as they are, it will be a miracle if any of us get a chance to run again, and that miracle has to start with me making the right choices. So…" He reached into his top drawer and pulled out a letter. "Due to family commitments, you can no longer fulfil your role, and you have come to the difficult decision that you're stepping down from office. Sign it," the PM said, pushing the letter towards him.

"Like hell I will. You can't make me, and if you try—"

The prime minister hit the intercom button again. "Mel, send in Douglas, please."

An impeccably presented, dark-haired figure in a two-thousand-pound tailored, black, three-piece suit walked into the office and straight up to the transport secretary. Douglas looked towards the PM who gave a barely perceptible nod before turning back to Richard. "Listen to me, you little twat. I don't give a fuck who your uncle is. Do you think he'll give a duck's fart about running to your side in support if these get printed? And I'm pretty certain your wife and kids won't be that impressed either." He pulled a small selection of photographs from a manilla envelope, featuring Richard in a number of compromising positions with a barely legal teenage male. He threw them down onto the PM's desk and they spread across the surface making a pornographic collage.

"Oh, dear God," Richard said, his legs suddenly becoming jelly as he flopped onto one of the leather chairs. "How … how did you get these?"

Douglas looked at him with incredulity. "How did I get them? That's your response? What the fuck does it matter how I got them, you creepy little pervert? Sign the fucking letter, get out of this office and take those vomit-inducing pictures with you."

Without hesitation, and without making any eye contact, Richard signed the letter, gathered his folders, gathered the photos, stuffed them back into the envelope and beat a hasty retreat from the office.

When the PM and Douglas heard the outer office door close, they both burst out laughing. "I swear, you are my idol," the PM said.

"Pish. It's like I keep telling you. It's not what you know, and it's not who you know. It's what you know about who you know that counts." The pair laughed again.

"Seriously, how the hell did you get those?"

"Friend of a friend," Douglas replied with a sly smile.

"Whatever. Is Elyse prepped?"

"Your lack of faith astounds me." Douglas pushed the intercom button. "Mel, send Elyse in, will you?"

A hard-faced but striking-looking woman in her late thirties walked into the office, pulling two sheets of paper from a leather folder. "I've been speaking to the ports authority, the CAA and the DFT all morning. When you sign these papers officially making me the transport secretary, we can get the ball rolling." She looked towards Douglas who gave her a wink.

The PM picked up a solid silver ballpoint pen and brought the nib within a few millimetres of the dotted line. He paused and looked first towards Elyse and then towards Douglas. "I suppose history will judge us best," he said.

"Good grief, Andy, I'll just be grateful if there's a future to allow us to be judged." No smile followed

Douglas's statement. As usual, he was apprised of the gravity of the situation long before anybody else. "Let's just hope that old British bulldog spirit gets us through this one, eh?" He picked up the signed sheets, nodded to Elyse, and the pair of them left the office.

Andy picked his mug up from the desk and took a drink. He grimaced as the now tepid fluid ran down his throat. He put the mug down and hit the intercom button. "Mel, you couldn't—" Mel entered the office with a steaming mug of coffee. She knew he didn't have anything scheduled for an hour, so, as their personal joke, she used the cup with "Do I look like a fucking people person?" emblazoned on the side. They both smiled as he took it from her. "What would I do without you, Mel?"

Mel had been with him ever since his first election campaign as the MP for Morley in Leeds. How many years ago was that? Sixteen—sixteen years. She would never work for anyone else. She wouldn't want to, and he wouldn't let her. It wasn't romance between them. She was ten years his senior and still turned heads, but their relationship was nothing like that. It was more like brother and older sister. He had nothing but the best for the country in his heart, and just working for him gave her a sense of patriotism she thought was long dead before the day she first auditioned for the job. She almost guided the awkward twenty-six-year-old through her own interview, he was clueless. By the end of it, she had pretty much awarded herself the job and a two K bump in the advertised pay. It didn't feel like boss and employee right from the very start. "You'll never have to do without me," she said, flashing that white smile that still stopped statesmen in mid-step. "Is there anything you need?"

"I don't suppose you've got any miracles to offer?"

"Things that bad?"

"We go back eighty years, Mel, to the beginning of World War Two, and I'd say maybe, maybe we'd have a cat in hell's chance. People were different back then. There was more of a fighting spirit, a greater understanding of putting others before ourselves, but today, it's a different time, practically a different species. I honestly don't know."

"Y'know you can always tell me anything, don't you?"

"I know, Mel, I know," replied Andy as he watched her leave the office.

She had not been gone more than a moment when there was a beep followed by Mel's voice—all business once again. "Edward Phillips on line one for you, Mr Prime Minister."

Edward Phillips was the head of the British Secret Intelligence Service, MI6, and someone who tended to prefer his politicians veering to the right, but he liked Andy Beck, who, despite being a Labour man through and through, had shown more than a healthy respect for the armed forces and intelligence services during his tenure. "Edward," said Andy.

"Mr Prime Minister. I've just spoken to the foreign secretary."

"Ah yes. I know that reporting to me directly rather than her is a break from the norm, but somehow I think we're going to be breaking norms quite a lot from now on. Things are very fluid at the moment, and it's essential I receive pertinent information as and when it becomes available rather than waiting for it to trickle down."

"Yes, Prime Minister. She explained the situation and sent a signed directive across. Everything seems to be in order, sir, and I am at your service."

"Good. Now, what do we have?"

Edward wasn't a great socialite; in fact, social situations made him very uncomfortable, so he appreciated the *straight to business* approach. "About an hour ago, all the Kremlin's firewalls crumbled. As you can guess, there is so much data to wade through that it will take us months if not years to get to the bottom of everything they've been up to, but…"

"Yes?" Andy asked, showing a little more than statesman-like interest.

"As we suspected, sir, Russia was responsible for some of the cyberattacks at least."

"Say again."

"The hacks, sir, some of them were carried out by Russia and groups funded by the Kremlin. The NHS, some of the ISPs, and phone networks, and that's just what we've found so far."

The audacity! Russia had been suspected for so long, but now they had proof. *How dare they? How dare they do this to another world power?* Holding up a country like a street thug holding up an off-licence. There had been clues that suggested Russia, but the progress that had been made in diplomatic circles in trying to get Russia back to the table with respect to so many things had made most decision makers discount the possibility of their involvement. They had made such sacrifice, showed such willing, but now, now it was obvious they were hugging their old enemies, pretending to be friends only to get a better angle when it came to plunging a poisoned blade into their backs.

"Motherfuckers!" Andy hissed.

"Sir?"

"Sorry, Edward, please go on."

"Err … well, sir, that's it for the moment. The encrypted document regarding the hack was a few weeks old, and we'd cracked it before we got access to all the files. There are terabytes upon terabytes of information that will take us a long, long time to work through, but…" He tailed off.

"But what?"

"Well, sir, it's…"

"Spit it out, Edward. What?"

"There are a lot of encrypted emails from senior-ranking intelligence agents, scientists and members of the Russian cabinet. The subject line on all of them simply reads, 'Konets Sveta,' sir. We haven't been able to decrypt the email content yet, but the name alone is … concerning."

"Edward, pretend for a moment that I don't speak Russian and you're talking to a layman. What does 'Konets Sveta' mean?"

There was a pause. "Doomsday, sir. It means Doomsday."

# 2

"Mel!" Andy shouted as soon as he replaced the receiver. His PA rushed into the office with a pen and pad in her hand. Get me Doug, John, Theresa and Elyse—now!"

"Shall I say what it's to do with?"

"Just get them here," he replied, taking another drink from his mug. Without pause, Mel left the room, and Andy saw the lines on his phone begin to light up. He walked around and took a seat at his desk. He could not really focus on anything but absently scrolled through emails. He paused on one from the office of the communications director. "ZOMBIES" jumped out from the screen. "Motherfucker!" he said underneath his breath.

Within twenty minutes, the four people he had requested were assembled in his office. He gave them the full debrief he had been given by MI6.

"Ha!" said Theresa McCann, the foreign secretary.

"Ha! What?" Andy replied.

"Ha! The Russian Ministry for Economic Development has been trying to get me on the phone all morning."

"Oh, they have, have they? Listen! We know for sure they've been behind some of the hacks over the last few months. We can't pin anything else on them at the moment. So, we go with what we know. There have been unconfirmed reports of this infection hitting all over Russia. Moscow, Novosibirsk, Samara, Murmansk, Penza—" The phone beeped. Andy hit the intercom button. "I said no interruptions."

"I'm sorry, Prime Minister, it's Mr Phillips from MI6, he was most insistent."

Andy took in a deep breath. "Put him through," he replied, picking up the receiver.

"Sir, I've got a rundown of the first officially confirmed cases."

"Where?"

"I've got one hundred and one different cities with new ones coming in all the time. You want all of them?" Edward asked.

"Countries?"

"USA, France, Australia, Brazil, Denmark, South Africa, Indonesia, Russia, China, India, Japan—"

"Okay, okay, okay. So, it's hit the fan? Properly I mean."

"I'm afraid it has, sir, yes."

"Okay, Edward. Get all that information across to me. CC Doug into it, will you?"

"Yes, sir. Straight away, sir."

"Fuck!" Andy said as he replaced the receiver back onto the base unit. "Okay, this is it. We've got the first confirmed cases. The first confirmed cases of the dead coming back to life."

Elyse let out a nervous giggle. "I'm sorry," she said almost immediately. Andy started to give her a glare then caught himself, realising how ridiculous what he had just said sounded.

"None of us are going to be sleeping much over the next few days and weeks. Find a coffee pot to make friends with, all of you, you're going to need it. We're about to enter the fight of our lives."

The intercom beeped once more. "Prime Minister, it's Mr Bright," Mel said.

"Put him through, Mel," he replied, picking up the phone. "Xander! Get yourself up here! If ever we needed some spin, it's now."

A moment later, heavy footsteps could be heard in the outer office, and despite the door being ajar, it was rocked further on its hinges as Xander entered. He and Andy had worked together for years. They were old, old friends and they showed it by being as disparaging as they could to each other in private, but in public, Xander knew he was addressing the PM and acted accordingly. "So, what's the problem?"

"Well," began the PM, "not to put too fine a point on matters, it looks like we're experiencing a bit of a zombie apocalypse."

"I thought we were going to call them *reanimated corpses*."

"Funny fucker, aren't you?" Andy replied. "But look, on the upside, now the Russian covert services have gone into meltdown, our IT and ISP infrastructure is returning to normal fast."

"That's great news, the new series of *Stranger Things* starts tonight. I've not been able to watch anything uninterrupted on Netflix for weeks." A nervous ripple of laughter followed his words around the office.

"Listen, Theresa, get Letchckov or Petchckov or whatever the hell he's called back on the phone. They'll have been monitoring the same communications we have. They'll know there are no reports of infection here; they'll be wanting to set up trade channels in case we manage to stay infection-free. We are going to be the best chance of a lifeline for a lot of countries. We are an island nation with vast resources and huge wealth and capability. Our borders are going to be easier to manage than most countries' borders, and the smart political operatives will know that. Say what you want about the Russians, they're good chess players."

"Okay, but what am I going to say?"

"Find out what they want. They wouldn't come to us if they didn't want something. Don't commit to anything. We are going to have to set up a small committee. You, Doug, John," he said, nodding to the chancellor of the exchequer, "we're also going to need—" He hit the intercom button. "Mel, can you get me the health secretary, the defence secretary and the business secretary?" Andy looked at his watch. "Tell them we'll meet in the cabinet room in forty-five minutes." He took a drink of coffee. "Okay, you're going to be getting a lot of calls like his," he continued to Theresa. "You take them all, you get lists of what everyone's needing, and we'll take it from there. Go!"

"Yes, Prime Minister," she said, immediately collecting the small folder she had walked in with and exiting the office. "Elyse, we need to look at the logistics of shutting the ports, and all the airports. We need to look at locking the country down and how best to do it, causing the least disruption. We can't risk this infection reaching us. Speak to your people, give me the estimates of how many British nationals we have abroad. Find out how many inbound flights and inbound sea vessels there are. Get back to me asap."

"Anything else, Prime Minister?"

"Isn't that enough?" he asked, shrugging his shoulders. She left the office straight away.

"John, we'll talk after the meeting, but you and I are going to have to take a grip of this quickly. Get your guys together, I want numbers. As of yesterday morning, unemployment was standing at three and a half million. The hacking put a lot of people out of work and a lot of companies out of business, but that's nothing compared to what's about to happen." Andy looked at John and the others assembled in the room.

Always serious, always lost a little in his own reality, John replied, "You think the effects on commerce will be instant?"

"John, you do realise what's happening?" Andy replied.

"Of course I do, but—"

"The second this news breaks officially, people are going to push furniture against their front doors and board their windows up. On a planetary scale, this is the end of everything as we know it, and if we survive, it will be a miracle." Andy knew John was a genius. A real genius. You asked him what seventy-two multiplied by thirty-one was, and he'd work it out in his head as quick as a calculator. He was the perfect guy to have around a negotiating table because he would completely freak out the other negotiators with his grasp of figures. His weak point was his lack of people skills. He had no filter, and his thoughts became words without the benefit of politics. Andy knew how to manage him, though, to get the best out of him.

Pre-empting the prime minister's plans, "I'll get you the unemployment figures and the pension figures by age breakdown too."

Andy smiled. "Thanks, John. We'll live or die by economics here. None of this can happen without you." The chancellor seemed suitably placated by the statement and exited the office. Andy exhaled and rolled his eyes at Xander and Doug.

"Very prime ministerial," Doug said, mockingly.

"Oh, fack off!" Andy replied.

The statement received a small snigger from Doug and Xander. "This doesn't want to be a leak," Xander said. "This wants to be an official address. It needs to be statesmanlike as if we'd planned the management of this for years. The importance of what we are about to do needs to be measured and emphatic, not panicky."

"Hang on," Andy said, "we don't even know what the measures will be yet."

"Look," Xander replied, "that's just window dressing. What you say isn't half as important as how you say it."

"He's right," continued Doug. "This is all about leadership. The people need a leader, not a politician or bureaucrat. You need to think back to the campaign. That was what sold you; your power to lead the country. It's all well and good finessing the electorate, but pulling them back from the precipice, that's something else."

"I agree entirely," Xander said, looking at his watch. "It's three o'clock…" He paused. In that pause Andy and Doug could see a thousand cogs whirring behind his eyes. He took out his phone. "Astrid, get the heads of all the broadcasters to my office in an hour. Tell them they're going to get the biggest story they've ever had." He hung up without waiting for a response. "We need to own the news. I suggest our ISP and communication network problems continue for the afternoon." He hit another speed dial. "Dave, give me a second." He muted the phone. "You're going live at eight p.m. to address the nation," he said to Andy. "We want to do everything we can to control the story before then. For one day, let me pull a Beijing on the internet service in the UK. I mean, right now, it's intermittent at best, and we can't knock it out completely, but we'll pretty much mute it for most of the day until a little bit before the speech tonight. Look, all government comms, all the military, it will be business as usual. They're what count. All emergency services will be fine. Don't let your sense of civil liberty outrage get in the way of saving people's lives. For one day, people can do without the internet and email. Look how many times they've done without it in the last few months, but this time, it will be on our terms."

Andy looked towards Doug, who gave a small nod. "Okay, Xander."

Xander un-muted the conversation. "Dave, listen," he said, walking out of the office.

Andy and Doug looked at each other as Xander's

voice faded. "He's right," Doug said. "Nobody wants to play Big Brother, but I can guarantee we'll be saving lives by doing this. Panic is a funny thing. Once it takes hold, it doesn't dissipate. There'll be uncertainty and rumour. I mean hell, some of the public will have already seen the stuff on YouTube, Facebook and Twitter, but if we can put all that on pause until eight, we can get back control. The next few hours are crucial. Nothing says stability like a well-planned strategy. We outline the basics. Give them enough information to make them feel safe in our hands, but not too much to make them confused."

"You make them sound like children."

"You know how I feel about the electorate," Doug replied. "What was it Churchill said? The greatest argument against democracy is five minutes with the average voter." They both smiled.

"This really isn't about politics, Doug. We're on a war footing. Granted it's not the usual kind of war, but it's war nonetheless. I want to lead the country. I want to save it."

"You are such an idealist. You always were. We will have the greatest minds in the working on every aspect of this. By eight p.m., you'll be giving the nation a chance that I can guarantee no other country on the planet will have. I'm with you on this, Andy. As much as I joke, this is what we came into politics for, serving our country, and I can think of no better service than saving it."

The intercom beeped. "I've got the transport secretary on line one for you, Prime Minister."

Andy hit line one and then the speaker button. "Elyse, you're on speaker, I'm here with Doug."

"Sir, I'm still getting the figures together for UK residents currently abroad. I've spoken with Theresa. There are approximately one point three million British Nationals living overseas, but people out of the country on holiday and business, that's going to take some time to get those figures."

"I'm putting you on hold, Elyse," Andy said. He looked at his watch, six minutes past three. "I'm going to pull the plug," he said to Doug.

"What do you mean?"

"I'm going to shut us down," Andy replied. "Mel!" he shouted, get me the health secretary here."

"He'll be arriving for the meeting soon," she called through the open office door.

"No, I want him here now," Andy replied before hitting the flashing line one button. "Elyse—shut down the ports, shut down the airports now. Tell them we are at threat level *Critical*. I want it done by five p.m. All inbound international flights and sailings are to be held on the tarmac and at ports until every single passenger has been given a medical. I want our airspace closed. All flights and sailings due to head here are to be cancelled until further notice. Understand?"

"Err … err … well, yes, sir. Five p.m., you say?"

"I didn't make a mistake promoting you did I, Elyse?"

"No, Prime Minister, absolutely not, sir."

"As much as we want to avoid panic, we're out of options. We need to get this done. Everything will become clear when I make my speech, and hopefully the whole country won't go into meltdown in the three hours in between this happening and me explaining everything to them. Right. I'm speaking to Zahid, the health secretary, in a few minutes. You're going to coordinate with him. The next few days are going to be scrappy. We will be under constant fire from the public, the opposition, the media, everyone, but we are doing the right thing for the right reasons, remember that."

"Yes, Prime Minister," Elyse replied before hanging up.

"Ballsy," Doug said, smiling. "On the subject of being under constant fire, you know Ashford's going to be really, really pissed that he's not being kept in the loop."

"He is. Your office is keeping him in the loop."

"He's your home secretary, shouldn't that be your job?"

"I don't want him around. He can do his job just fine without ever laying eyes on me."

"I'll make sure all the pertinent data gets to him."

"Thanks, Doug. All it takes is one case. You've seen the same unofficial reports I have. Jesus, it's been what? Twelve, thirteen hours? It's bloody mental how quickly this has happened. Right this second, who knows? We might have infected in the country, but we can't risk letting more in, so we've got to make bold moves." Andy looked down at the phone and hit the intercom button. "Mel, get me Theresa."

A few seconds later, the phone beeped. "Foreign secretary on line one, Prime Minister."

"You getting calls?" Andy asked.

"Non-stop," Theresa replied.

"Everyone you speak to, everyone, tell them we want as many medical reports as they can give us. We want to help them. We want to know the symptoms and as much about the causes as we can determine. Tell them we're inundated, but who we help first will be those who help us the most. Data, Theresa! Data is the best currency today. The rest of the stuff we can negotiate as we go. I'm seeing the health secretary in a few minutes, I'll get him to coordinate with you." Andy didn't wait for a reply, he just hung up. He looked at Doug, who was smiling.

"What? What is it?"

"When I first met you, this is the role I knew you were made for. There is no one I would rather have in your position to take us through this," Doug said proudly.

"Well, I haven't done anything yet. We might not have a bloody country by this time tomorrow, so let's not count our chickens. Look, things are just going to get more and more manic from hereon in. I need you and your people to liaise with the first ministers for Scotland, Wales and

Northern Ireland—keep them in the loop."

"And the Irish premier?"

"I've already been in touch with her, but keep her people up to date."

The intercom beeped. "Prime Minister, the health secretary has arrived, sir."

"Send him in, Mel."

# 3

Mya had never felt so alone in her life. Of all the times for this to happen, it had to be today. *Well, of course, it did.* Sitting by herself in the cockpit, she looked out across the runway to the fields and trees beyond. Behind her, she could hear the bone-shaking drone of the air-raid siren rising into the cold grey sky. On any other day, that would have seemed odd, but not today.

She let out a long sigh and closed her sad brown eyes. "You never could stick around, could you, Dad?" A single tear trickled down her face. She was thirty-six years old and had spent thirty-three of those years without knowing her father. When her mum passed away, he turned up at the funeral. Awkwardness had given way to anger, but he had stuck around and gradually a bond, albeit a tentative one, had formed.

Mya was not in a profession that lent itself to building solid relationships, but they had both persevered. *Had it been love?* Yes. Even when she was young and didn't know who he was, she had loved him. Not believing her alcoholic mother's stories of why he left, she had created her own image of the man. The reality was something very different, but she had loved him nonetheless. And as much as she hated him when he turned up at the funeral, she loved him as well. *Talk about fucked up.*

Now it was all a moot point; Mya was an orphan … again. Her mother had spent most of her life down at the pub, bringing home any man who would have her. So, right through growing up, Mya had neither a mum nor a dad to look after her. In many ways, she had been orphaned by circumstance. But now she was a literal orphan. This was much worse. All the things she had planned to say, planned to ask, all gone up in smoke. If it was any other time, she would have requested a leave of absence from work, but not today. Nobody could request a leave of absence today.

She opened her eyes and wiped the tear from her cheek. She had to put her game face on. She would grieve when there was time to grieve, but right now, she needed to dig in. There was a lot more at stake than her feelings, her welfare. *I'm sorry, Dad.*

*

The apartment was cramped, and the furnishings were mismatched. It told of two different interior designers—a woman who took pride in her good eye for style and a man trying to hold on to the past.

An air-raid siren began to scream again as a key turned in the lock. The grimy curtains let in enough of the grey light for the homeowner to see in the room without switching on the lamp. He closed the door behind him and turned the key before resting his head against the wood. He wasn't disturbed by the siren. In fact, part of him welcomed it. God, how he hoped a stray bomb would take him. It wasn't a sin in the eyes of God if he was killed by the hand of another. He headed further in and let out a small gasp as he saw a figure sitting perfectly still in one of the flowery armchairs.

"Yuri, Yuri, Yuri," came the English voice. "Long time, no see."

Yuri looked for a moment then went to sit in the chair opposite the figure.

"I expected you. I hoped for you in all honesty. This secret is too much to bear, but seeing you tells me it is not a secret any longer." Yuri wore thick glasses, his head was bald on top, but he had short cut white hair covering the rest of it. He was Russian but spoke perfect English with a Muscovite lilt. A few years before, if this man had been waiting in his apartment, it would have been a race to see who could fire a round off first. Their relationship had changed, and while there would never be complete trust between the two of them, there was certainly mutual respect and some kind of weird friendship.

The air raid siren continued. "Konets Sveta?"

"Yes," Yuri replied. "Konets Sveta. You must believe me, Sebastian, Konets Sveta … it was a mistake."

"Go on," Seb replied.

"May I get us a drink and take my coat off?" Yuri asked, beginning to stand.

"Of course," Seb replied, "we are old friends."

An uncertain smile flashed on Yuri's face before he struggled out of the chair and slipped off his coat. He walked towards the door and put it on a coat rack next to a long teal-coloured woman's coat with a fake fur collar. A last remnant, a comforting reminder of happier times. He walked over to a cabinet and opened a door bringing out a bottle of cognac and two glasses; Yuri poured healthy measures into each then grabbed the bottle as well and returned to the chair, handing Seb one of the drinks before sitting down once again.

"This goes back to Glasnost," Yuri began. "There were biological weapons research laboratories all over the USSR, but the one you are interested in was in Siberia, a bunker in a hundred square miles of snowy nothingness. Olga and I had just celebrated our fifteenth wedding anniversary when I was sent there to decommission it." His words became deafening in the room as the air raid siren came to a sudden stop. Decommissioning had a different meaning to Yuri and Seb than it did to an industrialist. "When I got there, there wasn't a single soul. Somehow word must have got to them. But you must realise this was a different time. The general feeling was that things were changing, that things were getting better. The KGB, though, they wanted the clean-up squads to remove evidence of the activities we had been pursuing that would have been frowned upon on the international stage. That lab ... that bunker ... my God, Sebastian, those poor subjects. Many had been put down, but the ones that weren't, they had been left to starve in their cages. We wouldn't have been more than a couple of days late, but we were late nonetheless."

He swilled the cognac around in the glass. It was nowhere near the right temperature to be enjoyed, but he took a drink anyway. "It was a big site. I had more than a dozen top KGB bean counters with me. Every specimen had to be accounted for. This was not something that could be left to chance. You can't risk a phial of pneumonic plague being sold on the black market. And this is where things took a bad turn." Yuri looked toward the wedding photo on the small side table next to where he was sitting. "Thank God Olga and I never had children."

"Go on, Yuri," Seb said, hanging on his every word.

"There was a set of samples missing. We went back again and again to see if there was any chance of a mistake, to see if they had been incinerated, but no. We are talking about a sample set no bigger than a deck of playing cards, every other... *every* other was accounted for, but this was gone. We contacted our superiors. They demanded we go over the entire place once more. Three days we spent in that facility, Sebastian. We could have spent three years and the result would have been the same. When we had satisfied our superiors that there was no chance these samples would be found, they told us to carry on with the decommissioning.

It took us over an hour to rig the explosives. During that period, I looked through the notebooks one last time. The technical material I only had a very limited understanding of, but there were some personal notes, and I found a diary." Yuri put his glass down and began to rise.

Seb raised his eyebrows. "Steady," he said.

"Do not worry, my friend," Yuri replied as he walked across to the bureau. He opened a drawer and pulled out a green silk-covered journal. There was a bookmark in it. He returned to his seat and sat down, opening the book to where the marker was. "I will translate for you. 'This new variant, it is like nothing we have seen. It is beyond our science, beyond our reason. It's as if it is touched by ruka d'yavola.'"

"The devil's hand. Touched by the devil's hand?" Seb said, and the hairs on the back of his neck suddenly prickled. At exactly the same time, a flurry of explosions sounded in the distance. They both looked towards the curtains and saw light coming through as each blast sounded.

"You see, Sebastian, within reason, a scientist can expect a certain type of behaviour or a certain result because most of the time experiments are done in increments. But this! This was something else."

"So, what differentiated this?"

Yuri licked his thumb and flicked to an earlier part of the diary. "Experiment seventeen-point-three-point-one–Prisoners A and B. Subject A—"

"Wait a minute. These subjects were human?"

"Testing on animals could only take the research so far," Yuri said, letting out a sad sigh. "You have no idea about some of the things I and others had to do, my friend. Prisoners went missing all the time. Nobody asked questions because nobody wanted to know the answers. I told you, these were different times." He turned back to the journal. "'Experiment seventeen-point-three-point-one – Prisoners A and B. Subject A was injected with the

29

contaminated strain of the hybrid Creutzfeldt-Jakob Disease/lyssavirus at ten thirteen. Within sixty seconds, Subject A had suffered cessation. Twenty seconds passed, and Subject A rose. His eyes were grey apart from shattered black pupils. The subject showed heightened aggression and no longer made noises consistent with that of a human but rather a low growl, more akin to an agitated canine. The dividing gate was raised between Subject A and Subject B habitats and instantaneously Subject A leapt on Subject B and took a large bite out of his neck. Subject B collapsed to the floor, screaming and desperately trying to defend himself. Subject B passed within seconds before reanimating in the same manner as Subject A. At this point, Subject A and Subject B shared no interest in each other, only their surroundings.' In twenty years as a research scientist, I have never seen such a thing. It is like science stopped and something else took over. The incubation period was impossibly fast. The aggression was uncontrollable. It was like something else was in that lab with us. I wasn't the only one to feel it, I can tell. It was a darkness, it was chistoye zlo." Yuri looked over the top of his glasses towards Seb.

"Pure evil!" whispered Seb, who swirled his cognac and took an early sip.

The bombs continued to drop in the distance. Yuri took another drink. "From all the labs, all over the USSR, there was nothing unaccounted for. It sounds farfetched, but it is true. The state was meticulous in its cataloguing. But that one sample set. That is the one blemish on our otherwise perfect record."

An explosion boomed, closer than the others. "Blemish might be understating a little, don't you think, Yuri?" The old Russian looked down at his glass. The two men sat for a while, listening to the bombs drop. Yuri took the journal and gently lobbed it across to Seb, who steadied it in his lap without spilling a drop of cognac.

"Take it back to your people. Maybe there is

something … anything … a clue I missed." Yuri poured more cognac into his glass and got up to fill Seb's.

"No more for me. I have a long journey ahead."

"We both have long journeys ahead of us, but you'll deny an old friend one last toast before he sets sail on his? My government is clearing the ghettos. That's where our first reported outbreak was. They think they can cut off the arm to save the body. They are doing the same in St Petersburg, Novosibirsk, Yekateriburg, all over. It will not work. My country is finished. You still have a chance, if you act quickly," he said, taking another long drink.

"I have a jet waiting," Seb replied.

"I would expect nothing else, my old friend." The two raised their drinks to each other, and both imbibed the rich amber fluid.

Seb put the glass down, placed the journal in the inside pocket of his coat and as he stood, picked up the pistol he had positioned down the side of the chair cushion and placed it in the back of his belt.

"After all this time, you still prefer your Browning to the Glock," Yuri said, smiling.

"If you have a reliable old friend, why would you ever want to trade them in?"

"A good point."

"You could come with me, Yuri. I could get you clearance, I could get you out of here," Seb said.

"No, my friend. The bombing will spread in wider and wider circles, and soon I will be with my Olga again. Until then I have fine cognac, enough shashlyik and stroganoff to feed an army. So, ya zhelayu tebe khorosho, moy drug." He raised his glass once more.

"I wish you well too, Yuri. My regards to Olga," Seb said with a sad smile as he walked across the room to the door. The sound of the bombs was muffled as he walked down the corridor. The hallway lights flickered. He pulled his mobile phone out of his pocket and entered a code then another. A text screen lit up. He typed, *Fifteen minutes*, and placed the phone back in his pocket.

As he entered the parking garage, the cold Moscow air made him shiver, but there was something else too. Seb lived by instinct; something was wrong. Then he heard it, a low, gurgling growl. He remembered back to the words Yuri had read from the journal, and he immediately reached for his Browning. He continued towards his car with the pistol raised. The dim light of the parking garage cast shadows everywhere, but it seemed half of Seb's working life had been spent in the shadows, so he was used to it. He sensed the charging creature before he saw it and he spun around ninety degrees to see what had once been a police officer sprinting towards him. Even in the subdued light, he could see the colour was off, no longer human, no longer lifelike, just a deathly grey. The skin, the eyes, this was the new enemy. He waited, fear taking a back seat, he was a professional killer among other things after all, and a foe was a foe.

Seb studied its movements, its single-minded focus unwavering. *No wonder these things are running riot, they'd be terrifying to any man in the street.* It was just a few metres away when he aimed and took three shots, straight at the heart. The beast flew back, knocked from its feet by the force before it sprang up once more. The calmness suddenly left Seb. "Jesus Christ!" he said, aiming once again and firing, four, five, six, seven. Each time the shot was close to centre; each time the bullet would have taken any ordinary man down, but the creature kept coming. At three feet away, Seb aimed at the forehead and an explosion of red burst from the back of the monster's skull. This time, it collapsed and did not return to its feet.

Seb kept his gun on it as he approached the body. He looked at all the red holes in the chest region. *God help us!* Looking down at the gun, he noticed his hand was shaking. He looked at his other hand, it was the same. Twenty-five years ago, he had made his first kill. He remembered shaking like this back then, but after that, it had got easier and easier. He stood with the body for a moment, watching, not yet believing it was dead, really dead. The sound of a car entering the garage brought him out of his daze, and he replaced the Browning into the back of his trousers. Seb walked to his vehicle and climbed in. He brought his hands up in front of him. They were still trembling. He gripped the steering wheel with all his might and took three deep breaths before starting the engine. He was a mile away from the parking garage before his breathing returned to normal and the shaking subsided. He stopped at a hastily erected checkpoint and a soldier asked him to produce papers. Seb showed his diplomatic credentials, and the soldier nodded, signalling for his colleagues to let the car through the barrier.

A few minutes later, Seb was heading out of the built-up city. He turned onto a narrow road that was in a state of disrepair before turning again onto a wider road that showed signs of being resurfaced recently. He put his foot down and the hedgerows blurred. The road came to a sudden end, blocked by a large metal gate. Seb got out of the car and entered a combination onto a keypad. He walked back to the idling vehicle as the gate swung open and the car headed through the gap. He checked the mirror to see the gate closing again. The road widened into a small car park. There were no bays, this was not a place for public parking. There were no signs to tell anyone what or where it was. He pulled on the handbrake and turned the engine off. He climbed out of the car and proceeded to the boot, where he collected a small holdall. The perimeter of the car park was surrounded by a high fence. He walked to a tall gate and entered a combination onto another keypad. The gate clicked open, and he stepped through. Beyond it was a runway with a Cessna Citation X+ jet waiting. Both it and the airfield belonged to an oligarch who had been bending over backwards to help the British and the Americans in the hope that when he launched his presidential bid, they would help manipulate the elections the same way the Russians had tried to do in their countries.

He climbed on board and pulled up the steps before heading to the cockpit. The pilot was a brunette, in her late thirties, dark features, with hair slightly longer than shoulder length and a smile that could light a cave. "You're late," she said, placing her headset on. Seb put the holdall in the cockpit storage locker and took the co-pilot's position. He let out a sigh and put his own headset on. The pilot turned in her seat to look at her companion. "What is it?" There was no response. "Seb, you're scaring me, what's wrong?"

He turned to look at her. "Mya, this is it. This is the end!"

## 4

"Don't you think it would be a good idea to talk to the cabinet secretary before you go charging off every which way?" demanded Nadine Parker, the cabinet secretary, as she entered the outer office.

"Look, Nadine," Doug replied, "all this crap is just unfolding. Minute by minute, we're finding out something new."

"Exactly! You need me. I can help facilitate. I've got eleven years in this position. I can get things done. I know you and I don't get on; I doubt we ever will, but have I ever given you the impression that I want to hinder this government?" She took off her glasses and glared at Doug as she wiped the lenses.

"No, no, you haven't," he replied.

"Is that Nadine?" Andy shouted from the office.

Doug was about to respond when Nadine called out, "Yes, Prime Minister." She walked past Doug and into the PM's office. Nadine was forty-one years old, but someone could be forgiven for adding another ten years. The position had been unkind to her. She was a civil servant through and through, meticulous and very knowledgeable, and she hated politicians trying to find shortcuts around procedure. She worked for the people; she was loyal to the country, not partisan but ready to enact what the government wanted, providing it was constitutionally justifiable and legal.

"Sit down, Nadine," Andy said as Doug appeared at the door. "Doug, do me a favour, head to the cabinet room and tell them I'll be a couple of minutes, will you?"

"Yes, Prime Minister," he said, winking and leaving the office, shutting the door behind him.

"You're right, Nadine. I overheard you, you're right. I need your help. You are a fantastic civil servant and a brilliant facilitator."

Nadine blushed a little and looked down at her hands. "That's very kind," she said in a soft tone. Andy Beck was very intelligent, very charming and had a JFK style appeal. He didn't like falling back on it, but he used it when it was necessary. Right now, everything in the arsenal was fair game.

"Listen, Nadine, I'm going to be brutally honest with you; we're in trouble. Not the government, the country; in fact, not just the country, the planet. We need to act. We need to act quickly, and we can't afford to go around the houses. I'm going to do some stuff … we're going to do some stuff that would get voted down in a heartbeat if I put it in a bill, but I can tell you now, all I am interested in is saving lives," he said, locking eyes with her.

Nadine looked uncomfortable and shifted around in her chair. "Go on."

"The fact is, it's true, Nadine. The stuff you might have heard; the dead are coming back to life. We've got operatives, right this second, trying to gather more information. I'm getting updates every few minutes from Edward. This thing is moving faster than you can believe, and if we allow it to reach these shores, that's it. I mean it! That will be game over. We don't have the infrastructure in place to deal with it yet. But we're lucky, this government has some really clever people working for it, and if we can keep this thing out for a little while, we can put the infrastructure in place. If we have to cut corners to do that, I'm prepared to cut corners. History can judge me; but if we mess this up, that's it. We're gone. That's not hyperbole, that's a fact."

She was the most senior civil servant in the country. She had heard it all, or at least she thought she had. "I…" She didn't know what to say.

"I admired the way you conducted yourself long before I took office here. What I'm asking you goes beyond what a PM should ask a cabinet secretary, but desperate times and all that."

"I'll do whatever you need, sir."

Andy smiled and let out an exaggerated breath. "Thank you. Thank you, Nadine, you have no idea what this means to me. Look, I've got a few of the ministers assembled right this second. It's basically for a quick briefing. Will you come along?"

"As I said, whatever you need, Prime Minister."

The pair stood up and headed out together.

*

Xander sat in his office scrolling through text messages. As he did, a new one came in from Andy. *Nadine on board. Do whatever you need to. We need to control the news cycle. Got every faith in you.* Xander slid the phone into his inside pocket and walked out of his office and into the meeting room. He had been lucky to get premises just around the corner from Downing Street. It always reminded visitors on whose behalf he was working and talking. As he walked in, the anxious conversations came to a halt.

A portly man with grey hair and a drinker's nose growled, "We're busy men, Xander, time is money."

Xander walked to the head of the table, clenched

his hands into fists and rested his knuckles on the thick wood. "We need a slot at eight p.m. The prime minister will make an address." None of the assembled heads of the various broadcasting companies said anything for a moment, but then the growler looked at the others and began to speak.

"It's that serious?" he asked, more conciliatory now.

"You've seen what we've seen on the internet," Xander replied. "Yes, it's that serious." Silence again.

"We've not seen much. Social media's virtually inaccessible, and I can't get the bloody internet on for more than two minutes without it going down. I thought things were meant to be getting better," Growler responded.

Xander just looked at him. "There's something else. Your news broadcasts. No footage of anything remotely to do with what is unfolding. Talk about it in general terms, you do not show any of the footage from the internet and if any of you have affiliates still operating overseas, nothing from them either."

"Now look here, making time for the PM, that's one thing, we're all happy to do it, but you can't tell us what news to report, that goes beyond the pale," said one of the other executives.

"Listen to me now, all of you. After tonight's broadcast, the world will have changed forever. If you want to keep on broadcasting, you do as I ask. This is about saving lives, trying to control the panic. You want to keep your broadcasting licences, you help us here and now, you don't work against us."

"You ask for our help and then you threaten us. That's not the way things are done," Growler said, getting up to leave.

"Things are changing, and these aren't threats. I see one piece of attack footage on the news before the speech tonight and you'll be off air within ten minutes. See how your advertisers like that. Your news reports need to be subdued. We are in a critical state, I expect all of you to cooperate." Xander stared at each of the assembled men and women before heading back out of the room, leaving them in stunned silence.

\*

Sombre expressions greeted Andy as he walked into the cabinet room. News had filtered through to the various departments about what was unfolding on the world's stage. Overtures had been made to the uninitiated and uncertainty reigned. He took his seat and took a breath. "Right," he began, as the cabinet secretary took her seat at the back of the room. He looked at her. He knew she was pivotal to making all of this work. "Nadine, please join us at the table. The people in this room are what stand between success and failure, winning and losing, and you are one of them."

He pulled the chair next to him out from underneath the table and gestured for her to sit down. As she took her place, Doug gave him the subtlest of smiles. "Thank you, Prime Minister," Nadine said as she shuffled her chair back into position.

"Everyone around this table I trust. Many of the things I'm going to discuss will not be made available to the rest of the cabinet. Many of the things I discuss can go no further than these four walls." His throat suddenly felt dry and he asked John to pass him the jug of water and a glass. John passed it across, but it was Nadine who stood and poured the glass for him. "Thank you, Nadine," he said, smiling warmly. "Okay, as we speak, Xander is putting the screws on the broadcasters, getting them to tone down their newscasts until eight p.m. when I'll deliver my address." He looked towards Doug, who gave him a barely perceptible nod.

"Although it appeared the national provision of internet service improved dramatically for a couple of hours yesterday and early this morning, it now seems that was just a flash in the pan. At best it's patchy, at worst, non-existent, but government, military and utility networks seem to be working much better than they were." Andy paused and took a drink of water. "The sheer scope of the measures we need to think about is overwhelming, but our primary aim is to stop the infection reaching these shores. To that end, I have ordered the closure of ports and airports." He looked towards Will Ravenshaw, the battle-hardened defence secretary. "Will, we need to protect our borders with everything we've got. We need the navy to patrol our waters; we need the air force to protect our skies. I am commanding the recall of all troops from overseas postings, that's nearly five thousand personnel. I've got a list of objectives that Mel is preparing right now. Myself or Doug will talk you through all of them, individually, but the main purpose of this meeting is to discuss currency and deals." He paused for a moment to let that information sink in and took another drink from his glass.

Nadine looked at him. "I'm sorry, Prime Minister, I don't think I understand."

Andy pursed his lips and nodded sympathetically. He was about to answer when Doug interjected. "It's like this, Nadine," he said, resting his elbows on the table and leaning forward. "We are the only major economic power that has yet to register a single outbreak of the infection. We want to keep it that way, so we're going to need certain things, and we're going to need to offer certain things to maintain our current position."

Nadine nodded, realising just how out of her depth she was.

"Before we start, have we heard from the US?" Andy asked.

"Yes, sir, briefly," Theresa replied.

"What does that mean?"

"We heard the president made it to a bunker, Prime Minister. The secretary of state, who as you know is visiting Ireland, has been given full autonomy with regards to any trade deals. That was all the information I managed to get. The US has been struck worse than anyone."

Andy shook his head sadly and looked around the other faces at the table who were equally disturbed by the news. "If you hear anything else you will let me know."

"Of course, Prime Minister."

"So," Andy said, looking towards the others and then focussing his attention on Theresa, "who wants what? And what are they willing to offer?"

"Well, Prime Minister, I've spoken not only to foreign secretaries but to some leaders as well and the primary concern for a number of them is safe harbour for themselves and their families so the situation can be managed more objectively." A number of people around the table including Doug and Andy let out exasperated laughs and shook their heads.

"Of course they do," Andy said, brushing his hands over his face. "Dear God, what's wrong with these people? They're the captains of their ships and they want to abandon them, leaving their crew on board. They make me so sick."

Theresa continued. "A good number of them have already volunteered medical and research data in good faith. We've been offered everything from oil shipments currently in transit to wheat mountains, to fishing rights, to supplies of antibiotics, to tanks, planes, scientists, you name it. We can pretty much call the shots. Offer as much or as little as you like in return, but if we protect them, they'll give us the world."

"Okay, let's backtrack," Andy said. "Wheat mountains? That can only be the French. They got a huge fuck-off subsidy for not selling the stuff, but they grew it anyway. How much have they got and where is it?"

"He said it's there, waiting for us in Dunkirk, sir."

"You are fucking joking me," Andy replied. "Is that little prick Dupont trying to be funny?"

"No, sir, I don't think so."

"And what is that, about eight hundred thousand

tonnes?"

Theresa shuffled some papers that were in front of her. "Yes, sir," she said, amazed. "That's it exactly."

"And all he wants for this is extraction for himself and his family?"

"Yes, sir."

"Spineless little shit." Andy looked towards Doug, who nodded once again. "Do it. Sort it," Andy said, looking towards Theresa and then across to Will. They both nodded. "And make sure there is minimal risk for our people. If we have to carpet bomb the surrounding area, then we do it."

"The Icelandic prime minister offered us shared fishing rights of their waters for military assistance in stemming the spread of the epidemic," Theresa said.

"You've got to be kidding me. She thinks quotas are still a thing? The world's population will probably halve over the next few days, and she thinks she can barter fishing rights? If we want to fish in their waters, we'll fish in their bloody waters. Who has something tangible to offer us?"

"The Netherlands, sir. Prime Minister Jansen has no wish to leave his country, but he has requested military vehicles and ammunition. He is offering a trade for some of his scientists and their families. The scientists are experts in agricultural innovation, including the design of energy-efficient, high-yielding greenhouses and new irrigation systems. He is willing to supply the raw materials for several hectares' worth of the said greenhouses as well as half of their current surplus of rape and sunflower. He believes these people will be key to rebuilding The Netherlands and the UK if we all make it through this, and he wants them protected."

Andy nodded. "Make it happen," he said, once again looking towards Theresa and across to Will. Nadine was frantically scribbling notes next to him, trying to keep up with what was said.

The meeting overran by an hour leaving the rest of the cabinet ministers nervous and agitated as they waited in another room. By the end of it, the UK had secured food, skills, materials, weaponry and resources to take them comfortably through the coming months.

The meeting finally came to an end, and Andy picked up the phone. "Show the rest of the ministers in," he said. That meeting overran as well. There were both blank and scared looks. The wider cabinet was not privy to all the plans, but it was important they were kept abreast of the essentials. They would all be called on at some stage to participate in the crisis. When that second meeting came to an end, it was seven forty p.m.

Andy left the cabinet room and Xander was waiting for him. "That took bloody long enough," he said, looking at the PM.

"Lot to sort out," Andy replied.

"Okay, this is your statement," Xander said, handing him some sheets of paper.

Andy stopped dead in the middle of the corridor and began reading. He nodded at numerous points in the text and then took a deep breath before entering one of the large conference rooms that had been suitably arranged with lights and cameras to broadcast his statement.

"I was hoping we'd have time to record this, but I think you're going to have to do it live, once we've got the lighting and sound levels right," Xander said.

Technicians and assistants shifted around the room feverishly trying to get everything perfect for the address. A clock on the wall with big neon numbers began a countdown, and the prime minister sat down. The director began a verbal countdown, which changed to a visual one as five fingers became four, became three, became two, became one, and action.

*My fellow citizens, these are grave times. Grave times demand grave measures, and it is for this reason I am addressing you this evening.*

*The deadliest virus our scientists have ever encountered is sweeping across the planet. It is unlike anything we have seen before.*

*Something that was previously science fiction has become science fact. The dead are coming back to life.*

*This virus is not airborne. It is transmitted by bites, scratches or any other ingestion of bodily fluids from a carrier. It is for this reason that I am taking the unprecedented measure of closing our borders.*

*As of seventeen hundred hours, I have invoked a strict ban on international travel. All our airports will be closed to international flights. Our ports will close, and the navy, coast guard and air force will be patrolling our waters to guarantee our safety. I have been in close contact with the Irish premier, and she has agreed the same. Britain and Ireland are two of the last places to have no cases of infection. I have recalled every serving member of the military back to our shores. Each one will be subject to a strict physical and medical examination and after a short period of quarantine will return to serving their country.*

*Every household in the country will receive an information pack about this virus in the next few days. In it there will be details on how to identify signs of the infection, what you should do if you suspect someone of being infected, and there will also be a list of emergency numbers.*

*Make no mistake, this is the greatest challenge this country has ever faced, and it is more important than ever that we face it together. It is for this reason that I am invoking another set of measures. As every citizen of this country will be aware, the downturn in international commerce has seen unemployment skyrocket. While we have endeavoured to protect our social security system the best we can, the situation is now becoming untenable.*

*So, I am conscripting all unemployed people between the ages of sixteen and forty to serve in Her Majesty's Armed Forces and all the able-bodied aged between forty-one and sixty-five who are currently unemployed will be drafted into the food, textile, arms manufacturing and utilities industries. I am reopening all mothballed coal mines and renationalising all transport, communication companies and utility companies.*

*I realise online communications have been increasingly erratic over the past months and so in an effort to facilitate the free flow of crucial information, internet service will now be free and available to everyone nationwide.*

*Our scientists are still receiving data from counterparts in several countries, and as ourselves and Ireland are the last remaining nations with a cohesive infrastructure, it has fallen on us to supply any state or country still trying to beat the outbreak with all the help we can. This is no time to be profiteering from the misfortunes of others, but the simple fact is we cannot afford to provide endless supplies of medicines, food and arms that we may very well end up needing ourselves. So, in return for our help, we have set up trade deals with the United States, Russia, Norway, France and a number of other nations still capable of operating on a basic logistical level. This will strengthen our own resilience in combatting this near-apocalyptic catastrophe and give these nations a fighting chance they would not have had before.*

*Although I am confident we have and are taking every precaution to avoid the infection reaching us, I have asked our best scientists and military minds to coordinate with COBRA in developing a response plan should there be an outbreak.*

*I believe as a nation we have the capacity to weather this greatest of storms. We have the strength to fight back and rebuild. Britain will prevail, it will survive this test, and it will become great again.*

*My fellow citizens, now is not the time to give up. Now is the time to stand tall; to be the best we can be. Your family needs you; your country needs you; your planet needs you.*

*Tomorrow is a new day. Tomorrow our war begins, and this is one I have no intention of losing.*

*Good night and may your God go with you.*

There was a pause for a few seconds as Andy looked sincerely into the camera. "And … cut!" came the command.

# 5

No sooner had Andy arrived back in the office than Mel transferred a call through to him. "Edward Phillips on line one, Prime Minister."

"Edward?" Andy said, picking the phone up.

"Do you have anybody there with you, Prime Minister?"

Andy's brow furrowed. "No, I'm just about to head down to—"

"I have something incredibly sensitive that I need to share with you."

"Just a minute." Andy walked across and closed the door firmly before heading back to his desk. "Go on."

"Sir, the virus was the product of a Soviet bio-weapons lab." Andy remained there for a moment with the phone pressed up against his ear. "Prime Minister? Prime Minister, are you still there?"

"I … I'm here. Are you sure?"

"Yes, sir."

"How do we know this?"

"We've acquired information from a witness in

addition to physical evidence, Prime Minister."

"And there's no mistake?"

"No, sir."

"So, you're telling me the Russians did this?"

"No, sir. I'm telling you that this virus went missing from a Soviet lab before the lab was officially decommissioned in nineteen ninety-two."

"Went missing?"

"Yes, sir."

"And it's stayed missing until now?"

"That's correct, yes."

"And we're sure it's not the Russians?"

"We can't be one hundred per cent sure of anything, Prime Minister, because we don't know how this got out there. But we have no reason and no data to believe it was the Russians. We've managed to decrypt a number of Kremlin emails from the past day that suggest they were as unprepared and as horrified as the rest of the world when this virus struck."

"My God," Andy whispered as he sat back in his chair. "We can't let this information get out."

"That goes without saying, Prime Minister."

"Edward, do we have any idea who could have done something like this? Who could have had the resources?"

"After the collapse of the Soviet Union, there were a few years when everything went to hell. Stockpiles of weapons were sold off to the highest bidders, and it took a long time to bring the situation under control. I know of attempts to secure nuclear material but never anything like this."

"What's your gut telling you?"

Edward let out a sad laugh. "My gut, sir? I'm afraid I'm not a very good judge when it comes to my gut. I think it makes more sense to look at evidence."

"I suppose that's fair enough. If you find anything else out, you'll keep me informed, won't you?"

"Of course, Prime Minister."

Andy hung up the phone and looked at his watch. He needed time to process this, time to come to terms with what he had heard, but there was no time. He would not be able to share this with Doug or Xander or even his wife. It wasn't because he didn't trust them, it was simply because this information was a burden. It was a burden to carry around and he wouldn't want to inflict it on anyone else.

There was a knock on the door. "Come in," Andy called.

"It's time, Prime Minister," Mel said, popping her head around the corner. "Is everything okay?"

Andy looked towards her for a moment. The hardest thing about the job was lying to the people you cared for. Lying to a country was nothing— a country was faceless. Lying to your friends, your loved ones, that was tough. A smile broke on Andy's face and he climbed to his feet. "Everything's fine, thanks, Mel. Everything's just fine."

\*

The Chinook flew low over the city. The Parisian streets were unrecognisable in the darkness. The grid had gone down again temporarily. Not just Paris but France had been hit hard by the infection. The ten SAS operatives and two MI6 agents pulled down their night-vision goggles as they were told by the pilot that they were approaching the Élysée Palace, the official residence of the French president and his family. They maintained silence as the helicopter landed in the ample space of the courtyard. The twelve operatives disembarked and immediately raised their rifles. The L119A1 CQB Carbine was a reliable weapon, and they needed reliability beyond anything right now. They struggled to believe their own eyes as a small army of growling grabbing creatures that had once been men and women in the employ of the French government came charging towards them.

"Remember," Seb said calmly through the mic, "headshots. Headshots are the only way to take these things down."

The storming horde was nearly upon them before the first bullets flew. It was just as well that they were wearing night-vision goggles. Colour made everything more real, and the green tint of the image made the blood seem far less like blood and more like they were playing some virtual reality game where they were not, in fact, blowing people's skulls to jagged pieces with their assault rifles. This crack team was not a bunch of new recruits, they were hardened special ops veterans. They had never faced an enemy like this before, but a mission was a mission, and the orders had been given. When the last face exploded in a splash of greeny-black, the team lowered their weapons. Two of them stayed with the Chinook and the other ten headed towards the palace. A pair of straggling monsters rushed out of the dark towards them, their growls cut short by two precise headshots.

*

Andy turned white as he watched the footage with the small group of ministers and advisors he had assembled. "Oh God," he said, picking up his mug of coffee and bringing it shakily to his lips. "And explain to me again why we're viewing this mission and not the others."

"This is the highest risk one, Prime Minister. Virtually all the other extractions are from isolated locations that we deem to be relatively secure. This one is in the heart of Paris, but there was no way around it. Dupont and his family got cut off," Doug replied. "Even if the virus doesn't reach us anytime soon, panic is going to be running through the very heart of the country. I know you don't like the idea of this, Andy, but we might have to look at censoring the content of what goes out. I know the internet is down more than up, but I think we should look at blocking some stuff entirely," Doug said, trying to gauge the look on the prime minister's face as he said the words. "What's done is done, we can't make people unsee the footage that has been broadcast already, but we need to take control of this situation. We can't instil confidence by you giving wonderful speeches then undermine everything by letting people see the reality of what's threatening us."

Andy stared at him blankly before returning his gaze to the large display screen in the otherwise dark Cabinet Office briefing room.

\*

The armed group advanced towards the palace, there were no more charging monsters and the horror of what the squad had seen still hadn't been fully absorbed. They reached the wide double doors the creatures had emerged from and began to sweep. "Okay," Seb said, "we're in. Where now?"

A female voice came through his earpiece. "The president and his family didn't make it down to the bunker. They are situated in a panic room. You can gain access through the library on the first floor. Head up the staircase, turn right, and it's the fourth door on the left."

Seb looked around to make sure the squad was still with him. He looked at Mya, who gave a nod to confirm she was okay. The huge building was shrouded in a heavy darkness, which suddenly seized them all in a vice-like grip as a wailing scream echoed through the upper hallways. Instinct told Seb to run up the stairs three at a time to help, but good sense kicked in. Whoever had screamed was being attacked. It was already too late for them; he had to focus on the mission. All eyes were on him. He pointed up the staircase and the squad moved off again, rifles raised ready for action. They reached the landing and turned right to see two creatures, the blood still dripping from their mouths, black in the green light of the night-vision image. An inhuman guttural growl began to emanate from the back of their throats as they charged towards the armed team. Shots rang out, and the two beasts were suddenly motionless on the floor. Their victim further up the hall was still moving around on the thick carpet. Maybe it wasn't too late.

"Medic," Mya called as she ran towards the woman. One of the SAS team broke free and followed her.

Seb was torn. All the information had told him that a bite from one of these things meant death then reanimation, but … it had all happened so quickly, what if the information was wrong?

*

The grainy images cast a solemn green light on everyone assembled in the Cabinet Office briefing room. From nerves more than thirst, Andy took another drink from his mug. The chief of defence staff stood by his side. Alistair Taylor had held his position for over ten years. He had seen war himself; he had seen some of the worst situations and atrocities he had thought possible, but nothing had prepared him for this. Nothing had prepared anybody for this. He watched as Mya and the medic advanced on the writhing figure.

"Should they be doing that?" Andy asked.

Taylor looked towards him. "Err … honestly, Prime Minister, I don't know."

The chief of defence staff was not a partisan role, but he had become a big admirer of Andy Beck. Taylor had seen PMs come and go; many had been nothing more than spineless bureaucrats, willing to do anything to win votes provided special interests were still willing to fund their party, but Taylor saw something different in this PM and his entourage. Beck always fought a hard game to do the right thing. He didn't always take all of Taylor's advice, but he did always listen.

"You don't know?" Andy asked.

"I'm sorry, sir," he said as the close-up image of the dark-haired woman in the business suit bleeding out magnified on screen. The medic's camera angled towards the wounds on her neck, and everybody in the room cringed a little as the black blood flowed.

*

"Stay with me," Mya said, supporting the woman's head. Mya shivered as she saw not pain but terror in the bleeding victim's eyes. Death was a certainty, most people feared it, but this death … what this kind of death brought was something else. Mya had seen a lot of action all over the world. She had seen a lot of people die, but she had never seen anything like this. More than any other time she could remember, she felt an urge, an instinct to help. Of course, it was due to her own loss, she knew that, but the compulsion was overpowering.

"Tue-moi," whispered the woman as blood bubbled in her throat. "S'il vous plait."

"What did she say?" the medic asked, tearing open a packet and removing some thick gauze.

Mya pulled back a little, the determination turning to sadness. "She asked us to kill her," she replied, swallowing hard. This was no time to get emotional, this was no time for … what was it the shrinks called it? Transference.

"It's shock; she's not bloody thinking straight."

Seb marched up behind the two of them. "Get out of the way," he said, raising his rifle towards the head of the downed woman.

The medic batted it away angrily. "What the fuck do you think you're doing?" he said, standing and facing up to Seb.

Seb swivelled his rifle and butted the medic in the face with it. The medic collapsed, and Seb turned the rifle back around before being knocked from his feet by one of the other soldiers. He went sprawling, and Mya shuffled out of the way, pressing her back against the wall. The soldier raised his own rifle, pointing it at Seb. "You lay a finger on one of my men again and I'll fucking kill you," he said just before letting out a high-pitched screech of agony as the woman who had been bleeding out suddenly took a bite from his calf.

"They're coming down the hall," shouted one of the soldiers.

"More on the stairs," cried another.

Seb gathered himself and watched the soldier who had knocked him down fall to his knees. A fountain of black blood sprayed in the green hallway.

"Oh fuck! Sarge? Sarge?" cried another.

Mya just sat in disbelief watching the virtual reality become true reality, the green tinge now full colour in her head. It was no longer cartoon-like black blood but red lifeblood that was flowing. She had suffered from nightmares her whole life, but nothing matched up to this.

The woman who had bitten the sergeant began crawling towards Mya, who was now frozen in horror. The other SAS troops, seeing their sergeant fall, began to fire at the advancing creatures. Control left them, each bullet was personal.

The sergeant started to convulse, and the medic scrambled towards him, blood dripping from his nose and mouth thanks to the rifle butt in the face. "Sarge! Sarge!" he cried as he felt the wind of a bullet pass his ear and drill straight through his sergeant's head. He looked back to see Seb. "What have you done?" he screamed incredulously.

Seb did not reply but shifted his aim and took a clean shot at the beast that was just a matter of inches away from Mya. The creature toppled sideways. He went across to his partner and grabbed her arm, roughly pulling her to her feet. "Get a grip!" he commanded. "You!" he said, turning to the medic. "Get on your feet, we have a mission. You get bitten by one of these things and that's it; you were at the briefing. We've all lost people we care about on missions, now let's not lose anymore," he shouted over the noise of the rifle shots and growling horde, but the medic just knelt looking towards the lifeless body of his fallen friend.

"They're coming too fast!" shouted one of the soldiers.

"Headshots, remember, headshots!" shouted another.

Another scream filled the wide hallway as one of the soldiers was pounced on by two beasts at the same time. Scared to hit his comrade in the crossfire, another trooper rushed to drag the attacking monsters off, only to get bitten himself. As he fell to the floor, clutching his arm, desperate to stop the bleeding, yet another creature attacked him. A pained screech cut through the gunfire as a third soldier got mobbed.

Seb understood what was happening and dragged the medic to his feet, the same way he had Mya. He looked at the doors. "Bibliotheque, this is it," he said and barged through, raising his rifle again immediately. He scanned the room to see nothing but walls of books and two large antique desks. "In here," he commanded as the gunfire diminished more and more. Mya rushed through the door first, still a passenger, still not able to take in the whole situation. The medic stumbled in after, in an equal state of shock. Seb headed back to the doorway and pressed his earpiece. "Fall back to the library, now!" He looked down the hall to see a hellish scene of carnage as seasoned warriors succumbed to fear and panic.

*

"Jesus Christ!" Andy said, scraping his fingers through his hair. Image after image flashed on the screen in a juddering blur of bloody terror. "For God's sake, pull them out. Do something, Alistair," he pleaded.

Alistair just looked at him, equally shocked, equally horrified. He'd known these men perform miracles all over the world in covert missions the average Joe in the street would not even believe, but to see this was heart-stopping. The gurgling growls and screams bounced off the walls of the Cabinet Office briefing room sending shudders through them all. Another shriek and another image went still.

"This is a massacre," Doug said.

Andy slumped down into a chair. "This is it. This is what my old science teacher swore blind would happen in our lifetime ... an extinction level event. This is it."

"We got through the Black Plague, we got through the Spanish Flu, we'll get through this," Doug said.

"You're honestly likening this to the Spanish Flu?" Andy asked.

"All I'm saying is no situation is unwinnable, and we've made all the right moves so far."

"Oh, you think so?" Andy said, getting back to his feet. "Tell these guys we've made all the right moves because I'm going to have to make some calls to families soon about some of the bravest men this country has ever seen who have died in scenes that make a bloody Lucio Fulci film look like a kid's movie."

Doug paused before replying. "I'm sorry, I was being insensitive."

"Do you think?"

"What I meant was politically we have made all the right moves."

"Who gives a fuck about politics right now?" Andy yelled, and all the heads in the room turned to look at him.

Doug didn't flinch. "We should all give a fuck about politics, Andy. It's politics that has closed our airports and shut our ports and harbours, ensuring the disease doesn't get into the country. It's politics that's reopening the mines to make sure we don't run out of power. It's politics that's manufacturing the weapons and bullets we'll need to use if, God forbid, this does ever reach our shores. We should all give a fuck about politics," he said calmly and firmly.

"You are such a smug, supercilious bastard sometimes, do you know that?"

"Of course I do, I had it engraved on my cufflinks to keep reminding me," he replied, pointing to each of his twenty-four-carat-gold accessories.

Andy gave him a stare before slumping back into his chair. "What the hell can we do?" he asked, turning to Alistair.

"I…" He began but suddenly fell silent as two of the still images started to blur with movement once more. The growling through the mics ripped through the darkened Cabinet Office briefing room, turning more than one of the assembled faces white with fear. "I want all mics other than one, two and nine on mute now."

No sooner had he said it than the room became quieter. More images began to transition from still to moving as the fallen soldiers started to morph into bloodthirsty ghouls.

"Oh dear God!" Andy said as images of the beasts joining the herd running down the hallway beamed onto the screen.

*

Seb went to push the door closed, but before he could, the medic barged him out of the way. "My friends are still out there," he screamed.

"They're all gone," Seb replied as the first of the beasts reached the doorway. Seb raised his rifle and fired. The creature flew back, falling to the floor. Another appeared, he did the same—another, and another, this one a soldier burst through. He fired again and again, backing further into the room, grabbing the medic by the scruff of his collar, nearly causing the rifle strap to slip from the medic's shoulder. The chance to close the door was gone as more and more bodies piled up, blocking the entrance. Seb kept retreating, dragging the medic with him into the room with his left hand while holding the rifle and firing with his right. Then he caught movement out of the corner of his eye. A camera in the top left corner of the large library panned towards him. "Open the door," he yelled. When they were far enough back from the entrance, he released the medic and pulled a fresh magazine from his vest, replacing the spent one. He raised the rifle again and continued firing at the stumbling beasts as they tried to gain entry into the room.

Just then, one stumbled through, tripping over two of its dead brethren and falling flat on its face, but like lightning it sprang to its feet once more and lurched towards the medic, who just watched in perplexed horror. This foul, hellish creature had been his friend. Their wives were friends. They had gone on holidays together, spent Christmases together, but now, in green-tinged fury, this friend was charging towards him with only one focus. The medic began to stumble backwards, for the first time really understanding what was going on. He fumbled for his rifle, still in shock but trying to access the part of his brain that was yelling, *Remember your training*. The creature grabbed hold of the medic's vest before the rifle was raised, and gnashing teeth were the only thing audible as the beast's face contorted with malevolence. Foul-smelling saliva sloshed as it opened its mouth to take its first bite, but the bite never came.

The creature crumpled sideways as Seb took a carefully aimed shot at its right Achilles tendon. Once the beast hit the floor and he was sure there was no danger of a headshot covering the medic in infected blood, he squeezed the trigger once again, and in a spray of dark liquid, the beast fell still.

The medic looked across at Seb then at Mya, who was still taking well-aimed shots at each figure that appeared at the door. In that brief moment, all the fogginess and confusion dissipated. He trained his weapon on the entrance and started to fire at anything that moved.

"Ouvre la porte," Seb shouted at the camera, but still no door opened as more beasts tried to gain entry to the library. The three of them tried to block out the demonic gurgling growls of the creatures. There was much they would need to block out to escape this situation alive.

"Ouvre la fucking porte, you spineless frog bastard!" yelled Mya towards the camera.

*

"Please tell me she didn't just call the president of France a spineless frog bastard," Andy said.

Doug smiled. "Oh, I like this girl," he said. "We should think about hiring her as a whip."

Andy just gave him a glare as he climbed to his feet once more. "Put me through to Dupont, now."

"Hallo!" came the frightened voice. There were sounds of crying children in the background.

"Xavier, open the door and let them in," Andy demanded.

"But those things are out there," he replied with much less of a French accent than he used when he pretended to be confused by the intricacies of a negotiation or the request for a favour he didn't really want to grant.

"Our people need to get to safety while we can reassess the situation. Now let them the fuck in!" Once again, all the heads in the room span round in shock as the profanity spat from the prime minister's mouth.

There was silence on the other end then a clicking sound followed by a whoosh as if air was escaping from some giant tomb.

*

One of the bookcases swung open, revealing a bodyguard holding up a Sig Sauer pistol. "Rapidement," he said, waving them into the panic room with his free hand. Mya, Seb and the medic took final shots towards the library entrance then rushed in, each raising their night-vision goggles as they entered the dimly lit enclosure. No sooner were they in than the bodyguard hit a button, which closed the door behind them.

The panic room was grander than the title suggested. It was approximately fifty feet long and twenty feet across. There were bunks set into the wall. There were glowing computer screens, video monitors, and an arms safe; it was like a miniature survival bunker. As well as the president's wife and three children, there were two bodyguards and a nanny.

"So now we are all stuck in here like rats in a trap. Bravo," Dupont said.

The medic went towards him, clenching his fist. "I've just lost seven of my friends who were trying to save you and your family, you little cunt." Seb quickly stepped between the medic and the scared-looking president as the bodyguards began to raise their pistols.

"Let's all take a breath," Seb said, placing a hand on the medic's shoulder. As he did, his earpiece crackled to life.

"This is Rescue One. We're going airborne. Multiple attackers are converging on our position. We have requested reinforcements, which are now en route. ETA forty minutes. Over and out."

Seb, Mya and the medic all looked at each other as the first creatures thudded against the bookcases desperate to find a way in.

6

"I thought that went rather well," Doug said as he and Andy walked back down the underground corridor to number 10 from the Cabinet Office briefing room.

"Give it a bloody rest," Andy replied.

"I'm serious. You were quintessentially prime ministerial in your handling of that situation. You had empathy; you dwarfed the French president, ordering him around like he was a naughty child. You did a good job."

Andy stopped and his two plain-clothed police bodyguards who followed him everywhere stopped several paces behind him. He shook his head. "How can you say that, Doug? Good men died today because of my decision. How can you say that?"

Doug put a hand on Andy's shoulder. "Listen to me. These deals we're making. Yes, it's shitty having to send our people in to save a bunch of cowards who are more interested in protecting their own skin than saving their countries, but what we're getting in return is … well, it's giving us a fighting chance no other country has."

"You make it sound terrible. We're not just saving

cowards, we're aiding with logistics too."

"Oh yes, yes, sorry, I forgot. Those aid pallets we're parachuting in will do no end of good. Dupont is a bureaucrat. Other than you, every fucking premier in Europe is a bureaucrat. You are not responsible for this. You are responsible for the British people, and if they knew the full extent of what was going on, they'd be hoisting you on their shoulders."

"Look—"

"No, shut up a second and listen. You feel responsible for everything; you take the weight of the world on your shoulders. You try to solve everyone's problems, but that's not your job, and it's not what the country needs right now. You … we, assembled a brilliant cabinet. We have the best people in place to govern the country through this, with the obvious odd exception, but they need to be led. You can't be distracted by things outside of your control. There are going to be some really, really shitty decisions ahead that no one in their right mind would want thrust upon them. Don't take the weight of all of them yourself. You've got me, you've got Xander, you've got the cabinet, and you've got an army of advisors to point you in the right direction. Ease your burden Andy, because if you don't, we're not going to make it out of the starting blocks."

"You do know I hate you, don't you?" Andy said, and Doug smiled.

The pair continued their journey, and as they walked through the door to the PM's outer office, Mel got up from her seat. She was about to start talking, but Andy put his hand up.

"I need to be back down there in thirty minutes," he said to her, "and I want the chief medical officer here as soon as possible."

"You've got a lot of messages."

"I bet I have."

"President Petrov has been trying to get in touch."

Andy raised his eyebrows. "I've got some stuff to

take care of, I'll meet you back in the cabinet room in twenty," Doug said. "Enjoy your conversation with Dmitry."

No sooner had Andy walked into his office than the intercom buzzed. "The chief medical officer is on her way, Prime Minister."

"Thanks, Mel. Will you get me Petrov?" He sat down in his chair and looked at the clock. Five past ten. That meant it was five past midnight in Moscow, that's if Petrov was still in Moscow. "And can you get me a coffee?" he added, pressing the intercom button again.

A line lit up on the phone. "President Petrov on line one, Prime Minister. The coffee's on its way."

"Dmitry," Andy said, hitting the flashing white button.

"Mr Prime Minister," replied the Russian premier.

"How are Vasiliya and the children?"

"It is kind of you to ask, Mr Prime Minister, but I think the situation demands that two of the world's most powerful men discuss something more than each other's families, don't you?"

Andy smiled at the directness of President Petrov. "I suppose you're right, Dmitry. Like how your country was responsible for so many of the cyberattacks on mine and others around the world. Like Konets Sveta."

There was a long pause. "Konets Sveta is a ghost from the past that has come back to haunt us all. It should not exist, but it does. It should have been destroyed a long time ago, and now … now it has come to destroy us. But hopefully not all of us."

"And the attacks, Dmitry?"

"I am not like my predecessor. I did not come from a KGB background, but the old faithful have much influence here. It is an embarrassment to say I don't have control of everything that goes on in the name of my government, in the name of my country. But to admit this would have made me look weaker than staying silent."

"Just so you know, Dmitry, the only reason we are talking is the fact that you have supplies that we will need," Andy said.

There was another pause. "I understand."

"Go on then. Why did you phone?"

"Twenty supertankers have been diverted to your shores as I speak. That is over forty million barrels of oil. As agreed, there are also thirty-two cargo vessels on their way containing everything from rubber and aluminium to wheat and soybeans. My people, the ones in rural districts where to the best of our knowledge the infection has not reached—"

"What about them?"

"I want to change our agreement, Mr Prime Minister."

"The agreement is the agreement."

"Please, Andy, my people are dying. I don't want extraction; I want to stay in my country. My family and I are in a giant fallout bunker north of the city, but alas, the infection has broken through. My armed guard are putting up a brave fight, but I fear it won't be enough. Part of our deal was for myself and my family to be given haven on your shores, surely if we no longer need that, it is worth a trade for something else." His voice was almost pleading.

"What did you have in mind?"

"I am sending five sets of coordinates. These are the places our scientists have calculated have the greatest chance of survival. If you could airdrop generators, food, medicines, and basic supplies they may stand a chance. They are in remote areas, the infection has not reached them, and if they have these things, it might mean that not all my people will perish. I am begging you; please will you help them?"

Andy's head shot back in surprise. Petrov had always been a hard-nosed negotiator, always tried to dominate and take the upper hand. He had never used the words *begging* or *please*. "Even if I say yes to you, what makes you think I'll actually deliver?"

"You and I have not always got on, but you have always been a man of your word. If you tell me that you will do something, I know that is the truth."

Andy let out a sigh. He was going to send in an extraction team, which, judging by the ongoing situation in Paris, would be costly to say the least. Five aerial drops of generators and supplies were nothing in comparison. "Okay, Dmitry. You'll get your airdrops."

"Thank you, my friend. Udachi!"

"Good luck to you too," Andy replied, hitting the call end button.

The intercom beeped. "The chief medical officer is here for you, Prime Minister."

"Bloody hell, that was quick," he replied. "Send her in."

A well-dressed woman in a dark business suit and glasses walked through the door. She was carrying a box and had a bag on her shoulder. She placed them down on a chair and walked up to Andy, who had come from around his desk. The pair embraced, and the CMO pecked Andy on the cheek before she returned to stand by the side of the chair.

"How the hell did you get here so fast, Liz?"

The woman smiled. "I was already on my way. I figured you'd need me tonight."

"You're not bloody kidding." He hit the intercom button. "Mel, bring us in two coff—" As he spoke, Mel walked through the door with a tray of coffee and biscuits. She placed them down on the desk and began to walk out again. "Thanks, Mel." He added milk and handed one cup to Liz, who sat down.

"How are the kids?"

"Fine, I hope. I need to call Trish. I've not really had time for anything in the last few hours, it's been mental."

"I was speaking to her earlier; she was just about to

go into surgery, so you won't be able to call her for a while anyway."

Andy felt a pang of guilt. He always made a point of phoning his wife before she was going to carry out a major op. "Damn, they did tell me; I forgot to call her."

"I think she'll understand, Andy. And how are you, more importantly?"

"Fit as a fiddle, why do you ask?"

"Funny man. I mean how *are* you?"

"God, Liz, what can I tell you? The world is falling apart around my ears. I've got life-and-death decisions to make every minute, and I can't even remember the last time I slept."

"I saw the broadcast; you were brilliant."

"I didn't feel brilliant."

"How long have we all been friends? Twenty years? I know you. If there is anyone who can get us through this crisis, it's you." She smiled warmly.

"I wish I had your confidence; I really do. It feels like I'm standing on the edge of a cliff that's crumbling beneath my feet."

"I'm sure you do. So, down to business. You wanted to see me?"

"God, yes. I'm going to need you here for some time. Do you think you can set up somewhere if Mel can find you a space?"

"I'm your CMO. I am at your disposal. Just give me a phone line and I'm sorted."

"You're a godsend. I've got to go back down to the Cabinet Office briefing room in a while. I want you to come with me. Obviously, you're going to have to sign some shit that says if you breathe a word of anything you see, you're going to the Tower of London for the rest of your life, but we've got some troops on the ground attempting an extraction. They're in a zone that is crawling with—"

"Zombies?"

"We're really trying not to use that word around

here. How about 'reanimated corpses'?"

"Okay," she said with a shrug.

"I want you to see these things. We're getting a lot of footage. I've already told Doug that I want you there. He's putting everything in place."

"Well, I'm happy to accompany you of course, but I've already seen them. The floodgates opened when your guys started making deals a few hours ago. We've had lab footage and lab work coming in all the time from what's left of the WHO research centres. France, Switzerland, the US, Australia, lots of places have been sharing what they've seen, what they've found. We're collating all the data. Everything from incubation times to pupillary response to light. We're having blood and tissue samples flown across too, but I may need your signature to authorise the release of those."

"Wow," he replied, "I thought all that stuff was going to take some coercing, I'm glad to see our guys are doing their job. Of course, I'll sign whatever you need. I'll also want projections. How will this thing spread? What's the worst-case, best-case scenario, etc.? How soon do you think you could work that stuff up for me?"

"It's already done."

"What?"

"Well," began Liz, "I can't say we ever planned for a zombie apocalypse—"

Andy brushed both of his hands up over his face. "God, I really wish people would stop using that word."

Liz just shook her head, mildly irritated at being interrupted. "Anyway, we have projections for many scenarios covering wide-ranging rates of infection. After speaking to counterparts in other countries, and going from the information we have to date pertaining to infection and mortality rates, I was able to adapt a model for a scenario that is the closest fit to this virus." She stopped and pulled out a laptop from her shoulder bag.

"Let me guess, it's good news?" Liz just gave him a look, similar to the ones his wife gave him when she was pissed off by one of his comments.

The computer screen came to life, and Liz began to scroll through a folder of documents until she came to a PowerPoint one entitled, "Doomsday." "This was the situation as of this morning," she said, hitting the touchpad. A map of the world showed on the screen. It was littered with an uncountable number of red and black dots.

"Holy shit! It's been just over a day since the first reports came in for Christ's sake. How can this be?"

"Hey, I'm just the piano player, I'm not writing the songs."

"What do the different colours signify?"

"Red dots signify a location where the outbreak has occurred. The black dots signify that we have lost touch with a location where the outbreak has occurred."

Andy took a drink of coffee. "Err ... we're in touch with every location where an outbreak has been reported?"

"When I say we, I mean the scientific community. We have been sharing data. Terabytes and terabytes of data," Liz said, pressing the touchpad again. Another map appeared with thousands more dots of both colours.

"Holy shit!" he said as she pushed the touchpad again. More dots came up, but a lot of them were black. She kept hitting the touchpad; each time, the scenario just got worse. "Okay, what are the chances of us finding a way to fight it?"

"Too soon to say. The problem is the speed of the spread of this thing. We've actually lost contact with some of our colleagues in other countries already. A lot of these guys were in bunkers. I mean that's scary, Andy," she said, folding the laptop closed. "This has all happened so quickly, and it's been so widespread. You understand there is more at work here than just the natural progression of a virus spreading. There is an unknown quantity, something that we're not privy to right now."

Andy's brow furrowed. "I don't understand, like what?"

"Well, if I knew that, it wouldn't be unknown, would it?"

"I mean what kind of unknown quantity?"

"I don't know, but in all my years, I have never seen or read about anything like this. The rate of infection, it's not natural."

"So, you're saying it's supernatural?" he replied with a smirk.

"I'm not saying anything, other than, medically, this shouldn't be possible."

"Well, that's useful," he replied, putting his mug down. He looked across at her. "I suppose there's a model in case this thing hits us or Ireland?"

"You don't want to see it," she said. "But we have already got a plan in place of how to deal with it if it hits. I've had preliminary discussions with the health secretary and he's quite keen that my department gets involved directly with the planning and logistics when it hits."

"If it hits," Andy replied indignantly. "This country is in lockdown," he added.

"Always the control freak." She opened the laptop back up and displayed the map again. "Look at this, Andy, look at the spread. It will be a miracle if we don't already have infected people in the country. I'm waiting to get a call any second. Yes, I saw your speech, but even you can't control this. It will hit, it's just a case of when."

# 7

Andy slumped down into his chair. "Listen," Liz said. "This is just breaking, but we're in a better position than anyone else. We're getting more data through, and we already have a plan in place for how we can attempt to minimise the risk of the spread. I'm assuming your speech, the bit about conscription, was discussing broad brushstrokes? You don't know specifically what people will be doing, what they'll be making, you just anticipated a need, yes?"

"We know specific areas that will require a huge influx of manpower to keep the country running, but the specifics are open to negotiation," he replied.

"Good. I could really do with a meeting with you, Zahid, and the people you talk to who make ideas come to life around here," she said closing, the laptop again.

"Regarding what happens if it hits?"

"Yes. I genuinely believe we can control it. I'm not just saying that to make you feel better, and the plans are quite radical."

"I need more info so I know who to have there."

"I'll get my guys to email the draft proposal across. It was still being worked on when I left the office." She took her mobile phone out of her bag.

The intercom beeped. "Prime Minister, it's time, sir," Mel said.

"Okay," he replied, getting up from his chair. As he and Liz walked through the outer office he turned to Mel. "Tell Doug to meet us down there, will you?"

Doug was already waiting when the two of them arrived at the door of the Cabinet Office briefing room. He summoned an officious looking woman in a grey business suit who presented Liz with a document and a pen.

"What's this?" Liz asked.

The woman was about to say something, but Doug jumped in. "Don't worry; it just says if you discuss anything of what you are about to see in this room with anyone other than authorised personnel, you're going to go to prison for the rest of your life—just standard boilerplate. Nothing to worry about," he said with the beginning of a smile on his face.

Liz took the pen, pausing with the nib over the dotted line. She finally signed and handed the pen and document back to the woman, who disappeared down the long corridor as quickly as she had arrived. Doug swung the door to the Cabinet Office briefing room open and ushered Liz inside. She took a few steps and then stopped before Andy caught up. He looked across at her as her mouth dropped open a little. "Impressive, isn't it?" he said. She didn't reply, just nodded.

Liz recognised some of the faces around the long, thick, dark wooden table. There was a general as well as the chief of defence staff, the secretary of state for defence, and a few others who she was not familiar with, but all were buried in documents or with their eyes staring at laptop screens. There were various camera feeds on the large screen that took up a good portion of the wall at the opposite end of the room to the entrance.

"The reason I wanted you here is so you can see these things up close, so you can understand exactly what you're dealing with," Andy said.

"I know what I'm dealing with. I've got hours of lab footage still to go through," she replied.

"To see a lab rat and a wild rat are two different things."

"Okay, but I think this is a waste of my time."

Doug came up behind the pair of them. He looked at his watch. "The second team will be arriving any minute. You should take your seats."

Within a moment of sitting down, the lights in the room dimmed, and more images appeared on screen. At the end of the table sat a uniformed soldier wearing headphones. He had a robust-looking laptop in front of him. He clicked on the mouse, and the large screen was suddenly taken up by one single infrared image. Paris by air, but unlike any shot seen on TV or film. Not a single streetlight, not a single house light glowed. The green-tinged screen showed a dying city. One of the most romantic, vibrant places on Earth had been reduced to a giant cemetery. Only the dead weren't in graves, they were tearing through the streets, making the gutters run red with the blood of two million Parisians. The camera image tilted as the helicopter changed direction.

"Is this the Apache or the second Chinook?" Andy asked.

Taylor answered, "This is the Apache, sir. It's going in to clear the way for the Chinook to land."

The whirring movement of the camera slowed as the Apache descended. Liz saw what she thought looked like the grand frontage of the Élysée Palace before the camera shot up again finally coming to a hover twenty feet above the ground. Yes, that was the courtyard of the Élysée Palace. "Who are all those people running towards the helicopter?" she asked.

"Calling them people might be a tad of a stretch,"

Doug replied. "The PM doesn't seem to like the Z word, so let's call them the respiratorily challenged," he said with a self-satisfied smirk.

Andy glared at him, shook his head disapprovingly and mouthed the word, "Twat!" which made Doug break out into a wide grin.

Suddenly the screen lit up in hundreds of flashes as a heavy machine gun began to fire at the advancing army of undead. Explosions of black erupted as creature after creature was mowed down. Some were cut in two, some lost limbs, but all continued towards the helicopter unless a headshot brought them down. After a few seconds, there was nothing left standing in the courtyard, and the camera panned up again as the Apache rose once more into the Paris night.

The screen went black before splitting into three images. Taylor stood up. "Archer!" he said.

"Go ahead," Seb replied.

"The second Chinook is about to land. Do you have any idea how many hostiles are outside the panic room and in the corridor?"

"We've been monitoring the cameras. We estimate around twenty. The majority are directly outside this door, but we've seen a couple milling about the landing area."

Doug's phone buzzed. He looked at it and got up from the table.

The large screen changed again, this time splitting into twelve images. The courtyard of the Élysée Palace was littered with dismembered bodies, but several of them were still moving, shuffling and dragging towards the Special Forces troops that jumped out of the Chinook. Even though they had been shown footage from the attempted rescue earlier, there was still a momentary pause as each soldier processed what they were seeing. Outstretched arms reached towards the soldiers as the creatures' vicious single-mindedness drove them despite their severed legs and damaged bodies. The pause finally ended, and shots began to ring out, putting the ghoulish beasts down for their final sleep. When there was no further sign of movement on the ground, two of the troopers remained with the helicopter, and the other ten ran towards the palace. Three more beasts stormed from the entrance and were quickly put down with headshot overkill.

"Oh my God, they're so quick," Liz said, breaking the tense silence in the room. Taylor shot a glance towards her. He wasn't happy she was in the room, but the PM made the decisions, and there was not much he could do about it.

*

The squad began to ascend the two staircases, five soldiers on each one, all the time scanning the landing and the grand foyer below. They reached the first floor at the same time. The intelligence they had gleaned from Archer suggested there were only a small number of the enemy in the hallway. The sensible option would be to try to take them out quietly then deal with the throng of the creatures outside the panic room. Each of the soldiers withdrew their knives as their feet touched the polished wooden floor. Almost immediately, two beasts from each end of the corridor began to blur towards them.

*

The tension in the room was palpable, and it wasn't just Liz who took a sharp intake of breath as the first monster attacked. The soldier went down as the force and ferocity of the attack took him by surprise. The camera image jerked on screen as the helmet-cam crashed onto the floor, but then the terrifying reality played out in detail as the technician at the end of the table clicked the mouse and the twelve separate camera images on screen became one.

The beast snapped its teeth like a rabid, trapped animal as the soldier did everything he could to keep it away from him. With each lunge, its head got closer. The general signalled to the technician, and suddenly a hellish cacophony filled the room until the volume was lowered and helmet mic was isolated. All the soldiers were battle-hardened warriors. They had seen combat many times, but everyone in the room heard the stifled cry of a frightened boy as the creature's eyes, black holes of horror in this already dark hallway, stared through the camera lens and shredded the very fabric of his soul.

A tear ran down Liz's cheek—fear, sadness, helplessness all contributing factors. Andy sensed it and reached across to touch her forearm reassuringly.

The fevered growl, more reminiscent of a ferocious guard dog than a human, thundered through the speakers before the beast bared its teeth once more and lunged towards the soldier's neck. Suddenly, there was a whir of action, and a boot smashed into the side of the creature's head, causing it to topple. The downed soldier rolled onto his side in time to see one of his comrades leap on top of the rabid monster and plunge his dagger through its eye socket, immediately rendering it still.

The technician clicked the mouse and the large screen separated into twelve separate feeds once more. Cameras angled up and down the hallway. There were bodies strewn everywhere but no threats. The team began to move towards the bone-chilling sounds once more. Two cameras kept angling back every few seconds to check there was no danger of attack from behind. There were bodies piled in the entrance of the doorway to the library, providing a partial knee-high barricade. All the creatures within were battering against the bookcases where their prey had disappeared. All the cameras were trained on the sergeant who held his hand up. The technician clicked the mouse, and suddenly heavy breathing could be heard through the large speakers in the room. "Alright lads," whispered the voice. "Remember your training. It's an enemy just like any other." There was a pause, and the ten men formed a semicircle in the wide hallway, around the library entrance. "Fire!" he shouted.

In that split second, more than half the creatures inside the room turned, and the technician adjusted the volume as the gunfire began to boom. The soldiers at the edge of the semicircle didn't have the same line of sight so aimed their weapons towards the door should any of the twenty-two creatures break through. Explosions of blood as black as oil spread over priceless leather-bound editions of some of the rarest books in the world. Pages flew from the shelves as bindings disintegrated in a hail of bullets.

*

"So much history," Dupont cried as he watched the scene on his CCTV monitors in the panic room.

"Motherfucker," the medic said under his breath. "Good men died for this prick, and all he gives a damn about are his fucking books."

"Keep it together," Mya replied, putting a hand on his shoulder, "it's nearly over." She could see the hate in his eyes as he looked towards the French premier. "Hey … hey!" she said, snapping her fingers in front of him. As if coming out of a trance, he looked towards her. "What's your name?"

"McKee," he replied.

"Well, McKee, if anything happens to him, they died in vain. Remember that. We don't choose our missions; we do what we get told. We don't always see the wisdom in what we get asked to do, but there's a bigger picture here, okay?"

The hate turned to acceptance, and he nodded as he turned his head away from the president and the screens.

"Okay," Seb said. He put the night-vision goggles back on but lifted the lenses and flipped out a powerful LED torch. McKee and Mya did the same. "When this door opens, our only aim is to board the Chinook as quickly as possible. He looked towards the president, the first lady and the nanny. "Keep the children moving and together, we don't know if we're going to come across any more problems." They nodded. The five French adults all put rucksacks on their backs. The president and first lady looked like they had never seen a rucksack before, let alone used one, and a small smirk appeared on Seb's face. The gunfire finally came to an end, and Seb touched his mic. "This is Archer, we're about to exit the panic room. We've switched to torches."

The twelve camera feeds suddenly switched to fifteen, and the green-tinged view on each of them was replaced with a more natural look as the powerful white torches lit the library and then the hallway as the group sped through the building and into the courtyard.

The tension had dissipated the moment the white lights were turned on. It was just a trick of the mind, as the situation was no less dangerous and an attack could still come from anywhere at any second. Eighteen living souls emerged into the courtyard as the first Chinook touched down at the side of the second. The Apache was still hovering above as the soldiers and the first family made their escape to the helicopters.

Seb and Mya brought up the rear, but Seb suddenly slowed and reached across to tap Mya on the arm, signalling for her to do the same. They both touched their earpieces and deactivated the cameras and mics.

"This is command," announced the female voice.

"Go ahead, command," Seb replied.

"Congratulations, the first part of your assignment is complete," said the voice as the first family and their entourage boarded one of the Chinooks.

"First part?" Mya asked.

"You didn't think we'd send two of our best agents on a simple rescue mission, did you?"

"Simple?" Mya replied.

"I think there's an echo on the line," said the voice.

"I keep hearing my words being thrown back at me."

"Go ahead, command," Seb said, becoming a little irritated.

"There's an air-gapped laptop back in the library. We need the hard drive," said the voice. "The Apache is going to get you out of there once you've completed your mission. Then we want you back at HQ asap. I'm sending details via an encrypted message now." The line went dead.

Mya looked towards Seb as the two Chinooks lifted off. "Remember I told you about the three months I spent undercover working in that flower shop in Chelsea?" she said. Seb nodded. "It was summer, and every morning I'd have to get up really early and head down to the flower market. The colours, the smells, they always brought a smile to my face. Those three months were the happiest I've ever been. I resigned shortly after that."

"What?"

"Yeah," she said. "I handed in my resignation letter, but they told me it was essential I stayed on for the next mission. It was a matter critical to national security."

"When isn't it?"

"Exactly," she replied. "I wanted that life so badly, but one mission became two and three and now look. My life's over, and my happiest memory is three months of impersonating a florist."

"What made you bring that up? Why are you talking like this?"

"Well, if today isn't one for reflection, I don't know when is."

Seb took hold of Mya's hand and looked at her in the glow of the torches they'd angled downwards to avoid glare. They had known each other for eight years and built up as close a friendship as one could in the world of secrets that they both inhabited. "I … I…" he stuttered, "I'm sorry, I didn't know you wanted out."

Their faces were just a few inches apart. "It's not your fault," she replied.

"Some of it is," he said. "I always used to ask for you when I needed a partner."

Rather than being angry, her lips turned up into the beginning of a smile, but just as quickly, she straightened them again so any observer could simply put it down to being a figment of their imagination. "Oh," she said. "I see. That's flattering. Suppose it's just as well. I had a shitty childhood, I never fitted in, the army and this is the only thing I've ever known. As much as I wanted a normal and happy life, I guess some people just aren't meant to be…"

"Aren't meant to be what?"

"Happy."

\*

"That text I took was from Xander, Prime Minister," Doug said. "He wants a quick meeting to update you."

Andy stood up. "Okay gentlemen, thank you very much," he said, nodding towards those assembled around the table. "We've got another COBRA meeting in about half an hour, Liz here will be briefing us on what the scientific community knows and proposes. For those of you this doesn't involve, thank you. The rest of you, I'll see you in a short while." The room began to bustle as laptops were folded and documents were gathered.

"Where should I go?" Liz asked.

"Mel's got an office sorted for you," Doug replied.

"I could really use my IT guy down here."

"This is Downing Street," Doug replied. "We've got IT guys coming out of our arses, use one of them."

"There's a good reason they're coming out of your arses as you so beautifully put it," replied Liz. "I want my guy. He's the best."

"Oh for God's sake, just get him here," Andy said. "Doug, arrange the clearance." Doug nodded and Liz smiled. "I'll see you upstairs in a couple of minutes," he said to Liz. She sat there for a moment then realised it was her cue to leave. When she was out of the door, Andy summoned Taylor across.

"Yes, Prime Minister?"

"I'm sorry I've not had time to read the briefs you sent across to me before I came down. How have the other extractions been going?"

"Particularly well so far, sir. Dupont was the only one who couldn't get to a safe zone. There have been no casualties in any of the other operations as of yet."

"I will get around to reading your reports Alistair, please keep them coming."

"I understand, Prime Minister."

"Also, could you get the contact details of the families I need to speak to across to Mel?" he asked as he headed out of the room.

"Yes, Prime Minister. I'll get my office to email them across."

# 8

"Give me some good news, Xander," Andy said as he and Doug walked into the office.

"Err … it's been a record year for Scottish strawberry farmers," he replied, watching Andy walk around the desk and plant himself firmly in the prime minister's chair.

Doug closed the door behind him and took a seat next to the spin doctor.

"Funny fucker, aren't you?" Andy replied. "So, what's the skinny?"

"Oh my God, you didn't just say what's the skinny? I need to talk to Trish about letting you watch too much HBO," Doug said.

Xander took a deep breath. "Okay," he said, placing a pile of folders down on the desk in front of him. "The TV address was a real triumph. Your approval rating has never been higher."

"You polled? You polled at a time like this?" Andy asked.

"Of course I bloody polled. We were on the phones

the second it was over. Granted we couldn't get the sort of numbers we would like, but something's better than nothing. It's more important than ever to know that the people feel secure. The last thing we want is political instability. If people believe they are in safe hands, there will be less panic, less risk of individuals, towns, regions deciding that they're better off fending for themselves," Xander said calmly. "The feedback was very reassuring. Over eighty-four per cent said they believed you to be a strong leader. Eighty-nine per cent believed it was a good move to put the country in lockdown. Forty-two per cent thought it would stop the infection reaching these shores, but here's the important one; seventy-one per cent of people believe you will be able to lead us through this disaster if the infection does reach Britain." Xander sat back and crossed his legs.

"Bloody hell!" Doug said. "Those figures are fantastic."

"I really need to see Trish and the kids," Andy said, his mind drifting momentarily.

"Trish is on her way back. The surgery went fine. The kids are upstairs whenever you want to see them," Doug replied.

"So, what are the papers looking like? *Zombie flesh eaters take over the world? Whoops, Zombie Apocalypse?* What are they saying?" Andy asked.

"I had a word with the owners," Xander replied.

"Oh, dear God."

Xander stood up and leafed through the folders on the desk. He opened one and spread out proofs for the front pages of all the dailies:

- *Beck's 'Fight on the beaches' moment!*
- *A call to arms. Beck invests his faith in the British spirit!*
- *Today our war begins. Beck has our backs!*
- *Andy's our man. We will be great again!*
- *Panic on the streets of London? Not Downing Street! Andy's the man with the upbeat plan!*

"They love me. They really love me," Andy said, pretending to dab away tears.

"For the time being," Xander replied. "As we discussed, the internet has got very patchy again." A smile crept onto his face. "The main social media sites are inaccessible. It's virtually impossible to send an email if you're a private citizen. Messaging apps are struggling as well. Basically, if you're Joe Bloggs, you're stuffed. Mission-critical agencies have normal services, although we have increased monitoring significantly."

"God! It's so *1984*. I hope this never gets out. It's the kind of thing they do in North Korea," Andy said.

"If this gets out, it's the last thing anybody will be worried about. Stop thinking like a politician," Xander said. Andy looked towards Doug, and they both started laughing. "What? What's funny?" Both of them just shook their heads. "So, in a nutshell, we own the news cycle. I've made sure all the TV stations are on board too."

"I don't want to hear how you did it, but thank you."

Doug burst out laughing and clapped his hands. "Brilliant! You're a fucking genius, Xander, I love it!"

"You two are just evil. You have no morals or scruples when it comes to winning, do you?" Andy said, looking at them both.

"Scruples are for losers," Xander replied, placing the front pages back into the folder.

Andy turned to look at Doug who sat with a wide smile on his face, drumming his arched fingers against each other. "Excellent!" he said in his best Mr Burns voice.

"Is there anything else?" Andy asked.

"I got a message you wanted me in on the next COBRA meeting about the scientific and medical response measures. Was that a mistake? I don't usually get involved in that kind of stuff," Xander said.

"It's more important than ever that we have the right words to address the nation when things start happening, so I'd like you in on the ground floor with this. I'm going to see my kids for a few minutes then we'll meet up with Liz and head back down to the Cabinet Office briefing room.

*

Andy entered the residence and two young children came running towards him. They each flung their arms around his legs. "Daddy!" they cried in unison.

"How are my girls?" he asked, shuffling free and kneeling down to embrace them. The three of them squeezed each other, and Andy smelt apple shampoo in their freshly washed and dried hair. He looked up and noticed the nanny standing there, regarding the heartwarming scene with a smile on her face. "What have you been up to, eh?"

"We've been making some new clothes for our dollies," said the smallest one. "Danielle has been showing us how."

"New clothes? Wow! Let me see," he said, smiling.

The two children released him and, taking one hand each, led Andy into their bedroom. The floor was littered with cut up clothing, craft scissors, threads and bobbins of various sorts and colours. Danielle followed them into the room and looked a little sheepish when Andy saw the mess. "Don't worry," she said, "I'll tidy everything up when we're done. I know they should have been in bed a long time back, but they didn't want to go until they'd seen you and Mrs Beck."

The girls let go of his hand, and each retreated to their own space where they picked up brightly coloured pieces of rags masquerading as dolls clothes. "Wow! You made these yourselves? You guys are so, so talented." Each of the children beamed.

"Hello?" came the call from the hallway.

"Mummy!" both of the girls shouted, running out

to greet her.

Andy lingered in the bedroom for a moment. "Thank you, Danielle. You don't know what a weight it lifts from me and Trish knowing that you're here with our girls. Have you spoken to your parents today?"

"Yes," she replied. "Just after your broadcast. They're fine. As fine as anyone can be, that is."

"That's good," he said, heading out of the room.

"I'll get started on this mess," she said with a smile as Andy disappeared out of the door.

Trish had always been a prize on his arm. Stunning, twice as smart as him, funny. Doug and Xander rolled her in front of the cameras at every opportunity. Andy was popular, but her polling numbers were off the charts. If Andy ever needed bailing out, she's the one they'd turn to, and it always worked. He stepped into the hall and saw the two girls wrapping their arms around their mum the way they had around him. He stood there for a moment; it was the tonic he needed. This is what he did everything for—his girls. Trish raised her head from the children to him. Their eyes locked, and the happiest of smiles formed on both their faces. He went across to the three of them. "Girls, why don't you go give Danielle a hand tidying away? Your mum and I will be in in a minute."

"Okay Daddy," they said in unison before running to their room.

Andy moved in close to his wife and threw his arms around her. They embraced tightly and kissed. It was a desperate and much needed expression of intimacy that both had craved more as the day had gone on. "I love you," Trish said.

"I love you so much," Andy replied.

"I suppose date night is well and truly screwed?" she said, smiling.

Andy looked at his watch. "Jesus! It's nearly eleven already. I'd give anything to spend some time with you, but I'm expected back down in the briefing room, then I'll have to—" She put her finger up to his lips.

"Andy, it's okay. I'm not at work tomorrow. When you come to bed, wake me. I saw a re-run of the speech and I'm so proud of you," she said, smiling. His face dropped, and she angled it towards her. "What is it?" she asked.

"I don't feel like I'm doing anything that anyone should be proud of. Good men died tonight because of my orders. I'm effectively curbing freedom of the press and speech. God, I've even—" She kissed him again.

"Did you do any of this for your own personal or political benefit?"

"No, of course not."

"Did you do it because it would help the people of Britain?"

"Yes."

"Then I'm proud of you, end of story. Now, get back to work," she said as someone knocked at the door.

Doug popped his head around the corner. "Hi, Trish."

Andy raised his left eyebrow. Although Doug, Xander and many of Andy's work colleagues had been to the residence a number of times, there was a strict rule in place that no business was to be discussed or carried out there. "What is it, Doug?"

Doug handed him a folder. "I've delayed the meeting. I thought you might want to make these calls from up here, with Trish," he said.

"The calls! Oh God! I'd forgotten about the bloody calls. Thanks, Doug. Yes. Yes, I would. Thank you." Doug nodded and retreated back out of the door. No flippant remarks, he knew how much this would pain his friend. Andy turned to Trish. "We lost seven men in an operation. I need to call their families. Will you sit with me?"

She kissed him gently on the mouth, pulled back and brushed her palm down the side of his face. "Of course I will."

9

"Okay, do we get any more clues? Or do we have to tear this place apart?" Seb asked, stepping over the dead creatures carpeting the library floor as he held the cellphone in front of him.

There was a pause then the same stern female voice from before answered. "The shelving units. There's one on the east wall that has a hollow back. It's in there." The line went dead.

Seb and Mya turned to the east wall. The giant room was covered from floor to ceiling in shelving. They angled their torches down and looked towards each other. "Any preferences?" Mya asked. Seb just shrugged. "Okay. I'll start bottom left, you start bottom right, we'll meet in the middle, then go up to the next shelf."

"Sounds like a plan," he said, and the pair got to work.

Bottom row, nothing. Second row, nothing. Third row, nothing. Fourth Row. "Here," Mya said. Seb shuffled over to where she crouched. They threw some of the priceless first editions onto the library floor in their eagerness to reach the hollow panel. They each pushed, pressed and picked at the back of the bookcase to no avail.

"Screw this," Seb said, knocking on the backboard in three places before punching straight through it. Mya grimaced as she could almost feel the wood break against Seb's knuckles.

"That's one way to get a job done," she said, shaking her head.

"What's wrong? Did you want me to do a bloody risk assessment first?"

"Ooh, we'll make a bureaucrat out of you yet." She smiled. "Yes, talk to me about risk assessments and asset risk against projected gains ratios. You know how that turns me on," Mya said, grinning.

"Funny," Seb replied, pulling the sturdy Toughbook style laptop from its hiding place. He dusted off some of the broken bits of wood and looked at it long and hard, turning it over and over. "There's no way I'm getting the hard drive out of this. This is a custom job. The unit's completely sealed. If I try to force it, we could lose everything." He opened it and stopped suddenly. "Holy shit!"

"What is it?" Mya asked.

"The keyboard, it's Russian."

"What?"

"This whole day just keeps getting weirder and weirder."

He slid the laptop in his rucksack and retrieved the mobile phone from his pocket, quickly typing in the unlock code before delivering the message - *Acquired.*

"The world has fallen apart around our ears. There are no governments, there are barely any countries anymore, yet we get sent back into hostile territory for a hard drive. You've got to wonder what the hell is on there."

The pair stood. They angled their torches down to minimise the glare. Their faces were just a few inches apart. "Sometimes, I think it's better that we don't know."

"You're not a little bit curious?"

"Not really. The only thing I am curious about is why you handed your notice in and never told me."

"It's personal."

"I thought we were friends."

"There's some stuff that's off-limits."

"Like what?"

"Like maybe I wanted a relationship, a normal life. Maybe I wanted to fall in love, none of which I could ever think about doing in this bloody job. Maybe if I left, I could have had those things, I could have opened my little florist shop and started a new life, maybe I could have met someone and fallen in love. Jesus Christ, Seb, I'm thirty-six, and I haven't had sex in close to a year. Do you know how depressing that is? All I wanted was a little bit of something to call my own, something for me, about me, and not just this job," she said, holding back her tears as well as she could.

"This is the job we signed up for, Mya."

"This is why I didn't tell you. You wouldn't understand."

"This probably isn't the time or the place. Let's get out of here, we can talk about this later."

"No. I don't ever want to talk about it with you."

"Fine." The pair retraced their steps out of the library and down the left-hand staircase before Seb grabbed his mobile. *Apache on the way*, read the text. The two of them slowed as they reached the entrance and brought their weapons up. There was a sound, the powerful droning of an engine, then suddenly a huge crash and the impenetrable gates adorning the palace were penetrated by a speeding snowplough. Behind it came a stream of other vehicles and panicked Parisiennes desperately looking for safety and an armed guard.

"Oh shit!" Mya cried.

*

Andy put the phone down and sat for a moment. A lump formed in his throat as the baying of the final widow still echoed in his ears. "I'm so proud of you," Trish said, taking his hand and leaning across to kiss him.

"Proud of me for getting brave men killed for a coward who deserts his own people?"

"No! Proud of you for doing what's best for your country." She let go of his hand and stood up. "None of these decisions will be easy, darling, but there is nobody who is better qualified to make them. There are going to be a lot more tragedies, the world is in meltdown. But if you save more than you lose, then that's a victory. If you make a decision, knowing it's the best you can do for the majority, then no one can ask more of you."

"I don't deserve you, y'know that?" he said, standing and taking her in his arms.

"Course I bloody know that; everybody does. I'm way out of your league. You're just lucky I was drunk when you proposed and I'm a girl who keeps her word," she said, and that magic happened, as it had done every day since they'd been together. She smiled that smile of hers and his heart began to race, while his mouth dropped open, just a little.

She still had the most incredible effect on him even after all those years. "I love you," he said. "I love you so much."

She kissed him long and hard on the lips. "I love you too. No decision you make in that office will ever change that. I know who you are inside."

There was a knock on the door and the mood shattered into a thousand shards around their feet. It was back to reality. Doug popped his head around. "I'm sorry," he said, realising he had interrupted a tender moment, "but everybody's waiting."

Andy let out a sad sigh. "Okay, Doug, thanks." Doug nodded and pulled the door closed.

"Remember, I'll be up no matter what time you come to bed," she said and kissed him on the cheek.

He kissed her back and started heading towards the door but then stopped. "I…" He paused for a moment.

"What is it?"

"You're one of the most noted medical professionals in the country. You're also the person I trust more than anyone. Come with me."

"To the briefing?" The shock was evident in her voice.

"This is going to be all about the scientific and healthcare response to this disaster. I can't think of anyone better."

"You've got Liz, she's second to none. I trust her implicitly."

"I know she is, and I do trust her, but I trust no one like you, and I'm way out of my depth with this kind of thing."

"But you've got numerous advisors, you've got Doug, you've got Zahid, you've got—"

"Doug's like me. He's a politician, he's not a scientist. Please."

"I'm just going to sit and listen?"

"That's all I want." His demeanour became immediately more relaxed. "I just want you there to listen."

"Looks like I can forget my hot bath and glass of wine, doesn't it?"

"I'll make it up to you."

"Oh, I know you will. You don't get me for free, wife or not," she said, smiling.

\*

Mya and Seb leapt back up the stairs three at a time. "I don't think anyone spotted us," Mya said.

Seb didn't answer, he was tapping frantically on the screen of his phone. "Courtyard compromised." The phone immediately lit up, and he put it to his ear.

"By what?" came the same curt female voice.

"Civilians. They've broken through the gates. Dozens … hundreds."

There was a groan on the other end of the line, the first time Seb had ever heard the woman distressed. "Where are you now?"

"Back on the first floor."

"Get downstairs, head to the kitchen. We're sending you a plan." No sooner had she spoken than an image appeared on the screen. "There's a disused dumb waiter. The shaft leads down to a secret tunnel system that has been there for hundreds of years but was used a lot during World War Two. Get to the tunnels and then await further instructions." The call ended, and Seb looked at the phone.

The voices outside were getting louder as a large group stormed towards the entrance. "C'mon, we need to hurry," Seb ordered as the pair of them ran back down the staircase and along the hallway, turning their torches off and reverting back to night vision as they ducked down the dark corridor to the kitchen. Eventually, they saw the double swing doors, and the two of them slowed. Ahead was the unknown; behind them was a frightened crowd, and they both knew only too well how fear changed people.

They eased the large doors open, ducked inside, and raised their weapons, ready for the onslaught. They stood there in anticipation but for nothing. The vast kitchen was silent. They moved along the various food preparation islands waiting to be set upon by some creature from their nightmares, but with each step they relaxed a little more. Seb tapped Mya on the arm and signalled that they needed to head to the right. There at the end of the aisle was a hatch in the wall. Seb lifted the door revealing the wooden box that would have transported a thousand meals to the upper floors in days gone by. He tapped on the wooden floor to gauge the thickness. It had remained unpainted and the slats looked worn and weak. He pressed down, and he felt the wood give a little. Mya brought a stool over from beneath one of the counters and climbed on it, grabbing Seb's shoulder to keep her balance. She placed her boot down, increasing the pressure until the wooden slats split then broke. It sounded loud in the confines of the shaft, but the noise wouldn't penetrate the heavy kitchen doors.

Mya climbed back down, and Seb got to work levering the remaining slats away. He angled up the night-vision goggles and turned on the torch once more as he put his head into the dumb waiter. "It's only about twelve feet," he whispered.

Doors were opening and slamming shut as the horde began to search the palace for an army of protectors who only existed in their hopes. Then came the sound Seb had been expecting, screams from people being attacked. He had little doubt that when the gates crashed to the ground, the creatures would be alerted far and wide. That's if they weren't already in hot pursuit of the frightened crowd.

Mya lifted her night-vision goggles and turned on her head torch too before shouldering her rifle and climbing into the shaft. She turned, grabbing a tight hold of the edge, and lowered herself as far as she could go before dropping the remaining few feet to the earth. "C'mon," she called urgently.

"Do you think you can take my weight? I'm going to have to slide this hatch door back down. We don't want anyone following us."

"Course I can; just hurry."

Seb climbed into the narrow shaft and turned back around, lowering himself until he felt Mya take hold of his feet and place them on her shoulders. When he was happy he had a firm footing, he reached up to push and release the hatch door before slowly sliding it down. "Okay," he said and pushed against the two sides of the shaft supporting himself until she was out of the way. When his path was clear, he shuffled down then dropped the last few feet into the tunnel. There was just enough room for the two of them to walk side by side, and after a few metres, they reached a stone staircase leading even further down below the Paris streets. They both looked back in the direction they had come from. "I don't suppose we have much of a choice," Mya said as she turned back towards the stairs.

# 10

Doug had received a text and already organised the clearance necessary for Trish to be a part of this special COBRA meeting, so he was the only one who wasn't surprised when Andy and his wife walked into Cabinet Office briefing room A together.

The rest of the assembly had been waiting for some time. Small talk wasn't on the menu considering the gravity of the events that were unfolding, but the attendees all conversed nonetheless. From the health secretary to the chancellor, to the cabinet secretary and the chief of defence staff to the press secretary and a host of special advisors, there were familiar and unfamiliar faces alike.

"Good evening, ladies and gentlemen, sorry to have kept you, but as you can imagine, things are a little extraordinary at the moment. I hope everybody has been introduced. As I'm sure you'll be aware by now, we are one of the last holdouts to this infection. Statistically, the odds of us remaining that way are slim, but I intend to do everything I can to keep this from ever reaching us." He paused and looked around the faces at the table. He could see none of them shared his belief, and a nervous smile crept onto his face. "Thankfully, despite what some of the press would have you believe, I'm not arrogant enough to have no contingency plans in place." He paused again and this time was greeted with polite laughter. "I'm going to hand the floor over to our chief medical officer, Elizabeth Holt." He nodded and sat down while all the eyes in the room turned to Liz.

She hadn't felt nervous or self-conscious in many years, but suddenly, with the eyes of cabinet ministers and senior military figures upon her, her throat felt dry and she reached for a glass of water. She took a sip and stood up. "Thank you, Prime Minister," she said, looking towards him and then towards her friend, Trish. She picked up a remote control and hit a button. On the large screen that earlier had shown the daring rescue of the French president, a title appeared, white on a black background, "The Reanimation Virus."

Liz pulled out her chair and began walking around the table. "What do we know so far?" she asked, clicking another button and changing the screen again. She walked up to the huge LED monitor and looked at it. "The virus has an unnaturally short incubation period. In fact, one could argue it doesn't incubate at all, it just spreads from one host to another like in a game of tag. You get bitten, you die, mere seconds pass and you reanimate. Nothing in history has spread this fast. Theoretically, nothing in nature should be able to spread this fast, which begs the question, where the hell did it come from?"

"What are your instincts telling you?" Taylor asked.

"I'm a scientist, I prefer to rely on data, but we haven't ruled anything out," Liz replied. "So," she said, looking towards the screen once more, "it spreads like wildfire, literally, and, from all the information we have received so far, has a one hundred per cent infection rate." She hit another button and 100 per cent came up on the screen for effect. She looked around the large table and usually unflappable people were loosening their shirt collars.

"Oh God!" Trish whispered, taking a tight hold of Andy's hand under the table.

"When the reanimates attack, they invariably aim for the throat, head or any exposed piece of flesh of their victims, but failing that, they will latch onto anywhere they can. Many of the bites inflicted are significant enough to cause the victim to pass in a matter of seconds, but even if that doesn't happen, every bite spreads the virus." She paused and took a drink of water, suddenly looking a little shaky, as if for the first time the gravity of what was happening had dawned on her.

"Are you okay, Liz?" Andy asked, looking a little concerned.

She nodded, took another sip, and then continued. "So, what does this virus do? Well, it kills, that's for certain, but then it reanimates. The body comes back to life, but not the person who was there before. Some of our colleagues in other countries have managed to capture and study a few specimens. There is no cognitive function as we understand it. There is merely a thirst to feed on the living. All those who turn show heightened states of aggression. They seem to possess the same if not an enhanced level of strength, and they seem less inclined to tire after prolonged bouts of activity. Now, obviously, all these are preliminary findings as the studies are still in their early stages, but ultimately we can deduce that we are dealing with something more virulent and deadly than we have ever dealt with before."

Xander was frantically taking notes; as press secretary, he'd have to figure out a way to put a manageable spin on this. "What are the chances of developing a vaccine?" he asked.

"A vaccine to stop a virus that turns people into relentless undead cannibals who rip out the jugular veins of the living with their teeth? Err … not great," she replied. Liz looked towards the defence secretary and the chief of defence staff. "So far, the only way we've established these beings can be put down is by severe brain trauma. A shot to the head, a stab in the head, or a violent blow to the head and they die, permanently I mean. The best intel we're getting at the moment is from a scientific team in the French Alps. They've got a number of specimens, including three people who sustained scratches from the reanimates."

"What symptoms are they showing?" Trish asked. She finally released Andy's hand and suddenly felt self-conscious as everyone turned towards her.

"Two out of the three are experiencing numbness, pins and needles and irritation around the scratch, but nothing more serious than that at present. The other, an older man who sustained a deeper wound, is suffering all those symptoms, plus a high fever, and he is dropping in and out of consciousness." Almost as if anticipating what Trish's next question would be, Liz carried on. "All three wounds were sustained within the last twenty-four hours. The scientists have been working closely with the military to attain as many examination subjects as possible. They have upwards of twenty reanimates under observation, in addition to the three scratch victims." She paused as her phone vibrated and lit up on the table. "Excuse me," she said, "this could be relevant." She picked up the phone and read the email. "Yes, it seems the elderly scratch victim has lost consciousness. We'll wait and see, but this could prove that a mere scratch from one of these things could be fatal. Of course, it could be that this older gentleman was just not able to fight off the infection, but hopefully, we will gather a wider sample base soon and be able to ascertain what it actually means to be scratched by a reanimate." Liz took another drink of water and placed her phone back down on the table.

"This is unprecedented," Trish said. Her friend just gave her a sad glance. "What are the projections for the spread?" Liz looked towards Andy, who nodded before the same world maps that he'd seen earlier came flashing onto the huge screen. The tension and fear in the room intensified, and Trish reached out to grab Andy's hand once more. "Oh my God, Liz, are these calculations right?"

"Trish," she said, "we're losing contact with more and more sites every few minutes. This thing is out of control."

"Christ!"

Andy stood up and stretched. "Okay!" he said, and every head in the room turned towards him. "It's grim, I get it. It's the single biggest catastrophe the planet has ever faced. We've put historic measures in place today that will minimise the possibility of this thing reaching our shores, but if it does, *if* it does, what do we do?" he asked and fixed his gaze on Liz.

"Well, Prime Minister, it's simple," she replied, and Andy furrowed his brow as if he'd missed something. "We've already done it with the rest of the world. We've quarantined them. That's what we need to do with an outbreak if it occurs over here," she said, picking up the laptop remote control once again. A list of bullet points appeared on the screen. "Firstly, this can't be just a medical response. It needs to occur in conjunction with law enforcement, the military and all levels of government, local and national."

"And what does that entail exactly?" Doug asked.

"Well," Liz said, "that's the very crux of this meeting, isn't it? Myself and my colleagues have a number of suggestions as to how to minimise the spread of the contagion, but they are utterly dependent on your willingness to employ and endorse them as a government. I can only suggest. I am an advisor, that's all."

"Okay," Doug said, "you've self-deprecated enough, now what do you suggest?"

Liz's eye twitched a little, and she took a deep breath before she answered. "Well, Doug, if there's an outbreak, we need to quarantine the town or city in the same way we would quarantine an individual. To avoid the spread, we would stop them coming into contact with anyone else. Now, to do that effectively, it has to be executed on a couple of levels. The venue of the outbreak should be isolated; all road, rail and track links to and from the town or city should be blockaded by law enforcement and the military. There should be an immediate lockdown, and all hospital patients barring those in dire need of specialist care should be sent home. The ones in dire need should undergo checks for signs of infection before being transferred to field hospitals set up just outside the quarantine zone."

"Shutting hospitals? I don't understand. Why would we do that?" Doug asked.

"Because at times like these, people who see their child or their loved ones with the slightest runny nose become convinced it is something more. The hospitals get overrun and kaboom! One reanimate suddenly becomes one thousand reanimates rampaging through the city. In the last eighteen hours, we have seen that happening time and time again. So, we shut the hospitals. We mobilise hundreds of medical units with armed guards. If people need urgent attention, they get it in their home. But, to be honest, if there's a strict lockdown, there will be a notable downturn in potential admittances anyway. The amount of alcohol and drug-related hospital visits to A and E is staggering. You remove that potential from the equation and the idea of shutting the hospitals becomes less outlandish."

"Where do we get all these trained medics from?" Andy asked.

"You could bring an awful lot of them out of retirement with your conscription idea. There are thousands of qualified doctors and nurses who no longer practice; there are paramedics who have gone into other lines of work. There are thousands upon thousands of people who we could recruit to help make this work. And all the time, by keeping people in their homes, keeping the villages and towns isolated, we minimise the risk of the infection spreading."

"But this infection spreads so fast. A city could be infected in no time at all. The measures you're suggesting would only work if a handful of infected were put down before it could get out of hand," Andy said.

"That's why this needs to be a multi-departmental operation. We would propose that regional placement of military personnel is rolled out for rapid deployment if an outbreak occurs."

"You're suggesting we put the country under martial law?" Andy asked.

"I'm suggesting we do whatever it takes to survive and this gives us the best chance. In the last twenty-four hours, we have seen unprecedented societal and governmental breakdown in some of the most advanced countries in the world. Employing these measures isn't the be all and end all, Prime Minister. This is an initial response to a disaster that has already taken the rest of the planet in its clutches. As we find out more, we can enhance and adapt, but right now, this is what I believe we need to do to make sure we have the best possible chance of subduing an outbreak," Liz replied. The pressure was beginning to show on her face, and without even realising it, a tear had formed in the corner of her eye and begun to roll down her cheek.

There was a pause as the information was absorbed by all the attendees. Andy and Doug looked around the room, trying to gauge reactions, but for once, neither of the seasoned politicians could. Xander was still scribbling frantically on his pad. Then Andy looked towards Trish and saw tears were in her eyes too. He reached across to her, and she took his hand in both of hers, caressing it as if it would be her last chance to do so.

Andy's mother-in-law had shown him a photo of Trish once. She was a young child and the arm had finally torn loose from an antique teddy bear she had owned since the cot. She had the arm in one hand and the rest of the bear in the other. There was a look of sadness and disbelief on her face that such a tragedy could occur to something she had loved so much. That same look now consumed her. Andy leant across and kissed her. He had been on autopilot all day, drifting from one meeting to next, one conversation to another. He had the weight of the world on his shoulders, but then again not really. When people spoke in terms of *the country*, or *the people*, it was always abstract, but now, seeing his wife with that look on her face, and imagining it sixty-seven million times over on the face of every Brit, he knew he had to do what he was born to do. He had to lead.

"Thoughts anyone?" he asked, standing up and placing his hands on the table. He knew it was way too soon for anyone to have had any thoughts, so he capitalised on the silence. He looked towards his health secretary. "Zahid," he said, "conscription papers are being prepared as we speak. I want your department to liaise with Nadine and take charge of identifying any suitable conscripts with previous medical experience."

"So, we're going ahead with this? We're going ahead with the plan?" he replied.

"We're going ahead with *a* plan, subject to change, but right this second, we need to get the wheels in motion," Andy replied. He turned to look at Taylor and Ravenshaw. "We've got all the overseas troops to take into account too, but right now, I want you to draw up plans for the deployment of forces we have in situ to key geographical locations that would give us the fastest response times for all the major cities and towns within the UK. I'm sure similar things have been devised in the past, so dust them off and adapt them."

"I imagine most of those were drawn up when the British armed forces were far greater in number than they are today, Prime Minister," replied the defence secretary.

"Yeah, well. We do it to scale. Soon we're going to have hundreds of thousands of conscripts ready to take up arms too. A good plan today is better than a great plan tomorrow. Time is of the essence, let's get this done, okay?" he said, looking Ravenshaw and then Taylor in the eyes.

"Yes, Prime Minister," they said in unison.

Andy turned to the cabinet secretary. "Nadine," he

smiled, and she smiled back nervously, "I need you to make all this work. I need you and your people to liaise with these departments, with Liz, with anyone else who you think needs to be involved. You've been doing your job longer than anyone in the room has been doing theirs. I trust you to do what needs to be done."

The unflappable bureaucrat suddenly coloured bright red. Nobody had publicly praised her so openly, especially not in such a pivotal meeting. "Thank you, Prime Minister, of course, Prime Minister, I'll get right on it," she said before pulling out a mobile phone and starting to text frantically.

Andy looked at his watch. "Okay, it's one fifteen a.m. We'll meet back here at eight a.m. I'll want full updates from each department." He looked towards Doug, Xander, and Trish. The three of them stood and followed Andy out of the room.

"Have you figured out how we're going to play this with the press?" Andy asked, turning towards Xander as they walked down the corridor. Xander was tapping feverishly into his phone too.

"I'm getting my guys together now. We'll have a strategy in place if this hits us. We'll inspire confidence from the outset," Xander replied before splitting away from the other three down a bustling hallway.

"I'll never get over just how bloody big this building is," Doug said. "It's like the TARDIS. All you ever see on the news is that one black door with a ten on it."

"Can you keep an eye on things for me?" Andy asked.

"Always," replied Doug.

"We'll meet at seven in the office, make sure Xander's there too."

Doug nodded and disappeared. Andy and Trish walked into the outer office to find Mel was still at her desk. "You have messages, Prime Minister," she said, not waiting for him to get all the way through the door.

"Anything that can't wait a little while? I really need to shut my eyes."

She paused for a moment. "No, I'm sure they could all wait a little while," she replied.

"Good. You need to go home and get some rest. We've got another long day ahead of us tomorrow."

"I'll get a few hours on the couch," she replied.

"Nonsense!" Trish said. "If you insist on stopping here, you'll use the spare bedroom in the residence."

"Oh, I couldn't do—"

"Shush! You can, and you will. I'll get it made up for you. Won't take no for an answer," Trish said before disappearing back through the door.

When she knew she was out of earshot, Mel asked, "How did it go?"

"We've got a plan, Mel, but then again, there've probably been plans for every monumental catastrophe in history."

"It went well then?" she said with no hint of a smile.

# 11

"I hate tunnels at the best of times, but when God knows what could be lurking in the shadows, I really, really hate them," Mya said as they continued their journey below the streets of Paris.

Seb remained silent. He was squinting into the darkness, searching for any sign of movement. They reached what at first looked like a dead end, but then they saw a door. Seb pushed the panic bar, and it swung open. They stepped through, and it slammed shut behind them. The heavy clunk of the lock re-engaging bounced off the walls of the tunnel. There were a couple of high-pitched bleeps, which signalled the battery back-up on the alarm was still operational. The two of them carried on and came to a flight of stairs. The torches only allowed them to see so far in front, but the cold silence and stillness were all that attacked them for the time being.

"Careful, stairs," Seb said, as he looked down into the blackness.

"More bloody stairs? Shouldn't we switch to night vision?"

"Drains the battery faster."

"So we're going further underground? Isn't our aim to escape?"

He looked at his phone. "This probably isn't the best time to mention this, but when we walked through that door, I lost our signal."

"Course you did, but you know where we're going, right?"

"Sure. We're going down a flight of stairs, further underneath the city, with God knows what waiting for us at the bottom."

"You're a real prick!"

It was a steep staircase, and the rusted handrail felt like it would give way in places. Eventually, they reached the bottom, and there was another door. This one didn't have a panic bar but a heavy steel wheel in the centre. It took some effort, but Seb managed to turn it, and they heard multiple locks disengage. The door swung open, and the two of them walked through. They noticed infrared sensors on the floor and as they reached the other side, the door almost silently eased back into place. It was then that they saw from this side it didn't look like a door at all but was masked perfectly into the tunnel's dark brickwork. The seam was virtually undetectable.

"I'm guessing this was an upgrade," Seb said, examining it closely.

"Seriously? That's what you're thinking about right now?"

"Are you okay?"

"I just want to get out of here."

"Fair enough." They walked a few feet and then stepped through an archway. The tunnel widened, and suddenly it wasn't as silent any more. There were distant echoes, too distant to identify.

"What was that?" Mya asked.

"I dare say we're going to find out soon enough."

"That fucking hard drive better reveal the meaning

of life for it to be worth this shit."

"Mya! You're starting to worry me," Seb said, angling his torch down and looking towards her.

"Look, I'll be okay when we get out of here," she replied. "I'm not good in tunnels."

"You mentioned you didn't like them, but it's more than that, isn't it?"

"Listen, when we get out of here, we can talk about this for hours, but right now, I just want to get out of here."

"We're going to be fine."

"Don't patronise me, Seb. Let's just keep moving."

There was a dead end to the left of the arch, so the pair turned right and walked along without saying a word; the distant sound of trouble sang a funeral dirge that echoed beneath the city. Seb kept pulling his phone out to see if the signal bars appeared, but none did. They carried on walking, but then Seb reached out and squeezed Mya's arm. "Infrared," he whispered, and in perfect synchronicity, they turned off their head torches and lowered their goggles. Everything immediately took on the familiar green hue.

"What is it?"

"Trouble," Seb replied. They carried on walking; then the narrow tunnel opened up into a vast pitch-black cavern.

"Where are we?" whispered Mya.

"I think we've just reached the Paris Metro."

"The underground?"

"Yeah!"

"Fuck!"

"No. This is good."

"Good? Good how?"

"The Paris Metro has one of the largest accumulations of stations in the world. It shouldn't take us long to reach one; then we'll be able to get out, contact our people and organise an extraction."

"That simple? And what about all the fucking noises we're hearing? You think that sounds like a happy ending?"

"Mya, you need to calm down and remember your training."

"Oh yeah? Well, I don't remember any fucking zombies during my training. Maybe I fell asleep during that lesson."

"Hostiles are hostiles."

"Have I mentioned you're a prick?"

"Once or twice."

"Hey! Do you see what I see?" she said, raising her goggles once again. Seb raised his too.

They continued along the tunnel, which was now lit up with small ground-level lights. It was not stadium lighting, but it was bright enough for them to walk and see what they were doing. There was a door on the left-hand side. Seb pushed down the handle and pulled it open. A small rat ran out, and Mya shivered. "This night just gets better and better," she said.

Seb stepped into the tiny room. There was a thick layer of dust over everything, but it had been some kind of storeroom in the past. There were sturdy metal shelves, all empty now, but the dents gave clues that heavy items had been placed there in days gone by. He headed back out, and they continued their journey.

"I'm guessing they've got a generator system set up to keep the lights on down here," Seb said.

"And I'm guessing we're approaching a station."

Almost as if it was a stage direction, a chilling growl echoed down the tunnel from up ahead, followed by another, then another. The pair of them raised their rifles as they continued towards the light. Suddenly Seb felt his phone vibrate against his thigh. He pulled it out and read the message: *Extraction, Sainte-Philippe-du-Roule zero six hundred local time. Apache had to return to base for refuelling.*

"Fuck!" Seb hissed.

"What is it?"

"We're here until six a.m. The Apache's returned to

base for refuelling."

"Fuck! So, what do we do until then?"

"We hide."

"What? Down here? With those things?"

"I'm pretty certain that station up ahead is Sainte-Philippe-du-Roule. When we head to the surface, we're going to have to deal with those things. I'd be happier knowing there's an Apache with some serious firepower waiting for us, so yes, we stick it out down here until then." He looked at his watch. "It's two thirty a.m. We should get back to that storeroom and get a couple of hours' rest before the chopper arrives. We're going to need all our wits about us."

"That room? With the rats?"

"It was just the one rat."

Mya looked up the tunnel to the bend. She could still hear the growls and only guess what the scene looked like on the platform. She let out a deep sigh. "I don't suppose we've got a lot of choices, have we?"

\*

There was a knock on the bedroom door. "Prime Minister?"

Andy forced his eyes open. The bedside light was still on. He had a brief laid out on the quilt, Trish had fallen asleep, nestled into him like a purring kitten. It took him a moment to get his bearings. There was another knock on the door.

"Yes, what is it?" Andy asked.

"Prime Minister, it's Doug. I'm afraid I need to give you a briefing. There's been a development. Several actually."

"Give me a minute," Andy replied. He looked down to see Trish still fast asleep. He moved the brief to his bedside cabinet, lifted her arm ever so slightly, and crept out of bed. He looked at the clock. It was just after four. He knew right then that there would be no more sleep for him, so he threw on his clothes, cast a longing glance back towards his beautiful sleeping wife, and left to face another day.

"Morning, Prime Minister."

"I need coffee," he said, heading straight down the hall and into the kitchen. "Want some?"

"Definitely," Doug replied.

Andy put a pod into the coffee machine, placed a mug on the stand, and pressed the start button. "Okay, so what couldn't wait?" he asked, looking at Doug. Before Doug could even answer, Andy asked, "Have you had any sleep?"

"No."

"Good!"

"Andy, it's bad."

"In the years I've been doing this job, I have never been woken up at four in the morning with good news," he replied. "Let me guess, there's a fucking comet about to hit us that will finish off the rest of the population that the zombies haven't gotten?"

"I think reanimated corpses is the preferred term," Doug replied.

"Very funny. When you call me Andy, I know it's bad. What is it?"

"In the past two hours, we've lost touch with more states than I can even remember. Most significantly Russia, Brazil, India, Japan, China, Indonesia, Pakistan, they're dropping like fucking flies. Oh, and before I forget, I've asked Xander to join us, he should be here soon."

"The last I heard, Petrov was in the shelter, it must be just a communications outage or something," Andy said, handing Doug his coffee.

"Are you seriously telling me that the Russians wouldn't have redundancy after redundancy in place to maintain comms? You did say that when you spoke to him, there had been an outbreak in the bunker too."

"Those bunkers are colossal. They're from Khrushchev's time. I can't, I won't believe they're out of the game. It will be a comms issue," Andy said, placing another pod into the coffee machine and putting his own mug on the stand.

"Okay, we can put a pin in that, but there's something else. Something closer to home."

Andy immediately turned his attention from the dark brown fluid dribbling into his mug to Doug. "What do you mean, closer to home?" His blood ran cold.

"We've lost contact with one of our nuclear subs."

Andy rubbed his hands over his face and through his hair. "Oh dear God," he said.

"Directly before losing contact, the communications officer sent the message that there had been an incident on board involving a reanimate, but the incident had been dealt with and the situation contained."

"Fuck!"

"Yeah."

"How many crew are on board?"

"Just over one hundred and thirty."

"Fuck!"

"Yep."

"Well. This is a great start to the day. Can't wait to see what giant vat of excrement is going to hit the blades of the wind turbine next," Andy said, taking his first sip of coffee.

"I'm going to hang every last one of these two-faced little fuckers from Tower Bridge by their scrotums," shouted Xander as he marched into the kitchen, flinging down a pile of daily newspapers.

Andy put another pod into the coffee machine. "I'll have to double-check with the attorney general, Xander, but I'm pretty sure we're not allowed to do that."

"When you read these, you'll change your mind," Xander replied. "We're going to have to think seriously about controlling the flow of news."

"You mean bring the press under permanent state control?" Andy said, smiling. "You are joking. Please tell me you're joking, Xander."

"Look, managing the press was a piece of piss in the past. If they had something juicy, I could bribe them with something juicier that was to our political advantage, but this… There is nothing juicier. There never will be. This is the end of everything, there is nothing else to report. What we need to do as a government is stem the panic as much as we can, but these fuckers are wanting to spread it more than ever to sell their arse-wipe papers."

Andy handed Xander the mug of coffee and pulled the first of the newspapers towards him. "Beck's Churchill Moment." "We're backing Beck." "Britain will be great again. Beck stands tall." "The end of times? Not for Britain."

"What are you talking about? These are great headlines."

"The headlines are great, but look at the fucking stories," Xander said. "They do nothing but incite panic. Yesterday was shock day. Today, the news will sink in, and these fuckers with all their statistics about infection rates and percentages, with all their stories about mass looting in other countries, with all their stories … with all their stories … they've just completely fucked us."

# 12

The quiet beep-beep, beep-beep of the digital watch woke Mya first. She could feel Seb's heavy arm draped over her. In the dark recesses of the tunnel system, the temperature was frigid, and they had nestled together like wolves for mutual comfort. For the first time since the news of the infection had broken, she felt safe. She was in a small, dark, dusty room that smelt of rat droppings and was way beneath the Paris streets, but at least there were no monsters trying to kill her. It was incredible how one lowered one's standards in a crisis.

Seb gradually stirred as the electronic alarm bled into his dreams. He pressed the stop button, and the two of them lay there for a moment, comfortable in each other's clasp. Seb touched Mya's arm gently. "I'm awake," she whispered.

"We'd better get going." He sensed her hesitation. "I won't let anything happen to either of us. We're going to get out of here, and we're going to get back home."

"To what?"

"To whatever. First things first, get your game face

on; we've got work to do."

*

Andy took another sip of his coffee. "Look, let's head down to the office and look at our options," he said.

Xander picked up all the newspapers, and he and Doug followed the prime minister out of the residence.

The three of them reassembled around the PM's desk. They placed their coffees down and sat back, crossing their legs, clasping their fingers together and silently contemplating. They were three of the most politically astute and media savvy people in the country. The government's policies had won the election in second place to Beck's image. They knew that how they looked these days was more important than what was said. But if what was said was said in the right way, then it was like a rolling stone. Public opinion and the politics of a nation was all to do with soundbites and portrayal. Actors on a stage, that's all they were. Thankfully for the country, Beck and his cabinet, well, most of them, were only interested in doing the very best for the people of Britain, despite having cracked the secret to getting elected.

"What you're suggesting is a coup," Andy said.

"Don't be so bloody stupid," Xander replied. "How can it be a coup? You're the prime minister; this is an elected government. We're discussing a measure that will reduce the chances of panic on the streets, of lawlessness and uprising due to uncertainty. If other countries had done this, they might have stood a chance. You saw the footage, Andy. You read the reports. It was panic and anarchy that was as much to blame as the virus. And the thing is, you said it yesterday, we are at war. Dress it up any way you like, but this is wartime and censorship of the media in the public and national interests is not unprecedented. If people get broken up about their civil liberties and rights to free speech, let's see how they'll feel when there's rioting in the supermarkets and their families are going hungry."

"I'm with Xander on this one hundred per cent. The press are doing what they do best. Even now, even with all this shit going on, they're still more interested in numbers than they are in reporting the truth, in actually looking at the real story … what's going on … what we're doing. Panic sells papers," Doug said, "and these bastards are having a fire sale."

Andy reached forward and picked up the coffee from his desk before relaxing back into his chair. He looked towards Doug and then at Xander. "It is a coup," he said quietly, too quietly to be heard.

"What?" Xander asked.

"It is a coup," he said again, louder this time. "It's a coup against democracy and freedom. We can't silence the press and still say we're a free country."

"But at what cost?" Xander demanded. "If the bastards carry on down this route, I can guarantee we're going to lose a grip on this thing. There will be civil disobedience, and nothing will polarise the country more. All our good work will be just flushed away."

"Let me speak to them," Andy said.

"Speak to who?" Xander asked.

"The publishers, the owners. Get them down here this morning. I want to talk to them."

"Not a chance."

"You've got to be joking," Doug added.

"No. I want to speak to them. I'm going to try to appeal to their sense of civic duty."

"What is wrong with you?" Xander asked, standing and beginning to pace around the room. "You've met these people before. You know they have no fucking sense of civic duty."

"And while you're at it, get the station owners in here too."

"Are you not hearing me?"

"Andy, Xander's right; this would be a really bad

move," Doug interjected.

Andy looked at his watch. "Make it lunchtime. We'll get them in here for lunch. This is how we win. It's how we won the election; it's how we'll win this."

Xander shook his head. "Look—"

"No," Andy said, putting up his hand to stop him. "You think I don't hear you? You think I don't understand you? I understand, Xander. We'll try it this way. I'm not saying we won't end up doing it your way. But with your way, there is no way back. This way, at least there's another option. Now, get them all in here for lunch. Get—" The intercom beeped, and all three of them jumped. Andy hit the flashing button.

"Just so you know, I'm at my desk if you need me, Prime Minister."

"Mel? Thank God! Please, I need you."

Seconds later, Mel was in the office with a notepad. Xander and Doug both nodded and smiled brief, albeit polite smiles. Andy's face lit up. *Finally, someone who would not argue with him.*

"What do you need, Prime Minister?"

"We're going to have a large gathering of newspaper and station owners here for lunch. Inform the kitchen. We'll have a buffet, nothing too formal, I'll need to mingle. We'll need plenty of booze, and make sure we've got a good supply of after dinner mints spiked with arsenic in case it all goes horribly wrong."

Mel smiled, jotting everything down. "How many are we looking at catering for, Prime Minister?" Andy looked towards Xander and Doug. "We want to make sure we've got plenty of our people working the room."

"Fifty," Xander replied.

"Make it eighty," Andy said. "And get me Harry O'List on the phone."

"Now?" Mel asked.

"Straight away."

"But Prime Minister, it's not even four thirty."

"Desperate times," Andy said, clapping his hands together.

Mel shrugged and disappeared back out of the office. Xander and Doug looked towards one another, baffled. It was Doug who spoke first. "Err … why are you wanting to speak to a music video director at four thirty in the morning when we're trying to fend off the apocalypse?"

"Harry did incredible work on our campaign videos. We need some of his magic again now."

"Are you going to enlighten us?" Xander asked.

"Come on, lads, when are you going to learn to trust me?"

"Do we have to answer that?" Doug asked.

"Right, we're back in the Cabinet Office briefing room at eight. I want confirmations from all the station owners and press owners before then. If they're not around, I want their proxies here with full autonomy. Make sure you impress on them they will not like the alternatives."

"Okay, boss," Xander replied.

"No problem, Prime Minister," Doug said, and the two of them left the office.

The intercom beeped. "Yes?"

"Harry O'List on line one, Prime Minister. He sounds a little the worse for wear," Mel said.

"Harry?"

"I'm warning you if this is a prank call again, I'm going to fucking sue Capital Radio," came the gravelly voice.

"Harry, it's Andy Beck … the PM."

"Prove it."

"That night I invited you to the residence, your date asked why the drinking fountain in the bathroom was right next to the toilet and so low down."

"Oh, fuck, it is you," Harry said. He coughed to clear his throat. "I mean … err … sorry, Prime Minister, what can I do for you?"

"I need you down here, now. You and whoever you need to make a video that's going to save our country before lunchtime today."

"What? What kind of video?"

"A video that needs to convince the British media to trust us. A video that's going to assure them that I am all that is standing in the way of this country descending into complete anarchy. Will you help me, Harry?"

"I err…"

"Your country needs you more than ever."

"Err…"

"This is the most important thing you are ever going to do in your career."

"Err…

"We've got the top media men in Britain coming, so Johnny Walker Blue Label is going to be on tap."

"Give me an hour," Harry replied and hung up.

Andy smiled and hit the end call button. He drained the last of his coffee and was just about to press the intercom button to ask for another when Mel walked in with two mugs. She placed one down in front of him, sat down in the chair Doug had occupied moments earlier and took a sip of coffee. "So?" she said.

"So what?" Andy asked.

"So, other than Trish, I know you better than anyone. You have to be strong in front of everybody else; you have to be this dynamic leader. You don't need to be that way with me."

Andy started smiling, but it faded fast. "I'm scared to death, Mel. I have no idea if what I'm doing is going to stabilise the country or cause a burst of mass panic that makes everything a thousand times worse. At least I don't have to worry about my legacy for the history books."

"Don't be so sure."

"What do you mean?"

"Don't be so sure there won't be more history books. Do you remember why I came to work with you?" she asked.

"Because I was the only one who'd hire you and I

paid more than minimum wage?"

"Oh, you are a wag," she replied with a smile. "I came to work for you because I wanted to do something with my life. Something that would benefit others, something for the community. Well, your constituency got a damn site bigger, but I see in you today what I saw in you back then. A man who will always strive to do his very best. An honest man, a decent man, a man who will never stop trying. That's what came across in that broadcast, that's what the people will see, and I can guarantee, that is what will stop them from being the worst they can be. You inspire people to be the best they can be. You always have. You inspired me. You still do."

Andy was about to tease her, but then he became overwhelmed as her words sank in. "I don't know what to say," he replied, his voice breaking a little.

"Well, there's a first." She stood, picked up her coffee mug, and Andy's empty one, then turned to leave.

"Mel."

She stopped and turned to look at him. "Yes?"

"Thank you. Thank you for what you said. You have no idea how much I needed to hear those words."

"Of course I knew. That's what makes me so good at my job," she replied, smiling.

Andy smiled too. "I suppose it is."

# 13

Seb and Mya left the confines of the small storeroom, and a wave of even colder air hit them. They walked along the tracks, grateful that the emergency lighting was still working. The distant growls slowly got louder as they continued towards the station up ahead.

Seb looked at his watch. "Twenty-five minutes," he whispered.

"We better get our skates on."

"Are you ready?"

"I really don't know."

"This is going to be like some fucked-up video game when we start. Just remember, we don't stop until we're breathing fresh air. Okay?" Seb looked across to Mya in the emergency lighting, and although he couldn't see her expression, he saw a nod.

"Okay." *This is it.*

They both came to an abrupt halt just before the arc of the more powerful lighting of the platform. They could see twelve of the creatures milling up and down, their bodies slow in the absence of prey, but their heads darting from side to side, their noses twitching like hungry animals.

Seb trained his L119A1 rifle on the reanimated corpse closest to them. The creature stopped in mid-step and looked straight towards him. There was no possibility it could see him, surely. He was in the dark, there was light interference, and they were still a good distance away. The beast did not break its gaze; instead it peeled back its lips in a fearsome snarl and began sprinting in Seb's direction. A chill ran down Seb's spine, the likes of which he had never experienced before. The monster leapt from the shoulder-high platform like it was no higher than a footstool, and not missing a stride, it landed on the track and charged towards him.

The rest of the pack, at first excited by the other creature's louder growl, then spotting what it had seen, also began to charge. They seemed graceful as they flew from the platform, like Hell's ballerinas, launching from light and into the shadows, landing in choreographed malevolence. Their pounding feet echoed loudly as they stormed towards Seb and Mya.

The assault team had not used the laser sights in the confines of the palace corridor, but now the two MI6 agents turned on the powerful red beams.

The pair of them remained statuesque but for the micro angling of their weapons as the first and second creatures approached. "And … engage," Seb said.

The pair of them had always worked well as a team. Although they had seen action many times, firstly in the armed forces and then working for MI6, up until the last few hours they had never been in what were essentially combat conditions together. But time changed all things, and now they stood side by side, almost touching. They both squeezed their triggers at the same time; as headshots made the first two beasts drop like sacks of coal, their bones smashed against the rails of the tracks.

Seb and Mya calmly aimed towards the next two— down. Next two—down. Next two—down. This was survival. This was everything. They had a mission, and world events, all that was happening outside the tunnel, meant nothing. It was a game of quickfire snakes and ladders. They had to ascend. They had to reach the end square before six a.m. local time, otherwise it was game over.

"Only seven billion to go," Mya said as the two of them ran into the warmer light of the underground station. They could hear the growls and thumping feet of other reanimates in the walkways and on the stairs and escalators, but for the time being, they couldn't see them.

Seb climbed onto the platform, raising his rifle again immediately; he aimed it towards the entrance while Mya joined him. "Ready?"

"Ready!" she said, and the two cautiously advanced. The red lasers danced on the dirty walls waiting for their next target to emerge, and the by now familiar growls sang a loud echoing chorus in the confines of the underground station. The emergency lights at the base of the walls and high on the ceiling cast enough clarity for Seb and Mya to see the macabre scene unfold as, suddenly, beast after beast flooded out of the corridors and from the parallel platform.

"Here we go," Seb said and fired at the first creature. The bullet blasted a hole through its forehead and exited amid a fan of brain, blood and bone, splattering over the face of the second beast, which Mya halted with another headshot. More reanimates emerged onto the platform, and suddenly Seb caught movement out of the corner of his eye. He broke his gaze from the ever-increasing throng of monsters massing on the platform and looked down at the tracks. "Shit!" he cried.

More beasts flooded from the tunnel up ahead and others who had found the access ramp were swelling the numbers already on the platform. Before they knew it, the whole tunnel was alive with movement. Hands were reaching towards them from the tracks, fingers desperate to clench onto a trouser leg or boot.

Seb and Mya continued firing. With each trigger pull, another beast fell, but the surging speed and sheer number meant the horde was getting closer, no matter how fast the two MI6 agents found their targets. They began retreating, desperately trying to give themselves more time.

Seb shifted his gaze once more towards the track. There were about thirty creatures massing, desperately grasping at the air. They wouldn't present an immediate danger unless he or Mya stepped too close to the edge or lost their balance, but the monsters' presence meant a quick escape through the tunnels was no longer an option. *This is turning to shit fast,* Mya thought to herself but didn't dare say the words for fear that vocalising them would somehow make it worse. A few more seconds and the first of the beasts charging along the platform would be upon them. Mya stopped firing for the quickest magazine switch in history. Seb knew it wouldn't be long before he needed to do the same. His shoulder blade hit something hard as they continued to retreat, and he turned to see a large vending machine. He immediately tipped it, the crash and sound of breaking glass temporarily drowning out the growls of the beasts. It left a gap of two feet between it and the edge of the platform. It meant any beasts who didn't go through that gap would have to clamber over the heavy snack dispenser, giving Seb and Mya some small modicum of respite.

"Quick," Seb said, grabbing Mya's arm and running back down the platform, pausing to drag a solid metal bench to a right angle with the wall, and causing another barrier for the creatures to negotiate. The pair of them continued to the rear wall next to the mouth of the tunnel. The creatures on the tracks followed them, step for step, their hands continuing to reach out like starving children from a Dickens novel, but Seb and Mya were just far enough away to avoid that danger for the time being.

They both brought their weapons up again as the first of the reanimates made their way around the vending machine, while others fell and stumbled. "You realise we literally have our backs to the wall," Mya said.

"Concentrate," Seb replied, firing and taking down the first beast, then the second, then the third, before finally swapping his magazine.

Mya quickly got her head back in the game, and while some of the creatures were still struggling as they clambered over the tipped snack machine, she made sure the funnel that it had created became just as impassable as body after body fell. Some piled, some slid off the platform onto the tracks.

Seb slapped the magazine in and took aim once again. Three creatures had managed to crawl over the wide, heavy barrier and their hands had just reached the tiled floor of the platform when the red beam of death from Seb's rifle found them. He and Mya moved onto the next wave, finishing them off in double quick time, before moving their aim further back as body after body fell creating a zombie blockade.

Gradually, the threat began to diminish. Although there was still a good number of the creatures on the platform and in the tunnel, for the time being there were no new ones joining them, and the desperate few trying to reach Mya and Seb struggled and stumbled, slowing their normal flighty pace to a virtual stop on occasion and giving the two MI6 agents ample time to find their targets.

\*

The intercom on Andy's desk beeped. "The chief of defence staff for you, Prime Minister," Mel's voice announced.

"Put him through," Andy replied.

"No. He's here, sir, in the office."

Andy looked at his watch. "This isn't going to be good news," he muttered to himself. He hit the intercom button again. "Send him in please, Mel."

Taylor walked in; there were no pleasantries, his

face looked tired and drawn. "I'm afraid I have some bad news, Prime Minister."

"Go on," Andy replied, slumping into his chair and gesturing for Taylor to do the same on the opposite side of the desk.

"I understand you were apprised of the situation regarding the HMS *Valiant* this morning."

"The nuclear sub we lost contact with? Yes, I was told."

"It was in port in Gibraltar at the same time as our aircraft carrier, the HMS *Indestructible*."

"And?"

"I'm afraid we've lost contact with that too, Prime Minister."

"Jesus Christ!" Andy replied. "How many crew?"

"There's a full flight crew on board as well as the ship's crew, sir. We're looking at close to sixteen hundred personnel."

Silence enveloped them both for a moment before Andy continued. "Do we have the last known whereabouts? Do we have any idea what's happened?"

"We're tracking the *Indestructible*, Prime Minister. It's still on course, but we can't raise it."

"Well, surely it's just a comms problem then? If it's on course, that means there are still people operating it."

"Well, yes, sir, but I'm afraid it's a little more complicated than that," Taylor replied. The chief of defence staff pointed to the water cooler in the corner. "May I have a drink, sir?"

"Of course," Andy said, gesturing towards the machine.

Taylor tugged at the column of plastic cups in the dispenser and several fell onto the floor. He bent down to pick them up, placing them back in the top of the dispenser only for more to fall out of the bottom.

"Just leave them, Alistair, I'll get Mel to sort it. Just get your drink."

Taylor looked at the blue plastic cups on the floor. He was not normally a clumsy man, but a combination of stress and a lack of sleep was obviously weighing on him. "I'm sorry, Prime Minister," he said, pressing the lever and filling his cup with cold water. He took a drink before refilling it and heading back to his seat.

"So?" Andy asked.

"Well, Prime Minister, as I said, we were … are able to see the *Indestructible* via satellite. It appears there was a battle of sorts on the deck of the ship."

"What do you mean, a battle? Are you saying she was attacked?"

"No, sir. Well … yes."

"What are you talking about? You need to start making sense."

"I'm sorry, Prime Minister. It seems there was an outbreak on board the ship, sir. There are bodies on deck. Some of them armed, some of them not."

"And how do we know it was an outbreak? How do we know it wasn't something else?"

"Our analysts have studied the images in depth. They are confident the evidence in them supports the theory that there was an outbreak on board, which resulted in a battle on deck with an indeterminate number of reanimated corpses." Taylor's throat went dry again as nerves got the better of him, and he took another drink from his cup.

Andy sat back in his chair, crossed his legs, clasped his hands together and looked at the family photo that faced him. As much as he loved his wife and two girls, there were sixteen hundred people on board that ship, all of them probably having someone loving them just as much. He let out a deep sigh. "So, where do we go from here?"

"This is the very crux of the matter, Prime Minister. Our deepest concern is that the carrier is heading back to these shores. We cannot let that happen."

"Okay. My head is obviously a little fuzzy due to a lack of sleep. If the carrier is heading back, then obviously whatever happened is over with. It's not like the bloody zomb—reanimates can navigate an aircraft carrier, is it? We'll simply quarantine the ship when it gets into port and take it from there."

"If we were in contact with them; if we knew what had gone on, that may be an option, Prime Minister. The fact is anything could have happened. Everyone on that ship barring a handful of crew might be infected. There may have been an outbreak as well as a mutiny. They could be planning to escape in some of the seventy-plus aircraft as we speak, in a desperate attempt to get back to their families. You've read what I've read; all it takes is one bite, and from preliminary reports, one scratch. There could be a thousand different scenarios as to why we can't raise them, but we must consider the worst. We're going to do a flyby. We are going to continue using everything at our disposal to regain communication and find out exactly what has gone on, but we cannot let that carrier into British waters."

"What are you saying?"

"I'm saying we *cannot* let that happen."

"Dispense with the riddles, Taylor. Tell me exactly what you are saying."

"Just what I said, sir."

Andy leaned forward, placing his elbows on the desk. He sunk his face into his hands and shook his head. "When I took this job, I prayed that I wouldn't be surrounded by spineless bureaucrats who would be so scared of doing the wrong thing that they refused to do the right thing. Now. Look where we are. I've surrounded myself with people only wanting to do the right thing, and that is the very last thing I want to do."

"I'm sorry, Prime Minister. When you reach this level, the true burden of command is realised," Taylor said. "I've agonised over this."

"Okay, so what are our options?"

"Well, sir. The *Indestructible* cost over six billion to build. That's not taking into account all the F-35s and the

Apaches on board. We are looking at a colossal monetary value. The ship is a cornerstone to any military plans we have implemented since it was built."

"So, what are you saying?"

"I'm saying—" He stopped and took another drink. "I'm saying if our continued attempts to communicate with it go unanswered, the safest thing to do is to immobilise it while it is a good distance from us. It seems extreme, but these are extreme times."

There was a long, long pause before Andy spoke. "Immobilise it? Attack our own people? If we do that, isn't there a chance we could destroy her? That it could sink?"

"We believe we can do it without that happening, Prime Minister, but nevertheless, it is a possibility."

"Right now, I'm not thinking about the money. I'm thinking about the sixteen hundred people on board and their families at home. Listen to me. I'm not going to take anything off the table. The most important thing is that we keep this country free from infection. I need you to get together with your people and present me with three options. We already know what the third one is." Andy looked at his watch. "We've got the COBRA meeting at eight. Let's meet at seven thirty."

"Yes, Prime Minister," Taylor replied as he stood and left the room.

Andy sipped his coffee and thought for a moment. When he came to office, he knew he'd have to make tough decisions. He knew at some point he would probably send the armed forces into harm's way, but he never thought for a second that he would have to think about what he might now have to order.

"Knock, knock," Trish said, walking into the office in jogging pants, trainers and a loose-fitting Springsteen T-shirt.

"Hi," he said, and for the first time since seeing her the previous evening, his heart lifted. "You're a sight for sore eyes."

She closed the door behind her, walked over to where he was sitting and sat in his lap, wrapping her arms around him. "You okay?" she asked.

"Not by a long shot."

"Anything I can help with?"

"Not unless you've been lying to me all these years and you are actually Diana Prince," he said, kissing her on the cheek.

"Again with the Wonder Woman thing," she said, smiling. "You want me to dye my hair black and put on the costume?"

"Is that a trick question? How long does it take to dye your hair? Because I've got about ninety minutes before my next meeting. This costume you mentioned, does it come with the Magical Lasso of Hestia?"

"You are such a perv," Trish said, and they both laughed. It felt good. It felt good to feel normal after everything that had happened … was happening.

He kissed her again. "I love you. You have no idea how much."

"What's wrong, darling?" Trish asked, seeing the frightened little boy in his eyes that only she was ever privy to.

"I might have to make the worst decision of my life in a few hours. I'm wracking my brains trying to think of an alternative, but nothing is happening up there."

"What decision?"

He pulled back and looked at her long and hard. She was so beautiful, stunning in fact. He loved everything about her. If he made this decision, he wouldn't be able to forgive himself, so would he want to put that burden on her? On the other hand, she was the only one in the world he could share this with. He looked across at the door.

"Trish, I might have to order an attack on our own aircraft carrier."

"What?" It wasn't anger, or sadness, or betrayal, but confusion that swept over her face.

"There's been an outbreak on board. It's on its way here. We can't reach them by radio. We don't know how many are infected. All we know is there is infection on board the ship. I don't need to tell you what happens if we get one case, just one."

Trish gazed into his eyes. "You'll make the right choice; you always do. Whatever you decide it will be because you were trying to do the right thing for the people of this country. I have faith in you, and I will always, always love you," she said, squeezing him tightly.

"But the men and women on board that ship are people of this country too. Not only that, they have made their careers protecting this country. How could I live with myself if I turned my back on them?"

Trish climbed off his knee and perched on his desk. Andy swivelled his chair around to look at her. "Look at what's happened in the last twenty-four hours," she began, "the most powerful countries in the world have crumbled; we have managed to hang on by the skin of our teeth. You've acted quickly, but you've acted well too. You have good instincts, and you surround yourself with others who have good instincts." She leaned down, kissed him and turned to leave but paused at the door. "I love you. Just remember that when you start to doubt yourself. I love you, and the kids love you, and that's the most important thing in the world."

"You're right. You're always right."

"Of course I am," she replied. "Oh, and I'm totally up for that Wonder Woman thing on date night," she said with that little giggle that always made his heart leap. She blew him a kiss and left.

Andy remained with a smile on his face for just a moment before the intercom beeped. "Edward Phillips, Prime Minister," Mel said.

"Put him through," Andy replied.

"No, sir. He's here to see you."

"Oh fuck!"

# 14

Seb and Mya surveyed their work. There was no more movement on the platform. They had put down every last possible attacker. The creatures on the track still reached towards them, their clawing fingers desperate to touch, to scratch, to drag. The two of them looked down at the dark figures from their cramped, safe corner. They stifled the urge to make them cease their unholy gurgling growls. They had used up a lot of ammunition in their battle, and there was still a long way to go before they reached the safety of the Apache.

They began their march down the platform, not taking anything for granted and keeping their rifles raised. Suddenly, an arm reached out from beneath a pile of downed corpses. The creature lifted its head, turning its disfigured and bloodied face towards the two MI6 agents. Half its cheek was hanging off, ripped apart by a stray bullet. It bore its teeth like a wounded animal, ready to exact one last vengeful act. Mya pulled out her knife and plunged it into the beast's eye, stopping it in mid-growl. She withdrew her blade, wiped it on another creature's thick cotton shirt, and replaced it in its sheath before switching on her head torch. "Their eyes are weird," she said, stepping towards the tracks, making sure she was still out of reach of the beasts. "Look at them." She panned the light beam from face to face as Seb joined her.

They both surveyed the chilling mass of bodies for a few seconds. "It's like they've all got cataracts. But the pupils … what is it with those pupils?" he asked, watching the shattered black shards expand and contract wildly as the light moved from face to face.

"Creepy as fuck," Mya replied, straightening up and shuddering.

The two agents resumed their journey along the platform, their eyes dissecting every inch. When they reached the entrance, a cold gush of wind hit them, along with a wall of sound from above. There was the familiar murmuring growl of the beasts but also the odd shout and scream as Parisiennes were still trying to find safety from the deadly streets.

Seb took a look at his phone. "Damn, no signal again."

Mya looked at her watch. "We only have a few minutes."

"C'mon then," he said, and the pair of them exited the platform and ran out into the vast stair and escalator well. There was no sign of any creatures, so they shouldered their rifles and brought out their sidearms. They began to run, bounding up three steps at a time, the emergency lighting enough for them to see any potential threats. The staircase was steep, and they had already endured a massive amount of physical exertion, but books could have been written about the extremities both of them had suffered in the past for queen and country. They slowed as they reached the top. Between them and the exit were more creatures. They couldn't see them yet, but they could hear their gurgling, guttural growls.

They ducked down, using the last few stairs as

cover. "Okay, this is it, the last run for freedom," Mya said, bringing her Glock up. "Are you ready?"

"Ready."

\*

"I'm sorry to come here at this hour, Prime Minister, but there have been developments in Paris," Phillips said, walking into the PM's office.

"What do you mean? We wrapped up the Paris operation. We got Dupont and his family out."

"Yes, sir, that part of the operation was concluded, but that wasn't the entire operation."

"Oh? You'd better sit down and tell me what's going on."

"As you know, I had two MI6 agents in that team, Prime Minister. They went back inside to acquire a hard drive, which we believe could provide us with some vital intelligence about the virus."

"Let me get this straight. You sent two MI6 agents in to steal a laptop from one of our closest allies to acquire information about the virus that has destroyed his country. Why didn't we just ask for it? Why do you think for a second he would be hesitant to share information with us that could help everyone? You're still not making any sense, Phillips."

Phillips removed his glasses, rubbed his eyes, and squeezed the bridge of his nose. "It's complicated Prime Minister. Very, very complicated. To tell you about it would require more time than either of us has right now. I will send you a brief, but the crux of the reason for me being here is this. We had to abort the extraction of our two agents last night, the Apache they were due to meet had to head back for refuelling."

"Okay."

"They were due to be extracted—" Phillips looked at his watch "—well, right now, but the French base where the Apache headed to for refuelling has gone silent. We can't raise anybody there or contact any of our people."

Andy sagged back into his chair and stared at the MI6 chief. "How many did we have at the base?"

"As I understand it, Prime Minister, we didn't have anybody else at the base. The French were helping us out with the refuelling, that's all."

"They didn't ask questions?"

"Prime Minister, I believe the French have other things on their mind at the moment, and although the British and French governments have not always seen eye to eye, the top men in the British and French military have always had a good working relationship. Taylor was able to get one of his people to speak to one of their people to make sure every courtesy was extended."

"So, is there a bright side to this? Is there anything positive you can tell me?"

"Seb Archer and Mya Hamlyn are two of my best agents, Prime Minister. The last thing I would want to do is lose them, but the nearest help is several hours away, and they are in the middle of Paris, which has a population of over two million. And I'm guessing at the rate this infection spreads, a good percentage of those are no longer…" He tailed off. It was still so hard to admit what was going on, despite Phillips seeing more intelligence regarding it than the man in front of him.

"And the Apache pilots?"

"I'm afraid the worst has probably already happened to them, sir."

"Jesus Christ," Andy replied, rubbing his fingers over his stubbled chin. "There's nobody else? We've got nobody else who can get them out?"

"All our allies are either uncontactable or in complete disarray, Prime Minister."

"Unbelievable. Well, this has been a great start to the day. You must drop by more often, Phillips," Andy said, glaring at the head of MI6.

Phillips stood. "I'm sorry to be the bearer of bad

news, Prime Minister."

Andy ignored the comment. "That brief. Don't forget that brief. I want to know why we sent two of our best agents to their deaths."

"Yes, Prime Minister."

"The other matter that we discussed on the phone."

Phillips cast his eyes down to the carpet. "Yes, Prime Minister."

"Do you think we'll ever know who did this?"

"In all honesty, no. But … never mind."

"No, go on. But what?"

Phillips brought his head up to look Andy in the eyes. "Does it matter, sir?"

"What do you mean?"

"It's happened now. The world as we knew it has come to an end. Whether this was a deliberate act or some horrific accident, the result's the same. We just have to hope we can somehow keep this country safe."

"I suppose you're right."

"Will that be all, Prime Minister?"

"Yes. Thank you, Edward."

\*

Seb felt a vibration in his pocket. He pulled out his phone. "We've got a signal," he whispered and punched in his unlock code.

*MISSION ABORTED. LOST CONTACT WITH APACHE.*

"What the fuck?" he hissed. His fingers moved quickly over the phone's screen. "INSTRUCTIONS?" he typed.

The phone buzzed again. This time it was an incoming call. "You'd better have good news for me," Seb whispered.

It was the woman's voice from the previous evening, only now it was not curt and officious, there was genuine sadness in her tone.

"There are no possible extraction scenarios at this time. All I can suggest is try to make it out of the city. I'm sorry, Seb. Pass my regrets on to Mya, and please fix a GPS tracker to the hard drive in case the worst happens." The line went dead, and Seb turned off the phone and put it back in his pocket.

"What did they say?" Mya asked.

"They said we're on our own."

"Fuck!"

"Yeah. Okay, listen. We can't go back the way we came. The only way is forward. Let's get the hell out of this station and then find somewhere we can haul up for five minutes to come up with a plan of our own."

"A plan of our own? Like taking on an entire city of hungry flesh-eating zombies by ourselves?"

"Yeah. Yeah, something along those lines." He moved slowly up the last remaining steps until his head peeked over the top and into the main part of the terminus. The emergency lights allowed him to see across the concourse to the open doors. There were about twenty creatures milling around, sniffing the air like hungry animals searching for prey. He turned back to Mya. "Fit your silencer." They simultaneously reached into their vests and fixed the silencers to the end of their weapons.

Mya moved up the steps to join him. "What's the plan?"

"Not dying," he replied and took aim, firing at the nearest figure. The beast fell. There was enough noise for the creatures inside the terminal to become excited but not enough to alert any from outside. The remaining reanimates instantly began searching their surroundings for the source of the disturbance. One by one, they began charging in the direction of the two agents as the quiet shots popped from the weapons. One by one they dropped to the floor amid small eruptions of bloody tissue.

Within twenty seconds, all the hostiles were down.

Mya and Seb looked at each other in the subdued light. "We're getting really good at this," Mya said, handing Seb her gun, pulling a band from her pocket and tying her hair into a ponytail. She took her Glock back and began to step over the bodies towards the breaking day beyond the station doors.

"I was here a year or so back. There's a hotel not far away that still uses keys instead of cards. It would make a good place for us to formulate a plan," Seb said.

"Anywhere's better than here."

*

The intercom beeped again. "Xander Bright, Prime Minister."

"Put him through, Mel," Andy replied.

"No, he's here, Prime Minister."

"Doesn't anybody make appointments anymore? I'm the prime minister for Christ's sake," he shouted through the open door.

Xander ignored the comments as he barged into the room. "Listen, I've been thinking, you and Trish need to take the kids to school today. It would be great PR."

"What? No, I can't. We can't," Andy replied.

"Why?"

"Firstly, I'll be in a COBRA meeting, and secondly, we were going to keep them at home for a few days."

"You really are a fucking amateur sometimes, aren't you?"

"I'm not playing bloody publicity chess with my family, Xander."

"Look. You're wanting the country to believe it's business as usual. That they should go about their daily routines. Nothing is going to instil that confidence in them as much as seeing you do it. You want to lead the country through this? Then do it by example."

Andy sat for a moment, looking at Xander. "I said

I'd never play politics with them. I promised Trish I'd never do it."

"This isn't playing politics," Xander replied. "This is real, Andy. It's the most important period in our history. We're a flame flicker away from going out for good. Leadership, real leadership, is the only thing that is going to help us. If you believe we stand a chance, you need to prove it. If you don't, then pack Trish and the kids up now and head to a bunker," Xander said, walking around the desk, pulling the bottom drawer open and taking out a bottle of Glengoyne and two glasses.

Andy looked at his watch. "Err …don't you think it's a little early?" he said as Xander proceeded to pour a measure into each glass.

"Dutch courage."

"I don't need Dutch courage. There'll be more Special Branch in that school than there are pupils."

"I don't mean Dutch courage for that," he replied, "I mean for you telling Trish."

Andy took the glass, drained it, and poured another. "Hang on. The COBRA meeting."

"I'll sort it with Doug. We'll knock it back forty minutes. Actually, I suggest we make sure the other ministers are doing the same. I'll get in touch with the stations we know are still friendly. It will take the bite out of the morning news cycle."

Andy took a small sip from his glass. "Okay, sort it. But I've got a meeting at seven thirty that I need to take."

"Oh! Anything I can help with?"

"Not at the moment."

Xander took a drink from his glass and went to sit in the seat that was still warm from the PM's previous visitor. He looked around the office. They had fought so hard and so long to get into power. Xander had never felt like just a hired gun, Andy had always told him he was part of a team. They weren't just words either, Andy really believed it. If this job was the last Xander would ever have;

if these things were the last he would do, then he would die happy. He had a wife who loved him. He had excelled as a journalist, then an editor, and now he excelled as a director of communications. He had already won in life, but now, as part of this team, they needed to step up their game even more.

Andy took another drink. "So, what's going through that crazy head of yours?"

"We did well—you, me, Doug, the rest of them. We got a tough agenda out there. The public voted for it, and we started delivering." Xander took another drink. "We could have done amazing things."

"We are doing amazing things," Andy replied. "You're meant to be bulling me up, for God's sake."

"We are. But I just wish it was in different circumstances. A new beginning rather than an end."

"Don't you think this is the absolute best time to be in power?"

"Are you serious? The fucking world is in meltdown, and you think this is the best time to be in power?"

"Doug said something to me last night, and it really stuck. I don't mean these are the best times, quite the opposite. But this is the ultimate test for us. For the last few decades, the political world has become more and more populated by bureaucrats and controlled by special interests. We always said we were going to be different." Andy took a drink, put his glass down on the desk and stood up. Placing his hands in his pockets, he began to walk around the room. "Don't you think that if ever the country needed people like us, it's now?"

"Err…"

"Seriously, if the last lot were still in power, how do you think they'd have reacted? They'd have wanted a bloody referendum as to whether to close the borders. Three months to organise, by which time the only voters would be a bunch of fucking zombies."

"I suppose you're right," Xander replied. "The thing is, though, as much as I have always loved our political and philosophical debates, and as much as I love this one, there is one key thing you're forgetting."

"What's that?"

"No matter how much you procrastinate, you still have to head upstairs and tell Trish that we need some footage of you and her taking the kids to school."

# 15

Seb and Mya arrived at the hotel with little interference from attackers. As they had emerged into the street, a car alarm had gone off around the corner giving them their first small piece of luck of the day. The once luxurious hotel, part of what was a big chain, like so many businesses in the previous few months had gone into liquidation. It was just another victim of the countless cyberattacks that had crippled not just commercial entities but entire countries. Le Magnifique had been magnificent once, but now it was just a shadow of itself. Window panels had cracked in the thick, beautiful and heavy stained oak doors. Victims of vandalism or Parisiennes desperate to escape streets full of the undead; no one would ever know.

Mya reached into her vest and pulled out a small gun-shaped pick. She inserted it into the lock and pressed the trigger. Seconds later, there was a click. She crouched down and did the same with the ground level lock; then she and Seb looked out onto the street one last time before pulling the door open and slipping through. On the other side, Seb grabbed an expensive-looking curtain sash and tied it tight around the handles. He pushed hard against the doors, but they did not give.

The morning light was beginning to bleed through more, gradually illuminating the expansive lobby. Now the rush of breeze from the opened door had died, the air began to smell stale once again. The car alarm was nothing more than a dull wail in the background as the two of them walked past a row of dead plants. "I hope there's some food in the kitchen. I'm famished," Mya said.

They walked down a long corridor running parallel to the once luxurious, now dusty and grimy dining area. Business for liquidators had been booming all over the world, and they clearly hadn't had time to sell off the fixtures and fittings in this place. It was all as it was, just dirtier. Seb switched on his head torch, the light from outside was not strong enough to reach down the hallway. He pushed open the double doors to the large kitchen and the two of them entered.

The narrow high windows meant he could save his battery power as they split up in search of sustenance. The stainless-steel cabinets under the work surfaces had speciality equipment, the odd blender, but no food. They worked their way around the preparation aisles to a door at the back. "Wonder where this leads," Seb said, opening the walk-in pantry.

"Result!" Mya announced as she pushed past Seb and began to scan the shelves. "Baked beans, tinned tomatoes, tinned sweetcorn, jars of gherkins. Shit! No wonder this place went out of business."

"Don't knock it. You see a Pizza Hut around here? This will be the difference between us going back out onto those streets weak and hungry or going back out fed and strong."

"I suppose you're right," she said, picking up the catering-sized tin of beans. "And I suppose at least we're safe in here for the time being." She looked at the label for a while and put the tin back on the shelf.

"Let's take a look around the rest of the place before we chow down."

"But I'm starving," Mya protested.

Seb stepped back and saw something on the top shelf. He reached up and pulled down a box of breadsticks. "There you go."

Mya opened the box, tore the plastic wrapper, and fed two breadsticks at once into her mouth as if she was a human wood chipper. "God that tastes good," she said, offering the box to Seb. He took three but ate them in a more sedate manner before he headed back out of the pantry.

Mya followed, she looked back and got a better view of the top shelf. There were more boxes up there. Suddenly she felt less hard done by. They walked back up the corridor. There was no talk, they just ate and took in their surroundings. Seb turned and headed to the staircase where he swung open the heavy fire door, keeping it open for Mya to enter before letting it swing shut and switching his head torch on. They began to ascend. There were no windows in the stairwell, and it quickly became apparent how dim Seb's torch beam was getting. Mya switched hers on.

"These are lithium batteries. It's not like we can nick a couple from a remote control."

"What are you expecting to find?" Mya asked, her words barely intelligible due to the amount of food that was in her mouth.

"I just want to look around. You never know, there might be something that can help us."

"Like what? A helicopter?"

"Funny. Funny girl," he said. They reached the first floor, and as he opened the door, he noticed a fire axe in a case. "Like this," he said, smashing the glass and pulling the axe out.

"Why the hell do we need an axe?"

"How much ammo did you use getting out of the

station?"

"Quite a bit," she said, beginning to chomp on another breadstick.

"Exactly; me too. What we've got isn't going to last forever, so we're going to have to find some new weapons. If we run dry before we get out of the city, we're going to need something more than our knives."

Mya stopped chewing for a moment. She had acknowledged that she'd have to go back out there at some stage, but she hadn't actually thought about the journey ahead. Now with Seb's stark warning about running out of ammunition, everything seemed a lot more real once again. She swallowed the mouthful of breadstick and put the remainder of it back in the box.

"You're full?"

"Just lost my appetite."

Seb tried a door, but it was locked. "Stand back," he said and booted it open, shattering the lock and splintering the frame.

"Nice," Mya said, "really subtle."

"Got the job done, didn't it?"

Mya turned off the torch as ample light flooded through the windows. "Cool room," she said, walking in. It smelt better than the lobby. The expensive furnishings, although a little dusty, felt far less grubby than the ground floor of the hotel. "This was a beautiful place once," she said, running her hands over the thick towelling robes that hung from the back of the door. She spotted a mini bar in the corner of the room and went straight across to it. Her face lit up as she opened the door, revealing various soft and alcoholic beverages as well as sweets and savoury snacks.

"I thought you'd lost your appetite."

"Who said anything about eating?" she replied, throwing Seb a vodka miniature. "I say we rest up here for a while, get some sleep and then head out."

"The situation out there isn't going to improve with the passage of time," Seb replied.

"Look!" Mya said. "There was no rescue. HQ have said we're on our own. The streets are swarming with those things. We are both very, very tired, we're hungry, and we don't have a good plan. Here we've got food and shelter. It's the smart thing to do to take our time and figure out a good exit strategy."

"And what about our mission?"

"Right now, our mission is to stay alive. The hard drive is safe, let's make sure we are too."

*

The intercom beeped. "Harry O'List, Prime Minister," Mel said.

"Finally," Andy replied, "someone I'm expecting. Harry!" he shouted through the door. "Get yourself in here." Harry walked through the door wearing skin-tight black jeans, a *Vegan as Fuck!* T-shirt and a fake leather jacket. He took a packet of cigarettes out of his pocket and put one in his mouth. He was just about to light it when Andy spoke. "Jesus, Harry, you know this is a non-smoking building."

"Still?"

"Yes."

"Fuck! Oh well, don't wanna get thrown out first day on the job, do I?" Harry said, putting the cigarette back in its box.

"Come with me." Andy guided him out of the office. The two of them walked past Mel's desk and the young nerdy looking woman who was sitting on the couch with a laptop computer on her knee. He guided Harry down a corridor, past the two armed police officers, and out into the fresh air of the Downing Street garden. The sun was just breaking, and they went to sit on a sturdy wooden bench overlooking a small red rose ringed feature and an immaculately kept lawn.

Harry shook a cigarette loose from the packet once again and offered one to Andy, who immediately grabbed it. They both lit up and took a long drag, inhaling the nicotine deep into their lungs before exhaling blue plumes into the cold air.

"Harry, I need your help. I need the impossible from you," Andy said.

"That's why I'm here," Harry said, standing up. "You honestly think I'd be out of bed at this time for anyone?"

The pair of them continued to smoke for a little while in silence before Andy broke it. "The campaign might have been a doddle compared to what I need you to do now."

"I like a challenge."

"Well, don't say I didn't warn you." Harry sucked the last life out of his cigarette and threw the stub down on the ground, extinguishing it with his foot. "You're not going to leave that there, are you?" Andy asked.

"Apparently not," Harry replied, bending down to pick it up.

"Have you brought any staff with you?"

"That four-eyed chick we left with Mel."

"Four-eyed chick? Jesus Harry, do me a favour, try not to talk to anybody today. You have an incredible knack of rubbing people up the wrong way."

"Yeah. I remember from the campaign there were a few touchy types kicking about."

"Yeah, well, I don't think your *Official Breast Inspector* T-shirt helped very much."

"Some of these people don't have a sense of humour."

"Jesus, that's an understatement."

They retraced their steps through the corridor and into the outer office. Andy came to a standstill in front of the young woman sitting opposite Mel. He looked towards Harry, who pulled his phone out and started sending a text.

Andy shook his head. "I'm Andy Beck, the Prime Minister, and you are?" he asked, offering his hand.

The young woman climbed to her feet and shook hands. "I'm Carla, Carla Thorne."

"Pleased to meet you, Carla. Would you like to come into my office?" Andy said, looking towards Mel and nodding. Carla followed the prime minister through the door, and Harry trailed after, still texting.

Andy sat down behind his desk, and Carla took a seat on the opposite side. When Harry finally finished his text, he sat down too.

"All done?" Andy asked. "You don't want to text your mum? Or your sister? Or your tailor?"

"Naa. Mum and Sis are right lazy bitches, they won't be up for another few hours." He pulled at his fake leather jacket and gestured towards his T-shirt. "As you can see, I've got all my threads sorted. No need to text my tailor."

"God, I'd forgotten how annoying you could be."

Mel came into the room with two folders and put them down in front of Andy. "Drinks, Prime Minister?" she asked.

Andy looked towards Harry and Carla, both of them shook their heads. "Not right now thanks, Mel, but let Doug know that Harry's here will you?"

"Yes, Prime Minister," she replied and left the office, closing the door behind her.

"Before we go any further, I need both of you to sign these," Andy said, passing the folders to each of them. Harry pulled out a pen, opened the folder and signed the document straight away.

Carla opened the folder and looked towards Andy. "What is it?"

"This is a non-disclosure agreement. It says that you will be witness to sensitive information and material that have implications for national security. What it ultimately boils down to, Carla, is if you talk about anything you see here today, you're going to prison," Andy replied.

Carla gulped, pushed her glasses back up her nose

and scratched her signature onto the form. Harry took the file from her and gave it and his back to Andy.

"Right, so I'm guessing you're wondering what the hell this is all about. This afternoon, I'm going to be addressing the biggest media men in the country—newspaper and TV station owners, etc. I need to instil a sense of duty into them. A sense that they have a huge part to play in the success of this country being able to stave off disaster. I need to appeal to their sense of decency."

"Fuck me! You're not asking for much, are you?" Harry replied.

Andy ignored the comment and continued. "We have lots of footage from all over the world, not just of the zom—not just of the reanimated corpses but of the panic they cause. That is our biggest enemy right now, panic. So far, our borders are free from infection, but all it needs is a media frenzy telling everyone how we're all doomed, and that's it, game over." He paused and looked at both of them as the enormity of the task they had undertaken began to sink in. "I want you to make a short video. Use whatever tricks you need to. Show how it was the panic that saw country after country fall in a matter of hours. Sure, show what caused it, but emphasise what brought about the lightning-fast downfall of those nations."

"And how long have we got to create this Orwellian masterpiece?" Harry asked.

"I'll need to see it before we show them at around midday."

"Fuck me! Are you havin' a laugh?"

"Do I look like I'm having a laugh, Harry?"

There was a knock on the door and Doug entered. "Weh Heyyy! Dougie boy, how's it hanging?" Harry asked.

Doug shot a stare of disdain towards Harry then looked towards Andy, who had a grin on his face. "Find a room for them, Doug. Give them what they need."

"Yes, Prime Minister," he said, and the three of them left the office.

# 16

"Hi," Andy said as he gently closed the bedroom door behind him.

"Hi," Trish replied, her face lighting up to see him.

"So. You know you said, whatever I decide to do, it will be the right thing?"

"Uh-huh," she said as he lay down beside her, pushing the morning paper she'd been reading to one side.

"I think you and I should take the kids to school together today. I think we should be filmed doing it," he blurted before breaking eye contact with her and pretending to be fascinated by the headline of the newspaper she was reading. There was a pause, and he waited for the eruption. When it didn't come, he looked at her again.

"I think that's a good idea. It shows stability; it shows it's business as usual."

"Err … yes, that's exactly it."

"Y'know, you should try to get the other cabinet members to do the same. I tell you what, you should ask Xander to sort out getting a couple of high-profile celebs to do it as well. Make sure they quote a sound bite about how they feel safe knowing you're at the helm."

"Do you want a job?" Andy asked. "That's bloody genius." He took his mobile phone from his pocket and frantically texted Xander the message. "I was worried you'd go ballistic."

"We will have beefed up security there for the girls, won't we?"

"I'm going to have an army outside the school, and Superman's on speed dial."

"I'm thinking about clearing my calendar for the next couple of weeks," Trish said.

"What? You perform lifesaving operations, I'm not sure that would play well if you were putting them off just to play the dutiful wife."

"Firstly, I wouldn't be putting anything off. All the ops would go ahead. I spoke to Rick and Simone last night. They thought I might be needed here. I had six procedures due in the next thirteen days. They can carry them out for me. The country needs stability; it needs video bites of normality. Seeing us united, and strong, helping people not to panic and lose heart, that's going to save more than six lives."

"What the hell did I do to deserve you?" Andy asked, leaning across and kissing her on the mouth.

"I've told you before. It was that whole bad boy thing you had going on at uni. That barbershop quartet you were a member of, what was their name again?"

"Seriously. You are such a cheeky bitch," he said, beginning to laugh. "We were a progressive rock band. There were five of us, and we were called the 'Paradiddle Paradox', as you well know," he said indignantly.

Trish began to shake with laughter. "Stop it."

"What is it about that name? A paradiddle is a musical term. It was a clever name. It rolled off the tongue as well … Paradiddle Paradox," he said again, whimsically.

Trish made a high-pitched sound as she inhaled,

before bursting out laughing and nearly doubling over. "Stop it," she said again. "I'm going to pee."

"Unbelievable," Andy said, shaking his head. "Laugh away. We had a record label interested in us."

Trish shrieked, "A record label? Seriously, stop it!" Tears started to roll down her face.

"We did."

"That middle-aged bloke who fancied your keyboard player and had a CD duplicating machine in his garage?" She creased over, holding her stomach. "Oh God," she said, still howling with laughter. "Oh God, you need to stop now."

"I'm so happy my rock star ambitions brought you mirth," Andy said, a little bewildered.

"So, what was that barbershop song you did?"

"It wasn't bloody barbershop. It was an acapella track called 'Ice Cream for Einstein'," Andy said, sitting up and folding his arms.

There was a thud as Trish fell off the bed. Andy thought about helping her, but as the guffaws and hoots of laughter continued, he decided to remain seated.

"You … are … so … funny," she managed to gasp in between fits of hysterical laughter, while her face was still pressed against the carpet. "My pretentious nerd boy. Tell me you'll never change," she said, trying to bring her laughter under control again.

"It was timing, that was all. If our lead singer hadn't needed that emergency orthodontic corrective procedure, we could have made it big that summer," Andy said, looking thoughtfully at his hands.

For a moment, Trish sounded more like a donkey than a human as she hawed with laughter. It eventually subsided, and the bedroom fell quiet again. After another minute, Trish got up off the floor and perched on the bed, using the ball of her palm to dab away the tears. "In my life, I have never met anyone who makes me laugh like you," she said.

"The thing is I wasn't trying to make you laugh."

She let out a giggle. "I know darling, I know," she said, patting him on the leg.

\*

Mya had only managed to close her eyes intermittently. The plan had been for her and Seb to refresh themselves with a power nap and regroup—come up with a proper plan. She looked across at her colleague, who was still fast asleep.

She glanced towards the door. They had leant a chair up against the handle, just in case. There was no point in taking risks. She carefully climbed out of bed and walked to the window. The street below did not look like the war zone she expected. Litter collection had not taken place, it looked a little untidier than usual. If you looked carefully at the entrances and windows on the opposite side of the street, there were cracked panes but nothing that would suggest the end had come.

Her eyes moved further down the road, and then she saw it—God's taunt. Her punishment for everything bad she had done in her life, a reminder of what she could have had. An Interflora sign hung outside a bright yellow shop front with a large arrangement of dried flowers in the window. She let out a small huff of a laugh and went to lie back down on the bed. She put her head on the pillow, got comfortable and stared at the ceiling, remembering those few happy months she spent in Chelsea. What she would not give to relive just one minute of them now.

\*

"Don't worry," Andy said, "Xander is going to coordinate everything. I've got this meeting now; we'll both head out to drop the kids off, then we're back here for nine."

"Okay," she replied. "Be sure to come straight back up when you've had the meeting."

"I will," Andy said as his wet and dry shaver negotiated the contours around his face. "How do I look?" he asked, towelling off the remaining shaving foam.

"Handsome, intelligent and prime ministerial," Trish replied, leaning in to kiss him.

"Thank you, love," he said, returning the kiss.

She smiled. "I like that."

"Like what?"

"Love. You called me love. It's a very northern thing, isn't it?"

"I'm a very northern guy," Andy replied.

"Well, not quite," she replied.

"Look, my dad was a miner who got laid off when Thatcher was in power. My mum was from a middle-class background. Her dad was a successful insurance salesman, and they had money, yes; but growing up, we had hard times. I lived in a council house, and just because my mum talked a bit posher than most didn't mean I had it easy. Granted, in later life, when my dad retrained and became an engineer, things got easier, but I'll never forget who I am or where I'm from."

"I wasn't criticising. I wasn't being sarcastic. Genuinely, I like it. I love it, in fact. It makes me feel safe. It makes me remember the other side of your personality, the strong side, the fighting side."

Andy looked at his watch. "I need to get to this meeting," he said, buttoning his shirt up and kissing her again on the cheek.

As he stepped out of the residence, the two plain-clothed police assigned to him followed him down the corridor. He fumbled with his tie but eventually knotted it perfectly. The three of them headed down to the underground corridor connecting Downing Street and Whitehall before the two bodyguards halted at the Cabinet Office briefing room, and Andy entered alone. Taylor and three uniformed men immediately rose to their feet.

"Please sit, gentlemen," he said, as he took a seat himself. "So, what have you got for me," he asked, turning to look at Taylor.

"We've mapped out three scenarios for you, Prime Minister. If you're quite happy to proceed, I'll go through them."

"More than happy," Andy replied. "Go on."

"Okay," Taylor began. "What it boils down to is this…" He had a laptop and mini projector in front of him. He hit a remote button, and a picture of the HMS *Indestructible* flashed up. "Prime Minister, I would just like to say that we have had the best minds working on these scenarios and none of them are ideal, but we are not living in ideal times. We must remember what our key objective is, and that is to make sure the infection doesn't reach these shores."

"I understand that, Taylor. Go ahead."

"Now, sir, what we know so far is this. One…" He hit a button and facts and figures began to appear on the screen. "Including flight crew personnel, there are over sixteen hundred people on board that ship. Two: we have lost contact with them. All communication channels are down. Three: There appears to have been a battle involving reanimated corpses on deck. Four: The ship veered slightly from course for a while but is now heading back here."

"It veered from course? I didn't know that. What the hell does that mean?"

Taylor looked towards the seated men and then back towards Andy. He let out a breath. "These are just best guesses, sir, but the fact that we are not able to raise the carrier at all suggests to us a deliberate act of sabotage. Although we can't be sure about anything, there may be a power struggle in progress on board. There was no sound reason to move from the course other than a change of orders from within."

"This gets better and better. Go on. What are our

options?"

"Well, sir, we believe by far and away the safest route is to immobilise the ship as soon as possible. There are numerous options open to us to achieve this, which I can go into once a decision has been made. This involves the potential for a significant loss of life and the destruction of billions of pounds' worth of equipment. However, sixteen hundred lives and six billion plus pounds mean nothing at the side of sixty-odd million lives if there was the slightest chance that infection got to us."

"And why is that the safest option? This is a huge, hulking vessel. It's not particularly fast-moving. Couldn't we surround it in waters closer to home and quarantine it?"

"Sir, there is the very real danger of the aircraft on board being launched. There are over two hundred and fifty airports in the UK. I needn't remind you, all it takes is one case and that's game over. And that's to say nothing of life rafts. The nearer this gets to us, the greater the risk. We know there are infected on board from the satellite footage. Nobody on that ship can be allowed back into this country without going into quarantine, and the nearer they get to these shores the more of a risk that becomes. The fact that the communications seem to have been sabotaged suggests that at least one faction onboard that vessel is working to its own agenda."

"And the second option?" asked Andy.

"The second option is we retake the ship, sir. This, however, means that we will have to send a significant number of personnel into harm's way. Because we have no idea what is happening on board, there will in all likelihood be heavy losses, and we have to consider the very real threat that some of the significant weaponry systems on the *Indestructible* may be used to repel such a mission."

"And what's our third choice?"

"We continue our attempts to re-establish contact in the hope that we can negotiate a voluntary quarantine of the vessel."

"How would we do that?"

"We're still working the details out on this one, sir."

"When I asked you to have three options ready for me, I expected three options. Not two and a half."

"Yes, Prime Minister."

Andy sat back in his chair, his face suddenly long and drawn. "Does anyone have a cigarette?" he asked, looking around the table.

Taylor let out a small laugh. He pulled a packet from his trouser pocket. "I gave up twenty years ago, but I bought this packet yesterday. Looks like I'll be buying another one tonight."

"This is a strictly no smoking building, gentlemen, but as of right now, I'm giving you permission to light them if you've got them," Andy said, taking one of the cigarettes from the packet and placing it in his mouth. Taylor offered a light before igniting the tip of his own cigarette. Andy inhaled deeply before raising his head and blowing a tower of blue smoke into the air. He looked at the other three men then back to Taylor. "Nothing really prepares you for this kind of thing. I can only imagine what situations you gentlemen have faced in the past, but up until taking office, the only battles I ever fought were in the House of Commons. How long do we have?"

"Prime Minister?"

"How long do we have before making this decision becomes critical?"

"If the carrier proceeds on its current course and at its present speed, we estimate it will reach our waters within nine hours," Taylor replied.

"So how long does that give me before I need to make a decision?"

"Well, Prime Minister, it's not that simple. It depends on your decision. Regardless of what option you decide, I urge you to allow us to take immediate action should any aircraft attempt to take off from the ship."

"Well, yes, I believe that would be prudent," Andy

replied, "but I need some time to think about this."

"I understand, it's an onerous responsibility to have."

"Andy looked at his watch. Right, you and I are in the full COBRA meeting at nine, I'm going to have to head out now." He looked towards the other three men. "We'll meet back here at ten a.m. I'll have a decision for you then." The four military personnel all nodded and closed their folders. Andy thanked them, stubbed out his cigarette into a coffee mug and left.

The two police guards immediately began to follow Andy as he stepped out of the briefing room and headed down the corridor. One of them took out a packet of sweets and offered one to his boss. "Mint, sir?"

"Oh Jesus, thanks, Les," Andy said. "I almost forgot."

"That's what we're here for, sir."

"To keep my secret smoking habit from my wife?"

"To protect you, sir. We can handle Al Qaeda, but I'm running for cover if Mrs Beck launches an attack." Andy burst out laughing, and the two officers allowed themselves a small chuckle too.

"Fair enough, lads, fair enough."

They reached the outer office door, and the two highly trained, black-suited officers took guard while Andy walked in. "Mrs Beck phoned down, she said they'll be ready in ten minutes," Mel said.

"Okay, thanks," Andy said, looking at his watch. He went back to the door and popped his head around the corner to see his two bodyguards standing bolt upright, ready for anything. "Les, Darren, come speak to me for a moment," he said, heading back through the outer office to his own inner sanctum. The two plain-clothed policemen followed. Andy sat behind his desk and told the two men to sit. "I know both of you have signed confidentiality and non-disclosure agreements, but I'm not talking to you just because of that and the fact I need a sounding board. I'm talking to you because I know both of you were in the armed forces, you've worked for me for quite some time, and I genuinely have a lot of respect for the pair of you. I'd be keen to know what you think." He spent the next three minutes giving the two men a potted account of what had happened on board the HMS *Indestructible* as well as the three options.

"May I ask, sir? What is your gut instinct?" Les asked.

Andy cast a nervous smile before becoming a little emotional. He swallowed hard. "I want to save them. I want to try to save as many as we possibly can. All those men and women put their lives on the line for us every day. Don't they deserve at the very least not to be deserted in their time of need? Don't they deserve that, Les?"

Les looked towards Darren and then back towards the prime minister. "You can't justify to yourself ordering more personnel into harm's way to go on a treacherous rescue mission to save an unknown number of people?"

"Essentially, yes. As much as I want to," Andy replied. "The stats show the safest bet is by far and away rendering the *Indestructible* immobile as soon as possible, which could ultimately lead to it sinking. I'm not bothered about the billions of pounds, lads. I doubt we will ever need our warships again, there's nobody left to fight. I am bothered about the risk of the infection getting to these shores; but how can I knowingly abandon such brave men and women? How can I knowingly send more into such peril?"

"May I suggest something, sir?" Darren asked.

"Please, I was hoping you would."

"Prime Minister, these are extraordinary times. Why not do something extraordinary? Ask for volunteers within the armed forces. I know for a fact you'll get more men and women putting themselves forward than can fit on the ship."

"Sir, may I speak freely?" Les asked.

"Of course," Andy replied.

"I'm with Daz. Get a volunteer force in there. You wouldn't be forcing anyone, and you'd be honouring those men and women in the best way possible because I can almost guarantee you, you'll have more volunteers than you can deal with. Jesus, if I wasn't on an assignment, I'd bloody sign up," he said.

"I can always sign a release for you," Andy said, smiling.

"Most other assignments, sir, I'd say sign away. This one, I think it's worth sticking with."

# 17

"Here we are at Pine Wood Primary as the prime minsiter and Mrs Beck deliver their daughters to school," announced John Carr, the BBC's chief political correspondent.

There was a flurry of activity and shouts for attention from every direction as the couple walked up the short path to the school entrance. Both Andy and Trish knelt down and kissed their children before opening the door and ushering them in towards the waiting headmistress who, gratefully and happily, took their hands.

"Mister Prime Minister, Mr Prime Minister," shouted Carr as the loving couple walked back down the path.

"Good morning, John," Andy replied. "Do you have a question?"

"Good morning, Prime Minister, yes I do," replied the award-winning reporter.

Andy had been briefed by Xander that there would be at least one friendly reporter ready and primed to ask a question that would gain them political ground. He said, in all likelihood, it would be John Carr, so it was John Carr that Andy devoted all his energy to. "Go ahead, John," Andy said with the cheesiest of smiles on his face.

"Prime Minister, with the country in turmoil in the light of global events, do you really think delivering your children to school, which you have only done five times in the three years you have held your position, is a worthwhile expenditure of your time?"

Andy felt his phone buzz in his pocket. He brought it out and glanced at the message. It was from Xander, it read CARR NOT ON BOARD. *No fucking shit,* thought Andy. Despite being outside, everyone could feel the atmosphere thicken. As the door swung shut and the heels on the children's shoes could be heard clattering up the hallway, Andy turned towards the photographers, cameramen and journalists.

There were more shouts of "Prime Minister, Prime Minister" as he walked back down the path, holding Trish's hand tightly. As the couple reached the kerb side, he turned to address the cameras. The pair of them had asked to walk the twelve metres without the two bodyguards present, but, at the car, they stood either side of them. Les leaned in to the Prime Minister holding his walkie-talkie watch up to his mouth and pretending to talk into it. "Do you want me to take him out, sir? I can make it look like an accident," he whispered.

Andy turned to him, smiling and like a ventriloquist whispered, "I'll let you know in a minute." He continued to smile as his eyes went back to Carr. "That's a good question," he said, and all the shouts suddenly stopped so the journalists could hear his answer, "and believe me when I tell you that the team and I agonised over this," he added as a small ripple of laughter ran through the crowd. "As you can all imagine," he said, letting go of Trish's hand and walking forward. "My colleagues and I have very full plates today. I was working into the early hours of this morning, and I was up at four. Now, as well as being your prime minister, I am also a husband and a father. My colleagues who are at various schools this morning dropping off their children before they come into work are all politicians and public servants, and I'm proud to work alongside them. I felt it was important that we did this today. We need to remember who we are. We need to remember why we do the jobs we do. We need to remember why we chose this life. There is no better place to find that answer than at a school: the children, the loving parents, and, most of all, the hope. Schools have always provided hope. And the tools to help that hope grow into a reality can be found at every school in the country. So, to answer your question, yes, I believe it is a more than worthwhile expenditure of my time. I believe it is a more than worthwhile expenditure of my colleagues' time, and I hope the people at home feel the same." He looked straight into one of the cameras. "What starts as hope becomes victory." He looked towards the journalists. "Thank you very much for coming here today, but, as Mister Carr pointed out, I've got quite a lot on. If you have any questions, Xander will be holding a briefing later this morning, I'm sure he'll be able to answer them for you." Andy returned to the car, leaned in and kissed Trish before the pair of them climbed into the back seat. Les and Darren surveilled the surrounds before climbing in too.

"Had you prepared that or was it off the cuff?" Trish asked as the convoy pulled away.

"Xander was worried I might get hit with a question like that, so we jotted a couple of ideas down," he said before breaking out into a big grin.

"You are such a smarmy arse sometimes."

"Whatever gets the job done."

Andy's phone rang. "What the bloody hell was that, Xander?" he asked as he picked it up.

"I got it wrong," Xander replied on the other end of the phone.

"Yeah! No kidding you got it wrong. He's always been a little prick has that Carr. Take away his credentials for Downing Street."

"I understand you're upset, but that's really not a good idea."

Andy paused for a moment. He took a breath. "This is exactly the kind of shit we need knocking on the head. These people need to work with us, they don't need to be trying to trip us up for God's sake. Do they have any concept of what's going on? Do they?"

"Listen," Xander replied, "this is the whole purpose of the luncheon. We're going to try to win them over, right? And if that doesn't work, you have my permission to withdraw all their fucking credentials. But let's go in with reasonable heads on our shoulders, not storm in there in attack formation. Okay?"

"I'll see you in a few minutes," Andy said and hung up. He hit the speed dial for Mel. "Hi, Mel, can you get Taylor and his people to meet me back in the briefing room when I get back?"

"Sir, you'll see him in the COBRA meeting," Mel replied.

"Yes, I just want a brief chat with him before that."

"Yes, Prime Minister. Is there anything else?"

"No thanks, Mel, we're on our way back."

"Prime Minister?"

"Yes, Mel?"

"That was a great speech you gave at the school, sir. The networks are replaying it already."

Andy smiled. "Good to know. Thanks, Mel, I'll see you in a few minutes."

"What are you smiling at?" Trish asked.

"Nothing," he replied, sitting back in the comfortable seat.

"Y'know, if your head gets any bigger, you'll have to start driving around in an open-top car," she replied. Andy's smile widened. "I think we should bring my mum and dad down here, they'll soon give you a reality check."

The grin vanished from Andy's face instantly.

"Don't even joke about that, Trish." Andy suddenly noticed smirks on the two bodyguards' faces. "I don't need an excuse, I can get both of you transferred like that, you know," he said, snapping his fingers.

"Good luck facing the mother-in-law then, sir," Darren replied. For a moment, there was a pause, but then all four of them burst out laughing.

It was not a long journey to Downing Street, and cameras were flashing long before the car came to a stop. Les and Darren climbed out first and surveyed the area. Les put his hand up to his ear to listen to the sit-rep and then ushered Trish and Andy out of the car. They paused on the Downing Street step for a quick photo shoot then headed inside.

Les closed the heavy door behind them, and Trish and Andy both breathed a sigh of relief. "Right," Andy said, leaning in and kissing Trish. "Thanks for that, I need to head to the briefing room, got some business to take care of," he said, nodding towards Les and Darren before disappearing. As he emerged from the short underground corridor and into the wide Whitehall walkways, he saw numerous cabinet members in discussion with one another. He nodded good morning and made the briefest of pleasantries while Les and Darren followed him. On reaching the meeting room, Taylor and the rest of the group who had briefed him as to his options regarding HMS *Indestructible* earlier were waiting, looking nervous.

The three men paused at the entrance. Les and Darren took up positions at either side of the door, and just before Andy entered, they both whispered, "Good luck, sir," under their breath.

"Thanks, lads," Andy replied as he stepped over the threshold and closed the door behind him. Taylor and the others looked towards the Prime Minister as he stood at the head of the table. "I never served my country in the armed forces, and I am in a constant state of awe of anyone that has or does. To be willing to lay your life down to protect your country and fellow countrymen is the ultimate act of selflessness," Andy said, pausing and looking at each of the assembled faces before carrying on. "We all know what this virus is capable of. We all know the dangers if it reaches these shores, and under no circumstances am I going to let that happen." Immediately, all the men assembled looked down at their hands. They knew what was coming.

"Sir—" Taylor began, but Andy immediately threw up his hand to cut him off.

"I want an assault force to take back the ship." All the other faces suddenly shot up again, looking straight towards Andy, not sure if they had misheard. "This will be the most dangerous mission any of them will have ever undertaken, and it is against a foe that not one of these brave men and women would have ever conceived of. So, I want volunteers. Ideally, we'll be hoping for people from the Special Forces, but if there aren't enough recruits among them then we'll widen the net. They will have every resource put at their disposal. Before we talk about blasting the *Indestructible* to hell, we should do our best to save them, don't you think?"

"But, Prime Minister…" Taylor began.

"Yes?"

"The logistics of getting a volunteer force together in time, on such a scale, it's—"

"No!" Andy said. "I don't want to hear that crap. Last year, the Animal Rights Coalition announced a demonstration in Trafalgar Square, and within two hours, they had ten thousand people blockading the streets. This is the twenty-first century. I want this done, and I want it done now." He looked at the other men around the table. "If you come back to me and tell me there are no volunteers, I'll understand that. If you come back to me and say we don't know how to find volunteers, I most certainly will not." He turned to Taylor. "You and I are in the COBRA meeting right now, but I want the rest of your team on this, and I want to reconvene at ten thirty a.m. Thank you, gentlemen."

Understanding that was their cue to leave, the other men got up, thanked the prime minister and left the room. Taylor stood too. "Please give me a moment, Prime Minister, I'll be right back," he said and followed them out.

Almost immediately, Doug walked through the door, followed by a procession of people carrying folders or briefcases. They took seats around the table and laid out their notes in front of them.

The door opened again, and this time it was Xander who entered. "No, I'm obviously not making myself clear," he said, holding the mobile phone up to his ear with his shoulder while looking for a piece of paper in one of his files. "If he's not at this luncheon today, my first job of the afternoon will be booking a courier to make a delivery to his wife." Xander found the piece of paper he was looking for and placed it at the front of the folder. "Yeah! You know exactly what I'm talking about. She'd love those photos of you and him at the private party Mick held after the last day of the conference." Xander placed his folder down on the table and took the phone in his hand. He put a finger up to Andy and mouthed, *One minute.* "I wouldn't? I wouldn't? Jesus, how long have you known me? Of course I fucking would. Niccolo Machiavelli was my fucking hero, and those photos will just be the start. Now get him to the fucking luncheon—no excuses. And you can turn the tears off too, that shit doesn't work with me." He hung up the phone and placed it down on the table, suddenly realising all the eyes in the room were firmly fixed on him.

"Nice," Andy said. "Classy. Blackmail and threats. Great legacy we're going to leave behind."

"I keep telling you, there has to be a future before we can worry about a legacy. One thing at a time."

Taylor came back through the door and nodded at Andy, who reciprocated. "Okay," Andy said, "I've met with most of you in the past few hours. I wanted to have a meeting to establish where we are right at this moment. Sonya, I'll come to you first. All of you will know Sonya, but some of you might not have met her yet. One month as commissioner of the Metropolitan Police and already the apocalypse has struck. I have to say, I'm not impressed with your record so far." A ripple of laughter fluttered around the room.

"Yes, sir. I'm sorry Prime Minister," she said with a polite smile on her face.

"Seriously, thank you for joining us this morning. So, tell me where we are," Andy said, leaning forward on the table, making his two index fingers into a small steeple and placing them over his lips.

"Good morning," Sonya said, beginning to address the PM and the rest of the assembled team. "The statistics I am working from are for the Greater London area but are representative of the rest of the country. During the first three hours, after the prime minister's address yesterday, we experienced an unprecedented number of emergency calls." She looked towards Doug, and a thin smile appeared briefly on her face before it disappeared again. "My office had been liaising with Doug's throughout yesterday afternoon, and we had cancelled leave and drew on every resource at our disposal from auxiliary staff and special constables to more emergency line operators. Obviously, we did not inform anyone of the exact nature of what was happening, but we explained the current UK threat level was being raised from severe to critical." She paused and took a drink of water. "Although we experienced this anomalous number of calls, a lot of them were false alarms. Virtually everyone who had one too many yesterday was identified by some well-meaning busybody as a reanimated corpse," she said with a smile.

Andy broke into a smile too. "Go on," he said.

"Well, sir, we have a lot of community officers who have good relationships with Neighbourhood Watch commanders, and these contacts proved vital in weeding out a lot of the erroneous calls. Although we were sent on a number of wild goose chases, they did not overwhelm us.

There was a significant spike in real crime reported during that first three hours, I'm sorry to say. Panic seems to bring out the worst in people. There were increases in muggings, rapes, and burglaries; we ended up stationing teams at larger supermarkets and petrol stations as panic buying got out of hand and turned into mini-riots, but after this initial spike, things began to return to a more manageable level. I think when people realised they weren't seeing the dead get up and walk, they began to take stock."

"Okay, so, as of this second, what's the state of play?" Andy asked.

"Well, sir, it's still pretty much the same. I think for the time being we will be able to manage, but in the longer term, we will need more bodies. I've spoken to the home secretary," she said, nodding and smiling towards Paul Ashford across the table, "and he believes we can significantly increase our numbers within the next fourteen days."

Andy looked towards Paul. Their eyes met, and each of them saw nothing but an enemy. Andy had won the leadership election comfortably, but Paul Ashford was the closest runner-up. The man was full of dirty tricks, and he left the party damaged and reeling by a lot of the slurs that he levelled against Andy and his cabinet. Given a choice, Andy would never have selected him for any post, but Ashford had sway with some of the party elders. Rumour was that he had damaging files on most of them regarding their finances. Andy was very loyal to those who had looked after him, and when his mentor had come to him, almost pleading, Andy had no choice but to play the game. Ashford opened the file in front of him.

"With the conscription scheme you announced last night, our initial estimates suggest we could bolster front line policing by up to twelve thousand. In addition, we may be able to outsource some of the administrative duties freeing up more personnel," Ashford said before closing the file again.

"That sounds promising. What do you think, Sonya?"

"We could certainly do with the feet on the ground, Prime Minister."

"How quickly can we get the ball rolling with this?" Andy asked, turning back towards Ashford.

"As soon as you give the nod. I'd have started straight away, but you must have some technical problems in your office. I haven't had a call from you. I'd have thought the home secretary was one of the first people you'd have spoken to at a time like this."

Andy glared at Ashford. "As you can imagine, things have been hectic to say the least. I've prioritised and handed work off when I've needed to. Your office has been liaising with Doug, who has kept me up to date with everything. Thank you for your hard work on this, Paul, and I swear the second I need to talk to you, I'll pick up the phone."

Ashford's eyes flashed with rage for a moment before he remembered where he was. "Very well, Prime Minister."

"Thanks again, Paul; Doug will walk you out. I've told Nadine to expect your call."

"You want me to go now? Before the meeting is over?"

"Yes. I just needed an update from you. No point tying you up when there is so much important work to do."

"I … err … I should be here. This is important," Ashford replied, clearly taken aback.

"No! We're good. Thanks again. I'll be in touch with you later to find out how things are going."

Ashford stood, and his eyes burned with fury. He looked towards, Andy, then Xander, and finally Doug as his face got redder and redder. "No need to see me out, I'll speak to you later," he said to Doug before storming out of the room.

The nature of the relationship was common

knowledge among all the Downing Street insiders, but Liz and Sonja looked genuinely taken aback. Picking up on this, Andy tried to reassure them. "Things between Paul and the rest of the human population can be a little strained sometimes," he said with a smile on his face. "I hope he will give you whatever you need, Sonya, but if you have any difficulty, please contact Doug. Doug is an excellent expediter."

*

Seb sat in his boxer shorts at the end of the bed. He looked back towards Mya, who was lying on top of the sheets. She was in a deep sleep, and her heavy breathing was threatening to turn into snoring at any moment. He pulled the laptop out of his bag and for the first time took a proper look at it. It was not like anything he had seen before. *What the hell were the French doing with a Russian laptop?* "It doesn't make sense," he whispered.

"Huh?" Mya said, rousing from her sleep.

"Sorry. I didn't mean to wake you."

"What did you say?"

"I said this doesn't make sense."

Mya turned and pulled one of Seb's pillows across to prop her head up so she could look at him.

"What's confusing? We stole a Russian air-gapped laptop from behind a false wall in the library of the Elysée Palace, the official residence of the French president. Seems perfectly straightforward to me," she said with a smirk. "Why wouldn't the French president have a Russian laptop?"

"My guess is Dupont didn't even know it was there. He's not the savviest political operator at the best of times. I doubt if he'd have the brain to turn this on, never mind digest what was on it. But the Elysée Palace is a pretty secure place to hide something like this. It's not as if it can be easily infiltrated, is it?"

"So who do you think put it there?" Mya asked.

"My guess, our French counterparts."

"The DGSE? How? Why?"

"I'm not even going to attempt to turn this thing on. It wouldn't surprise me if the bloody thing's boobytrapped." Seb reached across for his trousers and fished out his mobile phone. He pulled open the case and removed a small pad, which he then stuck just to the left of the touchpad on the laptop before folding the screen down. He was just about to place the laptop back in his rucksack when he noticed a small, rough inscription etched into the hard plastic of the case.

"Konets Sveta," he said out loud.

"Huh?"

"Somebody has scratched Konets Sveta into the case."

"Doomsday?"

"Yep," he said, finally placing the laptop into the bag and carefully putting it down on the dressing table.

"This day just gets weirder and weirder," Mya said.

"Didn't I say that?"

Mya sat up, and Seb joined her, resting his back against the padded headboard. The two of them remained silent as they stared towards the bag.

# 18

"Okay, so, is there any other business for the time being?" Andy asked as he looked around the table. The meeting had gone on for over an hour, but there was a lot of information to take in, so it was only to be expected. All the heads in the room shook, and people began to gather their files and mobile phones.

Doug stood up. "As you can all appreciate, the PM is going to be spread pretty thin, so, if you need anything, please run it by me first."

"Taylor, Will, please stay back, I want a quick chat with you. Liz, do you have everything you need?" Andy asked.

"Yes, thank you," she said, heading out.

"Thank you for joining us, Sonya; that was your first of what I guess will be many COBRA meetings," Andy said, smiling.

"A pleasure, sir. You know where I am if you need me."

Andy smiled and nodded at the rest of the assembly before they all got up and left. Xander and Doug paused.

"Yeah, I want you two here as well."

Taylor and Ravenshaw were frantically checking their messages while Andy walked across to the coffee machine and poured himself another drink. "Y'know they say people who drink black coffee are more likely to be psychopaths, don't you?" Doug said, smiling.

"You need to be a bloody psychopath to want this job," Andy replied, taking a sip from his mug.

"Fair enough."

"Sir," Taylor said, beginning to stand, "am I okay to make a quick call before we begin this meeting?"

"Is it pertinent to what we'll be discussing?" Andy asked.

"Yes."

"Then go ahead," he said before taking another sip of coffee and sitting down.

"Are you sure you want me in on this one?" Xander asked.

"Yes," Andy replied. "If ever I needed something spinning, it's now."

"Sounds ominous."

"Is there anything about any of this that doesn't sound ominous?"

"You make a good point," Xander replied.

"Taylor has kept you apprised of everything, Will, yes?"

Will nodded. "He's kept me up to date. I didn't see any point in being in on the other meetings. I've been on conference calls concerning everything from the training of the conscripts to compulsory purchase orders of newly built housing estates near barracks to house them all. I think I might want to take early retirement," he said with a smile on his face.

"Fat chance. Listen, don't get too tied up with that stuff. Nadine is shit hot with the logistical side, and she's got a dozen deputies who live for that kind of crap."

Will smiled. "You don't have to worry, Andy. My

doctor said everything was looking good. I've got no intention of having another heart attack."

"So, you intended to have the last one?"

"God, I'd forgotten what a pain in the arse you could be. You're like my bloody daughters," Will said.

"Look, Will. I trust you with my life. You have always had my back, I'll always have yours. All I'm saying is don't take on too much. We've got people, okay? Lots and lots of people who are really good at what they do. Don't spread yourself too thin."

"Okay, son."

"Sarky bastard," Andy said, smiling. "How are your daughters, anyway?"

"Just like their bloody mother, bossy and demanding but with hearts of gold. They wanted me to tell you how brilliant you were last night by the way. They were really proud. Janice would have been proud of you. I know I was," Will said, looking down at his hands.

"Thanks, Will. That means a lot."

"I don't want to teach you how to suck eggs…" Will trailed off, pulling his hands from the table and into his lap.

"Go on."

"No," replied Will, "it doesn't matter."

"It does matter. It always matters. I value your opinion about everything."

"You're going to have problems with Ashford."

"We always have problems with Ashford," Xander said, placing his mobile phone in his pocket and pulling his chair closer to the table.

"That man has been one continuous problem ever since we took power," Doug added.

"I understand he's been a thorn in your side, but I think he's planning something. Sharks respond to vibrations in the water and the first sign he gets a whiff of blood, he'll close in," Will said.

"I agree, but we've not actually put a foot wrong

yet," Andy replied.

"Well…"

"Well, what?"

"You may have been a little heavy-handed with the media. Remember, he's well connected with some of the publishers and station owners. More to the point, his dad is well connected, Andy. I know you've got a meeting with them today and some people might have applied a little pressure to get the right people here," Will said, looking towards Xander, "but you need to be careful; these are influential people – powerful people – and the last thing you want is them painting you black at the time you need them most. If things turn bad, don't think for a second Ashford wouldn't try to capitalise on it."

"I know we don't get on, but surely he wouldn't try to take political advantage with all that's at stake."

"You are frighteningly naive sometimes, Andy," Will replied.

"Yeah, you really are," Xander added.

"Have to agree with them here," Doug said before turning to Will. "Don't worry; I've been monitoring everything that little shit has been doing. I've got logs of his calls, who he's been meeting, the lot."

"I could really have done without knowing that," Will replied.

"This is National Security we're talking about, and I'm not going to let some overprivileged, treacherous little shit like Paul Ashford put this country in jeopardy with his manoeuvring and meddling. He wants to go to the mattresses, we'll go to the fucking mattresses," Doug said.

"Great, now you've got him quoting *The Godfather*," Andy said, shaking his head.

"I'm just saying, Will, that Xander and I have got Andy's back on this. He might be too nice for his own good sometimes; that's not a problem we suffer from."

"Trust me; I believe you," Will said with a thin smile.

"Too nice? I've never had that levelled at me before."

"I didn't want to use the term 'gullible twat' in front of an old family friend," Doug said, to which they all let out a small laugh.

"Good. I'm glad you're on top of things," Will replied, just as Taylor returned to the room.

"Okay, first things first," he said, turning to Doug and Xander. "There is a situation." He went on to give a potted account of what had happened on the HMS *Indestructible* and the plans that they were putting in place.

"Jesus," Xander blurted.

"Christ," Doug added.

"Yeah well, you can see why we're going to need your help with this, whichever way it goes," Andy said before turning to Taylor. "So, what can you tell us?" he asked.

"There's still no word on the HMS *Valiant*, Prime Minister, but there is some good news."

"Well come on, spill it."

"We've been inundated with Special Forces volunteers for the rescue mission, sir."

"That's pretty humbling," Andy replied.

"Yes. Yes, it is."

"So, what's the plan?" Andy asked.

"Can you give me half an hour, sir?"

Andy looked at the clock on the wall. "We'll meet back here at eleven a.m." Andy said as he, Doug and Xander picked up their belongings and left the briefing room.

\*

Seb and Mya had dozed off holding their vigil of the laptop bag. They were so deep in their sleep that, at first, the sounds outside the hotel did not rouse them, but gradually, eyelids began to flicker, and a slow creeping awareness of their surroundings took hold.

Screeching tyres and frightened shouts started to fill the street below, and they both crept to the window, careful not to get spotted while observing what was going on. Approximately one hundred metres down the road in the direction of the metro station from which they had escaped idled a black van. The back doors were open, and a half-dressed woman was running up the street, away from the parked vehicle. A man was running after her, carrying a meat cleaver in his right hand and shouting something neither Seb nor Mya could make out.

"Aidez-moi! Aidez-moi!" screamed the woman as she continued to run up the centre of the road.

"Holy shit, we've got to help her," Mya said, running across to the bed and beginning to throw her clothes on.

"Wait!"

"Fuck wait! She needs our help."

"Mya! It's too late," Seb said, turning around to look at her.

Mya rushed to the window and only then saw what Seb had seen. Sprinting along on an intercept course down one of the side streets were a dozen of the reanimated creatures. Everything turned to slow motion as Mya watched. The first two beasts launched towards the woman at the same time, knocking her to the ground in a sliding tackle. Her screams for help immediately turned to screams of agony as the infected tore into the woman's flesh with their teeth. Seb and Mya angled their heads further down the street to see the man with the meat cleaver come to a sudden stop before turning to run back to the van as fast as he could. He was clearly no athlete, and the remainder of the relentless creatures with their lust for blood rocketed down the street after him.

Within seconds, one, two, three, four beasts were on him, biting, ripping at his fatty flesh while their victim let out high-pitched terrified howls and screams. Before the last of his cries had finished echoing up and down the street, the woman, his one-time victim, was back on her feet. Only now she was no longer the hunted, she was a hunter, looking for fresh prey. Along with the two creatures that had attacked her, she moved off, searching for her first kill. They headed down the road in the direction of the van.

Seb went across to the bed and began to get dressed. "Come on," he said.

"Come on where? It's all over."

"We're getting out of here."

"What the hell are you talking about?"

"The van—the engine's still running."

"But those things are out there," Mya replied, still watching them out of the window.

"If they're not gone by the time we get there, we'll take them out, but that van is our ticket out of here."

"And where are we going to go exactly? Nice trip down to the Riviera?"

"No, nice trip to Honfleur, or thereabouts anyway."

"Where's that?"

"It's a small city on the channel, with lots of boats."

"Err, Seb, you do know we're in Paris, yes?"

"That particular fact had not escaped me, Mya. We're in Paris. Honfleur is just over two hours away on the A-Thirteen. Well, two hours on a good day," he said, placing his vest back on.

"It's a hell of a long shot," Mya said, starting to put the rest of her clothes on too.

"Look. Right now, we're in the most populous city in the country. The second we're out of it, our chances for survival improve. We can do this, Mya."

Mya looked around the room then back at Seb. "Okay, but I want to go back to the pantry before we go. Deal?"

"Deal!"

*

"Edward Phillips has been calling, and Harry says he's got a first cut ready for you to view," Mel said as Andy, Doug and Xander walked into the outer office, leaving the two plain-clothed police at the door.

"Thanks, Mel," Andy replied as the three of them continued into the prime minister's office. "Actually, just give me a second," Andy said as he retraced his steps.

He popped his head around the door and looked at the two policemen. "Thought you might like to know, lads. We got more volunteers than we could handle. I appreciate your counsel."

"Our pleasure, sir. Glad we could help," Les replied.

Andy stepped back over the threshold to the outer office and leaned on Mel's desk. "How you doing?" he asked quietly.

Mel smiled warmly. "I'm doing just fine. Don't you worry about me."

Andy smiled and walked back into his own office. They all took seats, and suddenly Andy's stomach began to rumble." He pushed the intercom button. "Mel, can you get us some food, please?"

"You've got the luncheon shortly, sir."

"Yes, I know, but I'm starving. Just ask the kitchen to bring up a couple of rounds of sandwiches or something, would you?"

"Yes, Prime Minister."

The three men sat in silence for a moment. Their brains had been working overtime for the past thirty-six hours, so a moment of tranquillity was relished.

"So, what's happening with Ashford?" Andy asked.

"Don't worry about it," Doug replied, "we've got it covered."

Andy looked at them both and a heavy silence fell over the room. It lingered for a few minutes until Andy took a breath and stood up again. "Mel, where have we set Harry up?" he asked as he stepped into the outer office.

"Err ... I thought you knew," she replied.

"Thought I knew what?"

"Mrs Beck came down and invited them to set up in the residence."

"Oh shit!" Andy replied, forgetting everything else and running down the corridor and up to the third floor. Les and Darren sprinted after him as he almost burst through the front door. He heard Harry's gravelly laugh and Trish's donkey like hiccups when she found something too funny. "Oh God!" he said as he walked along the short hallway and into the living room.

"Sweetheart!" Trish said, getting up and throwing her arms around Andy as he entered. "We've been waiting for you for a while."

"Sorry, meeting overran."

"Don't worry, Harry's been keeping me entertained with stories about some of the after parties you had to go to when I was working," she said, beginning to giggle again.

"Oh good!" Andy said, giving Harry a glare. "So, Mel said you'd got something for me."

"Yeah!" Harry replied, switching on the TV. He walked across and placed a USB stick into the back before returning to the sofa with Carla. Trish took Andy by the hand and led him to an armchair where she sat, while he squatted on the arm.

The video began with a view of Earth from space. Slowly, all the land began to glow bright orange as if it was turning to lava, and the camera zoomed in on Europe. Great Britain stayed green, and an animation of a wall being built in the waters surrounding its coast began, while the rest of Europe glowed brighter orange before finally turning black.

Suddenly a montage of quick-changing video sequences started. CCTV footage from around the globe of people running for their lives. Each image lasted just a second before the next, then the next. At the end of the first extract, the screen went black before "PANIC ON THE STREETS" appeared in white lettering. The next sequence of quick-changing video clips started rolling. It showed more CCTV footage of people running down busy pavements and roads in built-up cities. It showed people getting knocked down, barging into shop windows and doorways, and the final clip was of a mother being pushed out of the way. She fell, losing the grip on her baby's pram. The pram toppled off the curb and got crushed by a lorry that was heading up the street.

"Oh my God," Trish gasped as she squeezed Andy's hand tight.

The screen went black again before "PANIC KILLS BABIES" appeared in white lettering.

A third sequence of video images began. This time, the CCTV footage showed people running in various underground stations. Multiple victims were trampled on stairs and escalators, even more were barged off platforms. The fast-paced clips came to a halt again as the screen turned black.

"PANIC KILLS MOTHERS" appeared in white before a two-second clip of a woman being forced off a platform into the path of a train. The screen went black again before "PANIC KILLS FATHERS" appeared, followed by a similar sequence featuring a man. "PANIC KILLS BROTHERS", "PANIC KILLS SISTERS", "PANIC", "PANIC", "PANIC". After each text image came a horrifying clip of someone dying a needless death.

The screen went black again before a slow fade in. This time it was a clip of extremely fast cell duplication being viewed through a microscope. The screen went black once more and "WE ARE IN A WAR" appeared in white writing. Crystal clear CCTV footage of a hospital corridor flashed on screen, and eerie, rhythmical orchestral music began to act as a chilling soundtrack to the images. A nurse was suddenly pounced on by a figure who proceeded to tear a chunk out of her neck with its teeth. Both Andy and Trish gasped and grasped each other's hands even tighter.

"Jesus wept," Andy said.

The nurse fell to the floor as the creature began sprinting down the corridor towards another victim. The black screen flashed again; this time the words "A WAR LIKE NO OTHER" came up. The footage from the hospital resumed, and the fallen nurse sprang to her feet like a rabid cheetah. Her head flicked from one direction to the other before she too bolted down the corridor in search of prey.

The screen went black, and the music began to increase in volume. "MAKE NO MISTAKE" appeared in white lettering; then it vanished just as quickly making way for "WE ARE IN THE FIGHT OF OUR LIVES". CCTV footage of a Spanish street appeared on the screen. Dozens of reanimated corpses were sprinting after a young woman. The screen turned to black and the music reached a crescendo. "WHAT HAPPENS NOW … IS UP TO YOU." The music finished and the screen turned to black one last time.

Andy and Trish were still squeezing each other's hands. Their eyes were fixed on the blank screen, almost disbelieving what they had just witnessed. The horrific silence continued for a few seconds then Andy looked across towards Harry.

"Was that the kinda thing you were after?" Harry asked nonchalantly.

For a moment, Andy just stared, and when he spoke, it was in a barely audible whisper. "Yes."

"Bangin'! Any chance of a fresh brew? I'm fuckin' parched!"

# 19

Seb and Mya paused as they reached the main entrance. What lay beyond that front door was hell on earth, and the relief they had experienced since setting foot in the hotel was now a distant memory as the reality of the situation enveloped them once more.

"Are you ready?" Mya asked.

Seb fixed the silencer onto his Browning and nodded. "Let's do this," he said, untying the sash, pushing open the heavy door and stepping onto the street. He immediately turned his head right, scanning the city landscape before looking back towards Mya. "We're clear," he whispered.

Mya walked through the door, and the pair ran across to a parked Renault where they crouched down to survey their surroundings. She cautiously popped her head around the side to get a good look down the street. Her eyes went beyond the van and focussed on the group of reanimated corpses who were heading away from them. "Come on," she whispered, taking the lead. The pair continued their low run diagonally across the street to another parked vehicle. This time Seb looked out to see where the hostiles were.

"Okay," he said, mounting the pavement. He and Mya were out of the line of sight of the creatures now but still stayed low, just on the off chance there were any other dangers present. They reached the van and quietly closed the rear doors before both climbing in through the open driver side. Seb handed Mya his bag with the laptop and a few scavenged bits and pieces from the hotel. She placed it in the footwell, and he gently pulled the door closed. "Here goes nothing," he said, putting the gear stick into the reverse position and easing off the handbrake.

The engine whirred as the van moved backwards and, suddenly, the creatures who had been heading towards the centre of the city spun around and began sprinting towards the noise before their eyes could even focus on what it was exactly they were running towards. Their simple brains identified an alien sound. Whether it was the voice of a human or a mechanical creature, it was not a sound they were capable of creating.

The van straightened, and both Mya and Seb shot glances into the wing mirrors. The infected were fast, but, as Seb put his foot down on the accelerator, they began to get smaller. He changed into second, and then third, leaving the old danger behind them and heading into an entirely new one. He reached into his pocket and pulled out his mobile phone, punching the unlock number in with his thumb.

"Shit. Battery's getting low," he said. "Still no signal either."

Mya immediately opened the glove compartment. "Ha! Maybe it's our lucky day," she said, pulling out a mobile phone charger. She plugged it into the lighter socket and grabbed the phone from Seb's hand, looking at the bag of connectors and finding one that married to the socket in the phone.

"Voilà," she said, putting the phone in the small

well behind the handbrake.

"That's something, at least," Seb said, checking both mirrors. "Now all we need is a bloody—"

The flash came before the sound, and it was only when the van was lifted off the ground and the searing heat of the blast flooded the street like a volcano's lava that the thunderous rumble drowned out the shriek of tearing metal. The van toppled on its side and grated across the tarmac and cement as the force of the explosion pushed it through the storefront on the opposite side of the road. The crashing glass flew through the smashed driver side window, heralding a bloody eruption that blinded Mya before a final jolt as the van collided with a concrete pillar knocked her into unconsciousness.

*

Andy sat alone in his office. It was not too long until he was due to go into the media luncheon, but he wanted a minute, just one, to himself. *One minute isn't too much to ask, is it?* He would not be a leader, he would not be a father or a husband, he would just be himself. He would be allowed to be afraid of what he had seen. He would be allowed to be horrified by what he had seen. Just one minute, one.

"Knock, knock," Doug said as he popped his head around the corner. "Are you ready to go? Trish, Harry and Xander are already down there."

Andy let out a shallow, disappointed sigh. One minute obviously was too much to ask. "Has everyone shown up?"

"From what I've heard, yes. I think they realised we weren't pissing about."

"This is a gamble, but I think we can make it pay off," Andy said. "Have you seen the video yet?"

"Yes, it's bloody fantastic. Kudos to you for getting Harry on the case. The little shit irritates the hell out of me, but he knows his stuff."

"Fantastic isn't the word I used. You didn't find it the least bit horrifying, gut-wrenching … heartbreaking?"

"Hey look, it's a tragedy what's happening, but it was a bloody brilliant video. It will do exactly what we want it to. That pram sequence—sheer fucking genius."

"You're a monster. You are an absolute monster. I made a pact with the devil the day I brought you on board," Andy said with no hint of a smile. "I suppose you've got a shrine to him at your flat, and you worship him every night?"

"Don't be ridiculous. The last I heard, he was worshipping me," Doug said and beamed a mouthful of white teeth.

Andy shook his head and stood. "Come on then, let's get this over with."

"Oh, by the way, I forgot to tell you, Her Majesty and co. are all tucked away safe, up at Balmoral."

"Good, that's … good," Andy said as they walked down the corridor with the two bodyguards following behind.

"You don't care, do you?" Doug asked.

"Her Majesty and the rest of the royal family perform a vital role," Andy replied.

"So, that's a no, is it?"

"Her Majesty and the rest of the royal family perform a vital role," Andy repeated.

"Uh-huh."

They both came to a pause outside the door to the function room. "Here goes nothing," Andy said as he pushed down the handle and stepped inside. Their entrance went virtually unnoticed as they milled through the busy room. Important looking publishers and TV station executives were engaged in conversations with MPs, some of Xander's well-trained media bots and Trish. Andy's face lit up as he walked towards her; he could tell she was wowing the three middle-aged men she was talking to. If it was not for the fact that politics bored her to tears, she would have made a great politician.

"Darling!" She leaned in to kiss Andy as he walked up to her. "Rescue me, please," she whispered in his ear before pulling away with a huge smile still on her face.

"Hello, gentlemen," Andy said, shaking hands with each of them. "Long time, no see."

"Well, your attack dog made it pretty clear that we didn't have a choice other than showing up," said one of the men.

Andy smiled, the same disarming smile he used when he was heckled in the Commons. He took hold of Trish's hand, and suddenly the three assembled media men remembered who they were addressing. "Well, I apologise if Xander may have come across a little vehement in his request for you to attend, but that was only because the very future of our country depends on it. The men and women assembled in this room are among the most influential people in Britain. I needed you here today because what lies ahead of us is something I cannot even begin to explain the enormity of. But look, we'll talk in a little while. There's a video presentation I want you all to see, and then we'll go from there. Fair enough?" The men nodded, and Andy walked to the front of the room and mounted the small podium that had been used so many times for televised addresses.

The room began to hush as more people noticed the prime minister was on the podium, waiting for them to finish their conversations. When the sound had died down enough for him to be heard, he began to speak. "Firstly, I'd like to thank you all for coming today. I realise this was short notice, but I would not have asked you here if it was not critical to the safety and well-being of our nation." Andy paused, expecting someone to come out with a glib comment about the manner in which their presence had been requested, but the room remained quiet. "I'm going to show you a video now. When it's over, there's a buffet, and

I see plenty of you are already aware there's a free bar," Andy said with a grin, getting polite laughter in return. "A good number of my colleagues are here too this afternoon, and they'll be circulating if you have any questions, but right this second, I'd appreciate your attention." Andy nodded at Harry, who looked across to Carla. The lights dimmed in the function room, and the video began playing, cast on the wall by a digital projector. The surround sound did not come into its own until the music began, but as the volume increased, so did the effect. Andy stood to the side. He had no desire to see the video again, he was still reeling from the first time, but he did want to see the audience reactions. These were battle-hardened newspaper men and women as well as TV station owners who had nerves of steel.

The temperature in the room was a steady twenty-two degrees centigrade, but Andy witnessed chill after chill run down people's spines as the video played. He felt a hand shuffle into his own and looked across to see Trish standing there, watching the audience, as he was. Gasps sounded as the pram toppled into the road, and one person let out a stifled cry. Mouths dropped open and every set of eyes in the room apart from Andy's, Trish's, Doug's and Xander's was transfixed by the ghoulish film.

When it came to an end, Andy nodded at Harry, who gave the signal for the lights to go back up. The room remained silent, and as Andy and Trish looked into the audience, they saw more than a single tear trickle down the cheeks of some of the hardest nosed men and women in the country. Andy broke the quiet as his footsteps echoed back onto the small wooden podium.

"I appreciate your attention, and I can tell by looking around the room that those images had the same effect on you as they had on my wife and I." Andy beckoned Trish to join him on the small stage. She stepped up and took his hand while he continued talking. "We all have families. We all have friends and people we care about. We can't allow this to happen over here; we can't allow this virus to get here; we can't allow panic to seize our nation. This is why I've asked you here today. There is no assembly of people in the country who have more influence and more sway on public opinion. I'm asking you to use that for the sake of the country and not for your own sakes. I'm asking you not to scaremonger, not to sensationalise. I'm asking you to work together with us to put the country's mind at ease, to give this country a chance that no other had. I'm asking you to join us in this war. Because in my heart—"he looked towards Trish and squeezed her hand tightly before looking back out over the audience "—I know we can be victorious. In my heart, I know we can bring out the best from the British people. In my heart, I know this does not have to be the end of everything."

\*

Mya struggled to see anything at first as warm blood still covered the upper half of her face. She could feel the cold tile floor against her head. The passenger side window had shattered, and she could tell without moving that at least one shard of glass had dug into her shoulder. She slowly looked around, her vision becoming a little clearer with each blink. The van was on its side, she remembered the explosion before she was knocked unconscious briefly. She remembered blood, not her blood. Seb had fallen on top of her. She looked up towards the airbag that had inflated. Seb had not worn his seatbelt, so the airbag would have done him no good. She pushed hard to try to move him.

"Seb!" she said, shoving him. "Seb!" she said again, pushing, trying to shuffle from underneath him at the same time. Suddenly, she became aware of sounds; the by now familiar guttural growl of the creatures. The van had crashed through a shop counter and hit the back wall by way of a concrete support. The bonnet and the roof both rested against the exposed breezeblock, creating a small enclosure through the shattered windscreen. The only way the creatures could get to Mya, for the time being, was if they climbed onto the side of the van and lowered themselves down. Everything she had seen so far told her that they did not possess a great level of intelligence and such reasoning would be beyond them, but she decided not to take any risks. "Seb!" she whispered and this time pushed and shimmied to the side, finally freeing herself. Seb's body flopped face down beside her. She had seen Seb live through a thousand situations that would have killed normal men. He was invincible in her eyes, but suddenly, she was concerned. She reached to feel for a pulse and drew her hand back quickly as she realised the blood that coated her face had come from Seb's neck wound. She turned his head toward her, and his lifeless eyes stared back. A small whimper left her mouth, followed by a louder cry. Suddenly, she became deaf to the growls outside as sadness overcame her. "No. No. No," she said over and over again in between baying sobs. "No." She shuffled her left arm underneath him and brought her right over the top to join them in an embrace as she rested her head against his. She continued to cry, even when the first creature began to struggle and crawl through the broken and buckled door at the back of the van.

*

Andy and Trish left the function about half an hour after the video was shown. There was a small army of polished operatives working the room, all marshalled by Doug and Xander. "I would have stayed if you wanted me to," Trish said, looping her arm through Andy's as they walked.

"I know you would," he said, looking across at her and smiling, "but I couldn't ask you to do that. You worked your magic in there, you did more than I could have asked, and now we'll leave it to Xander and Doug while I get on with the rest of the day."

"You know I'm here if you need me, don't you?"

"I know," he said as they came to a stop outside the outer office.

"I don't suppose you'll have time to grab a bite with us tonight, will you?"

"I'd love to, but I don't want to promise anything."

"I understand. The girls would love to see you though. So would I."

"I'll see what I can do," he said, leaning in to kiss her.

She kissed him back before turning and heading back to the residence.

Andy walked into the office, leaving the two bodyguards at the door, and stopped in front of Mel's desk.

"Have fun?" she asked with a smile on her face.

"What do you think?"

"I think you could probably do with some coffee."

"That is what makes you such a great secretary," he replied. "Any messages?"

"Ha! What do you think?" Mel said as she stood up and walked over to the tiny kitchen area.

"I think every day you sound a little bit more like Mrs Krabappel from *The Simpsons*."

"And just for that, I get the last piece of shortbread," she said, biting a chunk out of a biscuit.

"So?"

"So, there's a list on your desk. But Edward Phillips has called a couple of times. It sounded quite urgent."

The jokiness left the conversation in a heartbeat. "Get him on the phone for me please, Mel," he said, taking the mug of coffee from her and walking straight through. No sooner had he sat down than the intercom beeped.

"Edward Phillips on line one."

Andy picked up the receiver and hit the flashing button. "Edward."

"Sir, it appears our operatives in Paris are still in action. A tracker was fixed to the laptop, and up until a short time ago, they were heading north out of the city."

"I see, and what happened a short time ago?"

"Well. They stopped heading out of the city, Prime Minister."

"Do we know why? Do we know what they're doing? Where they're going? Have we been able to raise them on comms?"

"Not at this time, Prime Minister."

"Get back to me when you do," Andy said and hung up. He took a sip of coffee and looked at the list on his desk. He hit the intercom button. "Get me Theresa McCann please, Mel." Within a few seconds, line one was flashing again, and Andy took the call.

"Hi, Theresa, what can you tell me?"

"I was about to contact Doug with an update. All the foreign dignitaries who requested safe haven are now in situ. We have most of them placed in the Greater London area, although, due to the security requirements, some of them have had to be sent elsewhere. I'm afraid their desire to coordinate efforts in their own countries from a safe vantage point has wilted, sir. Most of them have reported they can no longer contact their representatives, their military, anyone. Although we don't currently have all the agreed trades in hand, we are in the process of banking them. I've been coordinating with Will, and a prioritised list has been drawn up."

"Excellent. Good work, Theresa. There were no more casualties?"

"No. The only sustained casualties were during the Paris extraction."

"Okay, is there anything else?"

"Well, Prime Minister…"

"Well what?"

"We've lost contact with even more countries. Don't get me wrong; I don't doubt that there will be pockets of survivors, and I'm sure there are a good few governments still operating in full or in part from bunkers, but frankly, they won't be left with any kind of countries to lead. This thing happened so fast. The infrastructures just collapsed, nobody was prepared for the speed, not just of the infection but the panic that took hold. And the endless cyberattacks over the last months on utilities and communications networks all over the world, well… I just … I…"

"Look, Theresa, we can't control what happened, we can only control what happens. Nobody has ever seen anything like this before. Like you say, there are probably survivors all over the place, but if they've got any sense, they'll be hunkering down. I know very little of this makes sense, but all we can work with are facts, and right now, we know there is no infection in the UK and Ireland. We know we're doing everything we can to keep it that way, and whatever is going on in other countries, we need to take care of what's happening in this country. The countries that have held their hands up for help, we have tried to help them, but we need to look after our own interests right now. When things are on a more even keel, we can look further afield for survivors, but it's our survival that is key."

"You're right, I suppose, but it doesn't make it easier. I've had ambassadors from virtually every embassy here asking if there is some way I can help get their extended families to safety. I mean, God, they've seen us evacuate our military and all our embassy staff, what the hell can I tell them?"

"Tell them that, at present, we simply do not have the resources and our priority is the safe evacuation of British military and embassy staff. It's been nothing short of a miracle that we've got as many as we have out. A good part of it has been due to the deals we've made with the governments in those countries. As more nations go quiet though, extractions are going to become harder and harder."

"You do realise, Andy, all the British holidaymakers abroad, all the people overseas on business—"

"Do you think I haven't thought about that for a

second? But where the hell do you start? The military and the embassy staff are in specific locations. The rate this thing has spread it's more than likely that—Trust me; I've thought about all of them, Theresa. Let's just thank God that overseas tourism has tanked ever since Spain's air traffic control system got hit by a cyberattack last year. Who'd have thought four crashed passenger jets would have actually worked in our favour? Anyway, like I say, there's nothing good about any of this, and I've thought about all of it."

"Of course you have. I'm sorry."

"No need to be sorry. We're all going to have doubts at a time like this. Look, you're doing a great job; keep up the good work and keep our goals in focus, we'll talk soon," he said, hanging up. "Mel, get me Nadine, will you?"

"She didn't call, sir."

"I know, I want to speak to her though. In fact, I tell you what, get her to come to the office. And then can you get me Taylor on the phone?" Andy said, looking at the next name on the list.

*

Mya did not know how long she had been holding Seb's body when she realised the growling of the creatures had increased in volume quite substantially. She angled her head and only then caught movement out of the corner of her eye. One of the rear doors of the van had crumpled badly, and now a reanimate was squeezing its way through the gap. Despite her tears and sorrow, adrenalin began to surge and she looked around for her weapon.

Suddenly, the beast's body fell clumsily against the metal wall of the inside of the van, but in no time at all, it had gathered itself, excited at the prospect of fresh meat. It began to speed crawl towards Mya. Failing to find her own gun or Seb's, she knelt up, watching the monstrous creature through the horizontal gap between the seats. She reached for her knife and remained poised in readiness.

A second later, the beast pounced, lurching through the space between the passenger seat and the roof of the van. The confines of the toppled vehicle played in Mya's favour. She parried the grabbing hands as the beast lunged for her and, although transfixed by the creature's flaring black pupils, the feel of Seb's dead body beneath her left knee sent a jolt of rage through her. She brought the knife up and round with the poise and venom of a trapped snake. Then—silence for just a second as she and the beast froze in time before both collapsed into heaps. Mya regained her strength and composure then pushed the creature through the gap and into the back of the van.

She wiped the blade clean on the upholstery of the driver's seat before placing it back in her belt. *Oh Seb.* She looked sadly at his lifeless corpse for a moment before reaching down with her left hand and stroking his head. The body was still warm, but she had seen enough dead bodies to know this was temporary. She looked around the compartment and saw Seb's bag with the laptop in. They had stored the L119A1 rifles in the narrow gap behind the seats. She pulled out her own then Seb's. Mya double-checked, but it was empty. She looked inside the bag, there were two full magazines. Hopefully, that would be enough with whatever was left in her own rifle to get her out of a scrape. She checked Seb's body and found the Browning, with the silencer still attached, underneath him. She placed it and the ammunition in the bag with the laptop then searched around for her own gun.

Her attention was drawn away from the search as another creature began to climb in through the door at the back of the van.

"Shit!" she said, pulling out the Browning and firing. The beast fell still, blocking entry for any others. Mya turned and began to boot the shattered windscreen, wedging her back against the passenger seat. It broke enough for her to fold open a corner and climb out into the small triangular space that had been caused by the bonnet and roof of the van wedging against the breezeblock.

As she climbed out, she noticed her Glock 17 lying on the ground, thrown free from the wreckage. She picked it up and reached back inside the van for the bag. As she took it, she looked at Seb one last time.

She backed out of the confines of the van's cab, placed the bag over her head and shoulder, then threw the rifle over her other shoulder before climbing onto the side of the toppled vehicle. Five creatures immediately rushed towards her with outstretched hands. Mya brought up her weapon and fired well-aimed headshots. Quiet pops brought down each of them.

When all movement ceased, she jumped down onto the tiled floor. Now she was out of the confines of the van, she reached around and felt the wound on her shoulder. The piece of glass had fallen loose in the melee. It did not seem too deep. The storefront was completely destroyed. Mya looked across to the building on the other side of the road, which was in an even worse state. The explosion had occurred on the second floor, which looked like apartments. A fire had taken hold, and, for the first time in a while, Mya smelt something beyond the dried blood on her face and the rotting flesh of the beasts. It was gas. It had been a gas explosion, and by the smell of it, the danger was not over yet. She went to the front of the store, popped her head out and looked up and down the street. For the time being, it was clear to her right, but to her left, she could see figures in the distance heading towards the smoke.

Mya looked back at the van one final time and began to jog down the street. She would complete this mission for Seb or die trying.

# 20

"How are the preparations going?" Andy asked, holding the phone up to his ear with his shoulder while taking a sip of coffee.

"Everything's in place, sir," Taylor replied.

"So, why haven't I had a call?"

"I was waiting until closer to the time, Prime Minister."

"I don't understand; if we're ready, why aren't we launching the mission?"

"It's to do with the range of the helicopters, sir. The personnel will be carried by Chinooks as you well know, but the Apaches don't have the same range. We're waiting until the *Indestructible* is a little closer before commencement," Taylor replied.

"I see. And what happens in the meantime if there's an attempt to launch one of the aircraft from the *Indestructible*?"

"We have the ship under satellite surveillance; in addition, we have four Typhoons circling, ready to attack, should they need to," replied Taylor.

"I see," Andy said. "Good. Good work. I'll expect to hear from you shortly then."

"Yes, Prime Minister. Thank you, sir."

The intercom beeped. "Nadine Parker is here for you, Prime Minister."

"Thanks, Mel. Send her in, please."

Nadine walked into the office with her tablet and stylus at the ready. She stood by the side of the chair in front of Andy's desk until he gestured for her to sit.

Andy sat back and took another sip of his coffee. "Thanks for coming, Nadine. Would you like a drink?"

"No thank you, Prime Minister."

"I just want a progress report, Nadine. The conscription. It's a long time since our country has done anything like this, I need to know what's going on."

"Well, sir, despite it being a long time, several amendments to the procedure have been made over the years in case the requirement arose. The last time it looked possible, if not probable, was when Russia invaded Afghanistan in seventy-nine. There was concern that it was the beginning of a land grab that could lead into Europe. As time went on and with the advent of more complex computers and the availability of software that could more easily match age, health and other qualifying factors to job roles, further amendments were made to the policy and procedures with regards to the conscription process."

"Okay," Andy said, beginning to wonder if Nadine was actually human and not some bureau-bot designed specifically to communicate in civil service policy-speak.

"Well, sir. The result is what we are working with today, which seems complicated but really is no harder to understand than the software that they have in place at some of the larger, online recruitment firms."

"I see," Andy replied, not seeing at all. "So, in a nutshell?"

"The conscription process is in full vigour, and I have had meetings with various cabinet members including

Paul Ashford and Will Ravenshaw, in addition to Liz Holt and other senior figures that your office briefed me to meet with. The upshot of this, Prime Minister, is that although you outlined the broad brushstrokes with regards to the conscription process in your address, the system we have in place now will be able to identify skill sets that we can use to the greater advantage of the position we now find ourselves in."

"I see," Andy said again, praying for the phone to start ringing.

"Yes, sir. So, after speaking to Sonya Richards, for example, I was able to get one of our analysts to break down all personnel who had left the service within the last seven years for anything other than health or disciplinary reasons. This gave us a wealth of names providing everyone from civilian emergency operators right through to front line bobbies on the beat. The upshot of this is that we are able to place several thousand people into vital positions they are qualified for rather than waste their talents." Nadine sat back in her chair proudly.

"So, what you're saying is we're matching skills to requirements?"

"Yes, Prime Minister, and furthermore, because we have this system in place, it will not be limited to the first round of the conscription process."

"You've lost me."

"Well, Prime Minister, let me give you a scenario— Are you quite alright, sir?"

"Err … yes. Yes, why?"

"I could have sworn I heard you groan. Are you in pain, sir?"

"Oh, don't worry, it's just my neck," he said, beginning to rub it, hoping to cover up the fact that he had let out an audible sound of desperation.

"You have a pain in your neck, Prime Minister?"

"Frequently."

"You should see a doctor. You may find a new chair

could help. It could be your posture. But you can never be too careful with aches and pains, sir."

"No. I don't suppose you can," Andy replied. "Anyway, you were saying."

"Yes. The software we have in place will be able to satisfy future needs as well."

"I still don't understand."

"Well, Prime Minister, say for the sake of example we decide to designate a thousand acres of land in Cumbria to become a wind farm. There are a number of turbine manufacturers, but such an order would probably require a significant boost to their workforces. If all unemployed people are conscripted, how will they recruit staff?" Nadine asked.

"Good point, I didn't actually think about that."

"You can't be expected to think of everything, Prime Minister, so we've come up with this," she said, tapping the screen and handing the tablet across to Andy.

*To all business owners.*

*As you will now be aware, all unemployed persons in the UK are in the process of being conscripted to various industries that will help strengthen our country's infrastructure. This is to ensure that we maintain public services and utilities and bolster our armed forces at this, the greatest time of uncertainty we have ever faced.*

*As your government, we are acutely aware that now, more than ever, nationalised industries need to work in partnership with the private sector, and indeed, there are certain manufacturers and service providers in the private sector who are required, if not vital to our efforts.*

*As such, we have initiated the RCP (Redeployment of Conscripted Personnel) Assessment Scheme. If you feel that your business is providing goods or services to local/national government organisations, utilities or providers and requires further staffing, you can submit form RCPAS1 into the Assessment Office at your local council. A decision will be made within forty-eight hours as to whether your business requires and/or merits redeployment of conscripted personnel.*

*If you are successful in your submission, you will provide details of qualifications and experience required to fulfil the role, and then a shortlist of prospective employees will be identified from our national database for you to interview. If you select a candidate, form RCPAS4 must be completed and returned to the Assessment Office. The formal transfer process will then begin.*

*(Please note: At this time, it is expected that transfers will take between fourteen and forty-eight days to complete.) For further information, please visit our website or contact your local RCPAS office. (A list of numbers and addresses can be found in the booklet accompanying this letter.)*

Andy read it and handed it back to her. "You came up with this?"

"My team and a couple of the software developers, sir," Nadine replied, taking back the tablet.

"That's ingenious, Nadine. Seriously, I'm impressed, that's a great idea. Very forward thinking."

Nadine suddenly turned bright red. "Thank you, Prime Minister, it was a team effort."

"You're in charge of the team though, Nadine. Seriously, well done. Please pass on my thanks to the rest of your people."

"Yes, sir. Thank you, sir."

The intercom beeped. "Edward Phillips, line one, Prime Minister."

Andy picked up the phone and covered the receiver. "I need to take this, Nadine. Thank you very much for your time, and would you email me a copy of that document I've just read?"

"Of course, Prime Minister. Thank you," said the cabinet secretary before disappearing out of the door.

"Edward! What have you got for me?"

"You wanted to be kept up to date."

"Yes. Go on!"

"Well, Prime Minister, they're on the move again. Judging from the speed, they're on foot, but they're heading north."

"Can we still not raise them?" asked Andy.

"Ever since last night, communications have been very patchy, sir."

"You say they're heading north. What's your gut telling you?"

"Well, sir. The first objective would be to get out of the city. Second, if it was me, I'd continue to head north into less populated areas. If I was lucky, I might happen upon a small airfield on the way. If not, I'd go towards the coast and try to find a boat to cross the Channel, sir."

"Can we launch a rescue? Can we go pick them up?"

"If they continue north, Prime Minister, we could send an Apache across, but right this second, there are too many variables to do that. It's out of the Apache's range."

"I still haven't received that brief, Edward," Andy said. The line went quiet.

"No, sir."

"Well?"

"I'll come across with it now, Prime Minister," Phillips said.

"Why can't you just send it to me? We have encryption."

"I need to step out for a little while anyway, sir. I'll bring it across," Phillips said before hanging up.

Andy sat there for a moment just looking at the receiver in his hand.

\*

After running flat out for two minutes, Mya ducked into a shop doorway. She let out a small gasp as she caught sight of her reflection in the window. The top half of her face was encrusted with dry blood. Tears had cut a salty trail through the red, and she looked like something out of a survival horror film. She stayed in the doorway long enough to catch her breath. She had dumped the night-vision goggles and torch, she was dressed in her trousers, T-shirt and assault vest. The Glock was in her belt, and the rifle was over her shoulder. She had the rucksack over her other shoulder with the laptop as well as the Browning and extra ammo. She had two bottles of water, a couple of small boxes of breadsticks, two tins of pineapple chunks and a packet of raisins. It was not haute cuisine, but it could make all the difference if she had to spend another night on the road.

She poked her head out to survey the street. The creatures that had been charging towards the sight of the explosion were no longer visible. In the other direction, the road was clear too. It was this path she would take, north, out of the city, leaving the worst day of her life behind her.

She started to walk up the road, more slowly this time. She would only get so far on foot; she needed a vehicle. Just then, two small figures ran across the road in front of her. They were just children; as important as it was for her to get out of Paris, she could not let two youngsters fend for themselves in all of this.

"Hey! Hey! Arret!" she called, but not in so loud a voice that the creatures near the blast site would hear her.

The figures stopped in mid-stride and turned towards her. A low growl began to emanate from the back of their throats as they changed direction and charged towards Mya.

"Oh fuck, no!" she said as she just stood there staring in horror. As the children got nearer, Mya could feel stinging tears forming in the corner of her eyes once more. She raised her weapon and fired, once, twice. The two reanimated youngsters dropped to the ground.

Mya stood there looking at them in disbelief. What was this virus? What could create such horror? Could the laptop she was carrying have clues as to how to stop it? She began walking straight up the centre of the road. If something was going to come out of a side street, at least she'd have time to see it.

*Of all the times to leave me, Seb. Of all the times.*

\*

"So, how did it go?" Andy asked as Xander and Doug walked into the office.

"I need coffee," Xander replied, loosening his tie and shirt collar. "Those guys can drink."

"Mel," Andy said, hitting the intercom button.

"Three coffees coming up," Mel replied.

"It went well," Doug said as he and Xander slumped into the two chairs on the opposite side of the desk. "The video did the job for us. People were genuinely taken aback. Your speech helped too; you played a blinder there. I was sceptical about bringing Harry in. I was sceptical about the whole idea, but I think it paid off and then some." The three of them sat for a moment with self-congratulatory smiles painted on their faces until Mel finally walked through the door carrying a small serving tray with three coffees on it and placed it down on the desk. They each took a mug and sat back in their chairs.

Andy looked towards Doug, while Xander sipped his coffee, desperately trying to counter the effects of the alcohol. "I'm concerned about what Will talked about," Andy said.

"With regards to what?" Doug asked.

"With regards to our beloved home secretary."

"Ashford? You worry too much," Doug said. "I told you, Xander and I have got your back on this, you don't have to concern yourself."

"But it makes sense what Will said. Xander spoke to these guys yesterday. He thought they were all falling in line. Granted, the front pages were favourable, but there was a lot of damaging stuff inside. I'm concerned they aren't willing to get behind us because something's afoot with Ashford."

"What are you worried about? It's not like he's going to make a leadership challenge. A—you have more party support than any other PM in about thirty years. B—the public love you as well, and C—his dad might have the balls and ambition, but he certainly hasn't. Look, so what if the media guys got a bit miffed at being ordered around and they mouthed off to Ashford's dad? They've been shown what's at stake. If they don't do as we ask, then we bring out the big guns," Doug said.

Andy took a sip of coffee. "I really don't like the sound of that."

"Look, I've told you. You've got enough on your plate. Let us worry about that little prick, and you worry about governing and shit."

Xander suddenly started to giggle. "Shit."

"Oh Christ, I've got Beavis and Butthead in my office. How much did you two have to drink?"

"Err … I'm a bit hazy on that. They started serving this stuff with pineapple chunks on a cocktail stick. I fucking love pineapple, I do," Xander said before he started to giggle again.

"We've still got a long, long day ahead of us and I need you two on top of your game. Drink plenty of coffee, plenty of fruit juice; eat something; have a cold shower. Do whatever it takes, but sober up for Christ's sake."

\*

A loud explosion rocked the city once again. It was some distance away, but the sound still resonated through Mya's very bones. To her surprise and relief, she had not seen any more of the reanimated corpses since she had put down the two children. She was still on the same road heading out of the city, and the adrenalin was still pulsing through her. Anything could happen at any time. It was like being in the middle of a war zone. No, worse. Mya had been in the middle of plenty of war zones, but she had never experienced this heightened level of anxiety before. It was almost as if two worlds were meeting—the real world and the world of make-believe, where nothing was as it should have been and the dead came back to life.

Mya saw something move and whizzed around, pointing her Glock in the direction of the figure. She lowered it again just as quickly as a large, hapless dog stood there with its tongue lolling out, just watching her with wild but happy eyes.

"Hello there," she said, breaking out into a smile. "What's your name then?"

She knelt down and began to stroke the dog, who licked her face enthusiastically, causing Mya to laugh. "Well, you're a friendly one, aren't you?" she said as she hunted for a name tag on the chain collar the dog was wearing. "So, no name, huh? Are you hungry? You hungry—" she looked down towards the dog's genitalia "—boy?"

Mya reached into her bag and brought out a packet of breadsticks. She tore open the plastic and fed one to the dog, who chomped through it like Cookie Monster with a bad case of the munchies. "Oh boy, you are hungry, aren't you?" She pulled out another, and the same thing happened. After half a dozen, the dog got some of the biscuit caught in the side of his mouth and made a comical face trying to dislodge it. Mya placed the box back in the bag and stroked the dog's head with one hand, while gently reaching into his jowl with her thumb to dislodge the soggy biscuit. The dog let her without any sign of irritation or aggression. Its googly, happy eyes just watched her like a child seeing a cartoon for the first time. Mya smiled. "Where are you from, little boy?" She looked up and around, there was no sign of anyone. The buildings in this area were commercial. Wherever this dog had come from, it was not around here. She pulled out one of the water bottles from her bag, unscrewed the top and tipped it into her cupped hand. The dog lapped the water as fast as she could pour it. Finally, when its thirst was quenched, it sat back on its haunches with its goofy tongue still hanging out.

Mya indulged herself for a few more seconds, stroking and fussing the mongrel, who she could only guess was so happy because he had not seen a living, breathing human in some time. Eventually, she broke out of her daze and stood up.

"Well. It's decision time, boy. Are you staying or are you coming with me?" She stood looking at the dog for a few more seconds and then started walking once more. She did not look back, she just put one foot in front of the other, but an ear-to-ear smile swept across her face when she felt a warm nudge against the side of her leg.

"So. You decided to join me. What are we going to call you?" she asked. "Are you a Bubba?" The dog just carried on walking. "How about Max? No. You can't be a Rover. Your eyes remind me of Animal from the Muppets."

The dog looked up before looking down again. "Is that it? Is that what we're going to call you? Animal?" The mongrel did not respond but just carried on walking by her side. "No. How about Muppet?" The dog looked up with that goofy panting smile. "Muppet it is then."

Mya looked down at her new friend and smiled as the pair of them continued walking up the middle of the road. "Y'know, at some point, boy, we're going to have to find a vehicle. You might like walking, but I've had my fill for a while." Muppet continued by her side, not reacting to her words. "Not very talkative, are you? So, you're more a listener than a talker. I can live with that. In fact, you might just be my perfect man."

## 21

Andy looked at his watch. Edward Phillips would be arriving with him any moment, and then his curiosity would finally be satisfied as to what was on that hard drive. What was worth risking the lives of two top MI6 agents? The intercom beeped. "Alistair Taylor on line one, Prime Minister."

Andy picked up the phone and pressed the flashing line. "Alistair? Go ahead."

"Sir. I really don't know what to say exactly," Taylor began.

"You do understand how a telephone works? If you don't know what to say, this could be a very short conversation."

"Yes, sir, sorry, sir. What I mean to say is we've had news."

"News about what?"

"About the *Valiant*, Prime Minister."

"And?"

"Sir, there was a major fire on board the *Valiant*. There was damage and loss of power for some time. The communication room was cut off, which is why they went silent."

"And?"

"And they're back with us, Prime Minister," Taylor replied excitedly. "They have suffered significant damage; they will not be able to submerge again until full repairs have been carried out, but, thankfully, our worst fears did not come true."

Andy stood up and walked to the window. For a while, he just stood there staring out into nothingness. "That's fantastic news, truly fantastic."

"Yes, Prime Minister."

"Were there any fatalities?"

"No, Prime Minister. Three crew suffered third-degree burns, a number of people are being treated for smoke inhalation, one crew member suffered a broken ankle, but, incredibly, there were no fatalities."

"And no more reports of the infection?"

"No, Prime Minister, after the first instance was taken care of, that was it."

Andy breathed a long sigh of relief. "Thank you for letting me know."

"A pleasure, sir. I'll be in touch again shortly, we'll be approaching the launch window soon."

"Good. Thank you."

No sooner had Andy hung up the phone than the intercom beeped again. "Liz Holt is here to see you, Prime Minister," Mel said.

Andy hit the intercom button. "Send her in."

"How are you doing?" she asked as she walked into the office and gave him a warm hug. "That was from Trish," she said, smiling.

"She only lives upstairs. She could come down and do it in person."

"She doesn't want to get in the way, and I told her I was going to drop in and see you anyway," Liz said, smiling.

"It's always good to see you, Liz. I'm used to swimming with sharks, it's nice to have an old friend around."

"Hey, I'm four years younger than you, not so much of the old."

"You know what I mean."

"Have you got a few minutes?"

"Err … it will be a few, I'm waiting for someone, but I'm all yours until he shows up."

She took the bag from her shoulder and pulled out her laptop as well as a few files. "I just wanted to give you a quick update on where we are."

"Okay."

"Military and embassy personnel have started arriving back in the country. We have teams of doctors and medics, as well as over three hundred Royal Marines on site to manage the testing and quarantine."

"Okay," Andy said. "Which sites are we using?"

"We're using just the one," Liz replied.

Andy raised his eyebrows. "Just one?"

"Yes. I spoke with my team, conferred with Zahid, and we had a meeting with Will and the chiefs. I have to say, Elyse, your new transport secretary, impresses me. She's pulled out all the stops for us. It's all being put into a detailed memo to you as I speak, but, essentially, Stornoway Airport fulfils all our needs. It is remote, there is plenty of space to set up a field hospital and temporary accommodation. It is also an ex NATO base and has one of the longest runways in the country. We have requisitioned it from the operators for an indeterminate period. The regional Search and Rescue team that was based there has been relocated to Benbecula, and we have two mothballed luxury ocean liners heading up there right now."

"Okay, I was following you right up until the ocean liner bit," Andy said.

Liz smiled. "Okay, so the quarantine is a two-part process. We have several thousand military and embassy personnel overseas who are all arriving here in increments. We have appropriated the huge hangar at the airport for the testing facility. Western Isles Hospital and the local authorities are helping us out with the loan of equipment until we can get all ours on site. Calmac Ferries have brought in an extra vessel just for our use, and we expect to be operating at full capacity later on today. The first minister has been incredibly helpful in expediting all of this. There is a large amount of waste ground at the airport. A lot of this can be used while in no way infringing on the runways or taxi areas."

"Used for what?"

"We have procured multiple static caravans, which will be under twenty-four-hour guard. These are for any personnel showing signs of being in any way under the weather. If they've got a sniff, an ache, a dodgy pupillary response, anything, they will be put into one of the temp lodgings for a period of seventy-two hours. We will do physicals and extensive blood tests and check all their symptoms against the information we have accumulated from our colleagues around the world. If there is the slightest chance we believe they are infected, we will immediately relocate them to a more secure facility. The personnel who are tested and show no signs of illness will be transported to one of the two cruise liners. They will remain there for seven days before being transferred to the next. We believe two weeks' quarantine will be sufficient to ascertain whether there is any danger of an individual being infected."

"You mentioned a more secure facility. What would that be exactly?"

"We have two containment units that have been specially fitted currently being flown up to the airport by Chinooks."

"I see."

"You have to understand, all of this is best guess stuff. We have seen from the footage what happens if someone gets bitten. We've seen what happens if someone gets a huge chunk of skin carved out of them by one of these thing's nails, but there are so many variables that we don't know about. Incubation times may vary depending on fitness, on pre-existing conditions, on depth of the wound, on lots of things, but two weeks should cover us for most eventualities."

"And what happens if there is an infection and it leads to an outbreak?"

"Well, then we start phase two."

"Phase two? What the hell is phase two?"

"If you've got somebody coming, I won't have time to go into it, it's complicated."

Andy suddenly became concerned that so many decisions were being made without his knowledge or approval. "He can wait. Tell me what's going on, Liz. I don't like being kept in the dark."

"Nobody's keeping you in the dark, you have all this to take care of," she said, gesturing around the office. "The measures that my people have come up with aren't anything new. There are an awful lot of shitty diseases out there, Andy, we've had to plan contingencies for an outbreak for a long, long time. You and your predecessors were never interested in the past because nothing ever looked imminent. Nothing has been done behind your back. This is years of research and testing by experts in the field. Granted, we are in new territory now, but we've got plans in place, which is more than any of our colleagues overseas had the chance to do."

"I'm sorry. You're right, but please tell me what the measures involve. I need to know."

Liz sat back, a little more relaxed. "Could I have a drink of water?" she asked, looking across towards the dispenser.

"Of course, help yourself," Andy replied. "So, go on, what's your plan if there's an outbreak?"

"It's complicated."

"Well, I would hope so. If it was simple, why would I need to surround myself with experts?"

"Phase two is another stage of quarantine, only this time it would be on a larger scale. There's a reason we chose an island, Andy," Liz said, taking a drink from her cup.

"Go on."

"Well, if there is an outbreak, we try to keep the quarantine zone as small as possible. The smaller the zone the easier it is to control. Within the zone, we enforce a lockdown, like the one I discussed with you before. Nobody will be allowed out of their homes. The hospital will be shut down. All patients who can be cared for at home will be cared for at home. An army of paramedics, nurses and doctors will be flown in to set up field hospitals on the perimeter of the quarantine area. Anyone who needs intensive medical attention will be cared for in there."

"You mentioned this before, and I'm still a little fuzzy about it. What is the virtue of doing this again?"

"The virtue is we've seen the recent CCTV footage and gone through reams of historical statistics."

"Okay, still not with you."

Liz let out a long sigh. "Okay. Remember the bird flu outbreak in ninety-seven?" Andy nodded. "Everyone who had as much as a sniffle went to A and E. What do hospitals have? Lots of people. Lots of people not always in the best of health, lots of people who struggle to run or fight, lots of visiting families. In all the CCTV footage we've seen from around the globe, the infection spread through the hospitals like wildfire. Then the areas around them became hot zones. If you close the hospitals, set up a shit load of NHS phone lines and have hundreds of trained staff on standby, you immediately remove one of the main causes of city-wide outbreaks. Think about it. A family visiting a sick relative. There's an outbreak, somebody gets bitten or attacked. They don't die and turn instantly but are halfway across the city before the effects take hold. Suddenly, it stops being a medical problem and becomes a mathematical problem. One becomes two, two become four, four become eight, eight become sixteen, and it all happens before you have time to tie the laces on your running shoes. That's why we need to impose a lockdown and shut down the hospital before we think about anything else."

"Okay, but I don't understand. I thought if you got bitten by one of these things, you turned straight away."

"If you get bitten and die, you turn straight away. You get a bite, you're gonna die, but if it's your arm or leg or something that doesn't cause immediate cessation, you stick around for a while. We're still getting fresh information in, fresh footage, fresh accounts. We're going with what we're sure of, we're going with the patterns we've seen, and we're going with models that have been designed to manage previous pandemics. But what you need to remember, Andy, is nothing has ever been as virulent or fast-moving as this thing. This is like nothing we have ever seen before. So, going back to your original question," Liz said, taking another drink of water, "phase two is setting up the smallest quarantine we can get away with after an outbreak. If there are cases outside of the zone, we have to widen the quarantine perimeter. So far, though, there have been no reports, no outbreaks anywhere in the UK. If there is an outbreak on the Isle of Lewis it can be managed, the chances of it reaching the mainland are very slim; hell, Calais is closer to Dover than the Isle of Lewis is to the mainland."

Andy's brow furrowed. "So you're telling me the reason you selected Stornoway Airport on the Isle of Lewis was because you wanted a proving ground for all your theories. It wasn't that you were sure all your ideas would work; it was because it was more easily contained if they didn't?"

Liz glared at him. "There are no absolutes with something like this. It was the safest option."

Andy sat back in his chair and brushed his hands over his face. "Jesus Christ!"

"These plans will work, Andy. I have every faith."

Andy let out a dismissive laugh as he reached into his bottom drawer and pulled out a glass and an almost empty bottle of Glengoyne. He poured himself what remained and took a drink. "Aren't you an atheist, Liz?"

"You know I am."

"Then having every faith doesn't really mean that much then, does it?" Liz stayed silent and just looked down at the floor.

"Okay. That'll do for now. I need to clear my head before the next meeting."

Liz collected her files and laptop before placing them back into the bag and standing up. "It will all go to plan. I know it will."

Andy took another drink. "Let's hope, shall we?" Liz thought about replying but just turned and left the office. Andy hit the intercom button. "Mel, have you got a second?"

Almost instantly, Mel appeared at the door. "Yes, Prime Minister?"

"Mel, where do we keep the whisky? And do we know where Phillips is? And can you get me Taylor on the phone?"

"The whisky is kept somewhere you will never find it so I can dish it out to you one bottle at a time. Edward Phillips left his office thirty-five minutes ago, and yes I can," she said, disappearing back out of the door.

She returned a minute later with a fresh bottle of Glengoyne and handed it over the desk. Andy regarded it in his hand for a moment then let out a long breath and placed it in his bottom drawer. "I suppose I'd better have a coffee," he said.

"Good boy," Mel replied, smiling. "Bad meeting?"

"I think the days of good meetings are over, don't you?" Andy looked towards the door and nodded. Mel closed it. "Honestly, sometimes I just feel like a stationary cog around here, the world spins around me. There are all these people, experts in their fields telling me what they think we should do, what our best options are, and they take all the humanity out of the equation."

Mel sat down opposite him. "Do you remember when my father died?"

"Yes, of course I do," Andy replied, looking a little confused.

"I'd only been working for you for six months. My dad and I were always very close. It devastated me, I felt like my world had fallen apart. Well, you had to be down here for an important vote in the Commons. You were actually scheduled to be here for a few days. You were due to be interviewed for the *Sunday Times*, a rising star they called you." Mel sat back and folded her hands across her lap. "Straight after the vote you were on the next flight from Stansted. You got a hire car at Leeds/Bradford and drove to my place. There was a houseful of guests, very few of them I actually wanted there, but you stayed. You stayed until the last one had gone. You were in the kitchen most of the night washing plates and glasses. You stayed out of the way, just watching over me, making sure I was okay. You never have to worry about your humanity, Andy." She stood up, walked around to his side of the desk and kissed him on the cheek. "I'm really proud of you," she said before heading back out of the office.

He sat there for a moment and felt choked with emotion. "Thank you," he whispered as he watched her walk out of the office. Mel had become like his family over the past years and to hear such tender words humbled him. After a few seconds, the intercom beeped, and he cleared his throat, desperate to regain control of his emotions.

"Alistair Taylor, line one," Mel said.

"Thanks, Mel, for everything," he replied before picking up the receiver and hitting the flashing light. "Alistair!"

"It won't be long now, sir."

"No, that's not why I'm calling," Andy said, as Mel walked into the room with a fresh coffee. He took a quick drink before continuing. "I've just had Liz in here."

"Yes, sir. She said she was going to try to meet with you."

"She gave me a brief outline of the plans that are in place for the quarantine. I'm not happy about the numbers."

"I'm sorry, Prime Minister, what numbers, exactly?"

"I want the people on that island protected if there's an outbreak. I don't just want a handful of troops there to guard the safety of eighteen thousand British lives. Liz told me there were going to be three hundred marines there, is that right?" asked Andy, taking another sip of coffee.

Taylor shuffled some papers around to find the figures before replying. "Err … yes, that's right, three hundred."

"Well, I want to show these people and the country that they matter. I want a show of force up there, Alistair, and I don't want any excuses. We have a job to do. We need to defend this country and the people. I want another seven hundred troops up there, A.S.A.P."

"Seven hundred, Prime Minister?" Taylor asked, flabbergasted.

"Yes."

"That's err…"

"That's what I want, make it happen," Andy said, hitting the call end button before Taylor got chance to respond.

The intercom beeped as soon as Andy had hung up the phone. "Prime Minister, it's Edward Phillips, sir."

"About bloody time, send him in."

"I can't do that, sir," came Mel's voice through the intercom again.

"Why not?"

"He's dead, Prime Minister. Edward Phillips is dead."

# 22

Mya and Muppet continued their trek north for what seemed like an age. Whenever there was a sight or sound that suggested trouble, they would duck behind a car or into a doorway to avoid it and wait until it had passed. Ammunition was at a premium, and with no sign of viable transport in sight, Mya wanted to hold on to every bullet as long as she could. All the vehicles they had seen were relatively modern, and there was not a hope that they could be hot-wired. The one saving grace was that the further north they travelled the less built up their surroundings became and, subsequently, the chance of running into packs of vicious zombies diminished.

An explosion rumbled behind her, and she spun around. There had been a few similar distant noises since her journey began, but this one was much closer. There was no way to determine what had caused it, but it was too loud for Mya's comfort. *The sooner we're out of this bloody city the better.*

Muppet stopped dead in his tracks, and it was a few paces before Mya missed the gentle nudge of his body against her legs. She turned back to look at the dog, who just sat down and stared straight ahead. "C'mon boy," she said, gesturing for the dog to follow her, but Muppet refused to move. "We really don't have time for this," Mya said, walking back and taking him by the collar. She gave the chain a gentle tug, but the dog still refused to move. Mya stood with her hands on her hips. "You hungry again? You want water?" she asked, beginning to reach into her bag, but then suddenly she stopped. A low growl started in the back of Muppet's throat, and he bore his teeth, not at Mya but at something up ahead.

Mya reached for her Glock. She trusted the instincts of a dog above her own any day of the week, and there was most definitely something amiss. Just then she saw it. Like a train heading around a mountain, a virtual army of reanimates stormed around the side of a building and onto the road she was heading down. She turned to look behind her and noticed plumes of smoke rising all over the city. "Oh shit!" she said, quickly looking around to see if there was any possible place to hide. Before, the two of them had only needed to avoid small groups, not so difficult if a person stayed still and quiet, but what was approaching them now looked more like dozens.

"Grrr." Muppet's growl gradually became louder and louder.

Mya remained frozen to the spot while her head danced from side to side, looking for any kind of refuge. Running back was not an option, nor was moving forward. She was heading out of the city, where had all these creatures come from? Their grunts and growls reverberated through the air, ricocheting off the surrounding walls, even drowning out their thudding feet as they got close.

"Okay, little one," she said, quickly trying the doors of parked cars, finding the third one open and lifting Muppet into the back seat. She unshouldered her rifle and placed that in too. It was going to be speed rather than bullets that got her out of this. "Try to stay quiet." They were about one hundred and fifty metres away now, and

Mya started to sprint back the way she had come. The area she was in was full of office buildings; then she spotted it, a green-and-white cloth canopy arching over the front of a small coffee shop. She glanced back and looked at the horde of creatures storming towards her. She ran straight past the coffee shop and to the office of a solicitor next door. Picking the lock was the last thing on her mind, and she blasted a couple of holes in the area to the left of the handle. She stepped back and booted the heavy, green wooden door in, and it gave way with a loud crack. What remained of the locking mechanism fell to the ground with a jingle.

Mya looked back; the beasts were no more than thirty metres behind her now. She ran into the building and up the steps, pausing on the landing. She had one shot at this, and without realising, she held her breath in anticipation as she looked back towards the open door. The noise of thudding feet and excited growls got louder as the throng of malevolent creatures approached; then she saw the first figure in the doorway. Its head whipped from side to side, searching, then it finally locked eyes with Mya. Its lips curled back, and for a split second, Mya thought it was in an evil grin, but then it let out a loud gurgling growl and tore up the stairs towards her, quickly followed by the rest of the rabid army.

She turned and sprinted up the second flight of steps. It was only then that she realised her plan was not going to work.

*

"What the hell do you mean he's dead?" Andy asked with his finger pressed down so hard on the intercom button that the end of it turned red.

Mel appeared at the door. "His secretary just informed me, sir. His deputy is on her way over here now."

"His deputy? Just hang on a second. What happened?" Mel looked at him blankly. "Where did it happen?"

"His secretary said it was at Vauxhall tube station."

"Tube station?" Andy said, sitting back in his chair. "And just what happened, exactly?"

"I don't know, sir. His secretary was in shock. His deputy should be here very soon."

Andy let out a long sigh. "Jesus Christ. This day. What the fuck?"

"I know," Mel replied.

They both looked up as two pairs of feet thundered across the outer office floor. "Edward Phillips is dead?" Doug asked as Xander followed him into the prime minister's office.

"I'm just hearing myself," Andy replied.

"What the hell happened?" Xander asked.

Andy shrugged his shoulders. "It happened at Vauxhall tube station."

"What happened?" Xander asked again.

"We don't know," Andy said. "Doug, could you get one of your people onto this, so we can find out?"

"Leave it with me," he replied, hitting the speed dial on his mobile phone and walking into the outer office.

"Mel, I'll need to speak to his wife. Can you get me her details?"

"No problem," Mel replied.

"Jesus," Xander said, flopping into one of the chairs opposite Andy. "This day."

"I know."

The intercom beeped. "Alistair Taylor on line two, Prime Minister."

Andy picked up the phone, "Err … hello."

"Mr Prime Minister?"

"Yes. Yes, Alistair, it's me, go ahead."

"Is everything quite alright, sir? You don't sound yourself."

"I've just been told that Edward Phillips has passed away."

"Ah, yes, terribly sad. I'd only just heard myself."

"I see," Andy replied, beginning to wonder just how old this news was. "What can I do for you, Alistair?"

"We're ready to go, Prime Minister."

"Who's ready to go?"

"The rescue mission, sir. The *Indestructible*. Everything is in place; we just need your final go ahead for the launch."

"Very well, go ahead," Andy said. "Keep me up to date."

"Yes, Prime Minister. When we've reached the *Indestructible*, sir, it may be prudent for a meeting with the chiefs in the Cabinet Office briefing room. We'll be able to hook up to a live feed, sir."

"Yes," Andy said, "speak to Mel, she'll help arrange it." He put the line on hold and placed the receiver in its cradle. "Mel," he shouted through the open door, "Taylor, line two."

Mel appeared at the door. "Yes, Prime Minister. Mrs Phillips is on line one, sir. She's been crying."

Andy nodded and took a deep breath before picking up the phone. He gestured towards the door, and Xander got up and pulled it to as he left the office.

"Gaynor? It's Andy Beck. I'm so sorry to hear this news. We're all in shock here; I can't even imagine what it must be like for you."

"Th-thank you, Prime Minister," came the quivering voice from the other end of the line.

"Do we know what actually happened, Gaynor?"

"N-No, sir. I was just told that there had been an accident at Vauxhall tube station and Edward was dead."

"I'm so sorry. We don't know what kind of accident?"

"No. They said they'd have more details for me shortly. The two police officers who came around were only young. I think this might have been their first time for this sort of thing."

"Police? That was pretty quick, I mean it's only just happened."

"Yes, Prime Minister," Gaynor said, clearly not interested in the chronology of the events.

"Well, look, I'll get my people to look into this, and as soon as we find anything out, I'll be in touch with you. Edward was a great servant to this country, I'm so dreadfully sorry for all of us but especially you. Do you have anyone there with you, Gaynor?"

"My friend is here at the moment, but my sister and niece are on the way."

"Do you need anything? Do you need help with anything?"

"No, thank you."

"Once again. I'm so terribly sorry for your loss," Andy said.

"Thank you, Prime Minister," she replied, breaking down in tears before hanging up the phone. Andy looked at the receiver for a minute before placing it back in its cradle. He shook his head.

"Why do I get the feeling I'm the last to know about this?" he muttered to himself.

\*

Mya's plan had been to reach the second floor, barricade herself into the office closest to the canopy from the adjoining cafe, then take her time to climb or swing across to it, cushioning her drop and then sprinting hell for leather while the creatures were still preoccupied with trying to get to her. As she reached the second floor, she found that it was undergoing major renovation. The offices were empty, and all the doors had been removed. Ten new ones with expensive glass panels had been leant against the wall of the landing awaiting fitting and a grey filing cabinet sat beyond them. A waist high bannister stretched the length of the hallway and as she shot a glance back, she could see through the gaps between the mahogany spindles the fast-moving, jostling figures tearing up the stairs after her.

"Fuuuccckkk!" she cried as she sprinted towards the end office. Mya could already feel the thud of the beasts' feet, and she knew she only had one shot. They were far heavier than she expected, but she toppled over the new doors, creating a diagonal barrier across the wide landing. She heard some of the glass smash and crack as the frames battered against the thick wooden bannister. Mya let out a combined grunt and scream as she hoisted the filing cabinet on top too before retreating further down the hall. A steady stream of creatures was still bounding up the stairs, and she knew there would still be more outside on the street, heading in. *I need to stall them as long as I can.*

She aimed her Glock and fired at the first reanimate trying to negotiate the diagonal barrier. It collapsed to the floor. She took half a dozen more well-aimed shots, and each time, another creature fell, making more stumble behind them. The gaps below and above the barrier were now blocked with rotting corpses, albeit temporarily. At the most it would give her a few seconds. Mya continued to fall back, firing and reinforcing the blockade further with each beast that fell. Then she shifted her aim and moved to the top of the landing. Three more shots and three creatures collapsed, causing a mini cascade in the stairwell, buying her more valuable seconds as she pointed her Glock back towards the growing door and corpse barrier. She took two more shots, downing another pair of creatures and making yet more stumble behind them, before replacing her magazine.

She backed into the office she determined was closest to the canopy of the cafe, nearly tripping up over a protective sheet that the decorator had placed paint cans, brushes and other tools on. As Mya reached the window, she took her eyes off the landing and looked down. A handful of creatures were still on the street trying to barge through the doorway of the building. She only needed to hold the horde off a little longer then all the reanimates would be inside and she could make a break for it. She aimed and fired once more, taking down another beast, but noticed more were coming up the stairs now as the creatures she had shot had been trampled. She looked down at the blanket and saw a large plastic bottle of white spirit. She dived to her knees and quickly shredded a corner of the thick material of the protective sheet with her knife. The sound of the toppled doors scraping as they were gradually pushed along the handrail, moving the barrier forward inch by inch, sent a shiver down her spine.

*Fuck! Fuck! Fuck! Fuck!* She poured some of the white spirit over the cut cloth before stuffing it back into the mouth of the bottle. Mya pulled out her lighter and lit the ragged fuse. It would be just a matter of seconds before the throng of malevolent beasts piled over the makeshift blockade and had a clear run at her. *Here goes nothing!* She hurled the two-litre plastic bottle through the air. Mya's arm and body arched as she put every fibre of muscle into the throw. The container left her hand; her torso fell parallel to the floor and she remained there, frozen. Her eyes followed the cartwheeling bottle through the air.

The monsters beyond were oblivious to the danger of the flames and what was heading towards them. Their primary goal was to overcome the obstacle and pile of bodies in their way and reach the sweet-smelling feast in front of them.

Such was the force of Mya's pitch that there was no arc. It shot straight like a bullet, hitting the first creature square in the chest and forcing the bung out of the top of the flimsy plastic bottle in a flaming cascade that made London's New Year fireworks look dim in comparison. Liquid fire spread through the air like a thousand burning dragonflies, and in the space of a heartbeat, half a dozen of the creatures were burning, setting more alight as they bumped and jostled. They did not react to the pain, as Mya had hoped, but as the skin on their faces burnt; their vision faltered slowing their progress and their advance towards their prey. One, wearing a bus driver's uniform, became completely blind as the plastic brim of his cap melted over his brow and eyes.

She took a breath, the first since she had flung the bottle, and stood up, rushing back across to the window. The last three creatures were barging through the office door. Mya looked back into the hallway and saw the barricade was still nudging forward as more beasts pushed and shoved to get onto the landing.

*Fuck it. It's now or never.* She placed the gun back in her bag and pulled the window open. Mya put her head out. The distance and drop between the opening and the canopy was further than she thought, but as a loud scraping followed by a floor-shuddering thud sounded out on the landing, she knew her time was up.

She climbed onto the windowsill before stepping out onto the narrow ledge with her right foot. She was in a half-crouch due to the opening's height. *Shit, there's no way I can do this. What the fuck was I thinking?* Mya's head shot around to the doorway just as the first thundering feet entered the room. Flames reflected on the gloss paint of the frame as the fiery demon crossed the threshold followed by four, five, six more. She felt her breathing stop for a second in dreaded anticipation as growls, gurgles and flaming crackles filled the office. The hellish creatures charged towards Mya with grabbing hands. Even from this distance, she could see their cavernous black pupils behind the flames dancing in fevered anticipation of reaching their prey.

Suddenly she became hypnotised, deaf to all the sounds, sights and smells. A stark realisation overwhelmed her as the first creature approached. Its mouth opened and closed as if it was already chewing on her soft olive skin. *Oh my God, this is it. I'm going to die.*

\*

The intercom beeped. "Carrie Marsh here to see you, Prime Minister."

"Who's Carrie Marsh?"

"Edward Phillips's deputy, sir."

"Ah, right, yes. Send her in."

A polite knock sounded on the door before it opened, revealing an impeccably well-groomed woman in her forties. She closed the door behind her and walked straight up to Andy's desk, extending her hand. "I'm Carrie Marsh, Prime Minister. We met once before, a long time ago, but I wouldn't expect you to remember."

Andy stood up, shook hands with Carrie, and gestured for her to take a seat. "Well, I'm sorry our second meeting is under such sad circumstances," he said as he sat back down.

Carrie let out a sigh. "I am too, sir."

Andy regarded her for a moment. The whites of her eyes were veined with red streaks; she had been crying, but her foundation and mascara were flawlessly applied, so she had grieved but now wanted to hide the rest of her feelings away from the world outside. "Edward was a good man. I'm still waiting for a full report on what the hell happened."

"Yes, Prime Minister. There's an investigation going on as we speak."

"Yes, a lot's happening as we speak, Carrie."

"Yes, Prime Minister. That's one of the reasons I came to see you, sir. Obviously, in good time, a replacement for Ed will be found. But I've brought the necessary documents with me for you to sign, which make me the acting head of MI6, just so there are no delays in key operational undertakings at this time. Under normal circumstances I would be speaking to the foreign secretary, but I understand you want us to report directly to you for the time being."

"That's correct, yes."

"Very well, sir," she replied, handing him the folder.

Andy nodded and leaned forward, taking it from

her. He opened it up and began to read through. "So, are you up to speed with everything Edward was dealing with?"

"Yes, Prime Minister; I believe so."

"He was on his way across here to give me a brief about a hard drive that two of our agents came into possession of."

"Yes, sir."

"You know about this?"

"Yes, sir."

"And you can tell me what we believe is on it?"

"No, sir."

"And why not?" Andy asked, raising an eyebrow.

"It was above my clearance level as deputy, Prime Minister."

"I see."

"I am aware of the current state of the operation. I know that we are hopeful the operatives Mya Hamlyn and Seb Archer are in possession of the laptop. We know the locator pad that was attached to it is active and is heading north. At the speed it is travelling, we are confident they are on foot at the moment, but, God willing, they will find transport soon and continue heading north. We have not been able to establish contact with them, but let me assure you, Prime Minister, I know Archer and Hamlyn personally. They are the best of the best. If any two people can succeed on such a mission, it's them."

"That's good to know. Let's just hope we can get them back safely. We've lost enough people already today."

"Yes, Prime Minister. They are two of the most rational and level-headed agents it has been my pleasure to work with. I'm sure they'll take every precaution necessary to complete their mission."

*

*Fuck it!* Mya could feel her eyes widening to the size of golf balls as she launched herself from the window ledge.

She felt the brush of a hand against her vest as the first of the creatures made a frantic last grab at her, but she was already in flight. She stretched out her arms, desperately trying to control the trajectory of her diagonal leap, and as her left hand made first contact with the thick green-and-white canvas canopy, she suddenly realised that this would be like hitting a trampoline. As the rest of her body became enveloped by the thick material, she had a vision of being catapulted across the road and hitting the wall of the opposite building, slowly sliding down the side like Wile E Coyote in a *Roadrunner* cartoon. She prepared herself for the sudden relaunch but heard a rusty creak as the old outer frame of the covering buckled and snapped at the far end. The brunt of Mya's force had been absorbed, but as the thick material fell to the ground, so did she. Mya hit the pavement with a heavy thud and lay there for a moment, winded and dazed. Eventually, she staggered to her feet but still felt her bones vibrating with the sudden jolt from the pavement.

Her body had cushioned the bag's blow, ensuring the laptop was safe, and Mya slowly turned to look up at the window she had launched from. Burning figures reached desperate hands out towards her, and for a few seconds, she just stood watching, still not fully able to grasp the fact that she had escaped. When she convinced herself, she was, in fact, alive and not dreaming, she turned and began to run back up the street. Muppet was barking as she approached, and when she opened the car door he nearly knocked her to the ground with an emotional welcome. Mya crouched down, allowing herself just a moment to have her face kissed and licked before gesturing for the dog to jump down and follow her. She reached into the car, grabbed her rifle and wasted no time in setting off. The way north was clear for the time being, and now they would make up for lost time. The pair of them ran, putting as much distance between themselves and the lawyer's office as their legs and bodies would allow.

Mya looked left when they reached the street that the rampaging creatures had emerged from. In the distance, two large buses had crashed. One was on its side, the second had smashed straight through the first one's undercarriage. She remembered back to the hallway and the sickening image of the bus driver having his eyes welded shut by burning plastic. A shiver ran through her, and she immediately looked back in the direction they had come from. There was no one and nothing following them, but she could see smoke billowing out of a window as the zombie kindling helped the fire take hold. If the plumes rose high, it would signal more of them to come out of the woodwork, so the sooner she and Muppet were out of sight the better.

"C'mon boy." She turned back around, and the pair of them began to sprint. "I think I'm all out of miracles for one day, we'd better not chance our luck."

## 23

"We need someone to witness this," Andy announced, having read through the documents Carrie had handed to him. He picked up the phone and dialled an internal number. "Doug, I need you to witness a document being signed. Also, do we have a photographer kicking about somewhere? Okay, good. See you in a minute." Andy put the phone down and looked at Carrie. "We'll get this out of the way and then we can get back to work. You will let me know if you find anything out about Edward, won't you?"

"Yes, Prime Minister. Of course, sir."

"Also, I need to be kept up to date with the situation in Paris."

"That goes without saying, Prime Minister. I won't let you down."

"I have little doubt." He smiled the thinnest of smiles and then hit the intercom button. "Mel, we're about to have a photo in here. You couldn't work your magic and make this place look a bit more prime ministerial, could you?"

"I'll be straight through, sir."

Within seconds, Mel was collecting empty mugs and glasses before returning them to the small kitchen area. She collated the papers Andy had on his desk and placed them in one neat pile. As he stood up to get out of her way, she straightened his tie. A glass with a film of whisky at the bottom sat on the windowsill. She picked that up, gave the office one final glance, and left.

"She's quite something," Carrie said, smiling.

"She's the best. I'd be lost without her."

"I doubt that, but I know what you mean."

Doug tapped on the door and entered. "Ah, excellent. Doug, have you met Carrie?"

"Doug and I have met on a few occasions. Nice to see you again," she said, shaking hands.

"Nice to see you, Carrie. Sorry about Edward. I know you two were close."

"Thank you."

Andy opened the folder containing the documents that needed signing. "Did you manage to find a photographer?"

"Of sorts," Doug replied, cringing a little.

"What do you mean?" Andy asked.

"Look. You can't blame me. It was Cameron who took all the bloody vanity staff off the payroll in two thousand and ten. I managed to get someone who's won awards though." He looked up towards Carrie. "You're going to have an award-winning film-maker taking your photograph."

"Oh God. How much Johnny Walker has he had?" Andy asked.

"A bit, but he's had a nap since then."

Harry stumbled through the door with a small satchel around his neck. "Are you going to be okay to take this photo, Harry? It's important," Andy said.

"Doth thou jest, sire? When I was working as a paparazzo, I'd be drinking all night in Spanish bars and I'd still get better celeb jug shots than anyone else the next day. You see the trick was to wait until they'd been for their morning swim. The water was still cold first thing and then—"

"Fascinating, fascinating story, Harry, but if you say another word, I'm going to have you executed and your body will be dumped in the Thames. I'm the prime minister, and this is the new acting head of MI6, so you know I can do it if I want to."

Harry sniffed. "Fair enough." He reached into his satchel and pulled a very expensive-looking camera out.

"Okay, Carrie is going to sign this, I'm going to sign it, and Doug's going to sign it. Then I'm going to shake hands with Carrie. We'll want pictures at all points. Do you think you can handle that?"

"Does a polar bear shit in a tree?"

Andy and Doug gave each other confused looks before deciding not to press the line of inquiry any further. The document was signed in all the right places. The photos were taken, and Doug guided Harry back out of the office, leaving Andy and Carrie alone once more.

"I dare say we're going to be talking quite a bit over the coming days and months," Andy said.

"I dare say." Carrie picked up the document folder and extended her hand once more. "Thank you again, Prime Minister. I'll be sure to let you know the moment I find out anything about Edward or the Paris situation."

"Thank you."

*

Paris had fallen into hell over the last two days, it was no surprise that shops and offices were empty, but Mya would have given anything to see a living human being. The more time went on the more she and Muppet had to avoid small groups of the reanimated creatures, and the more Mya questioned whether she was the last living, breathing human in Paris. The pair of them crossed another intersection, and then she saw it; a lone car parked on the right-hand side of the street. It was a vile colour, but she immediately recognised it as a classic Citroen Two CV. "Well boy, it's not a Bentley, but at least I'll be able to hotwire the bloody thing."

They approached the pea-green antique, and to Mya's delight, she did not even have to break a window, the door was open. As she became aware of the rust and other cosmetic issues like dented bumpers, a cracked rear screen, and a mismatched door on the other side, Mya decided the lock was probably broken, rather than the car being left open deliberately, but she was prepared to take whatever she could get. She opened the passenger side and gestured for Muppet to climb in, which he did in slow motion, sniffing every section of carpet in the footwell before finally taking his seat. She placed the bag and her rifle in the back and walked around to the driver side, took out a straight-edge screwdriver from her vest, and jammed it into the ignition, pounding the end with her fist. "Let's hope this does it, boy, otherwise we're doing this the hard way."

She turned the screwdriver and held her breath. The engine began to cough and splutter before finally rumbling to life. She put her foot on the accelerator to make sure it did not stall. She knew by using the screwdriver she would have damaged the ignition cylinder, and if it didn't start, she would have to use the old faithful way of marrying up wires and risking getting one hell of a shock. Mya pulled the door to and looked in the mirror to make sure the sound of the engine had not attracted any unwanted visitors.

She looked around the controls. The thing really was an antique, the positioning of the handbrake and the gearstick would take some getting used to, but it was driveable. The Citroen slowly pulled away, and Mya immediately checked the mirrors once again. Sound and movement were surefire ways of getting detected by these things, but hopefully this would help them get out of Paris, and then they could find proper transport.

*

Carrie Marsh climbed into the waiting car and settled in the back seat before nodding to the driver to set off. Her phone began to buzz immediately. She removed it from her suit jacket pocket and answered.

"Yes, I'm officially acting head, and I'm telling you now, I did not like lying to the bloody PM as my first official act. What have we found out?" Carrie listened carefully as the car turned onto the next road. Despite the broadcast, people were still getting on with their lives. The streets were quieter for the time being, but that would change. Whatever anyone thought of this government, they had done an incredible job of avoiding mass panic and rioting, for the time being anyway. "So, in a nutshell, nothing; you can tell me nothing. Send me the footage … no, surprise me on my birthday, yes, I mean now. I'll call you back when I've got it." She hung up the phone and reached into her pocket for a small Bluetooth earpiece and mic. She placed it in her ear and waited for the video file to load. The earphone made a quiet *bing* sound, which was the signal that the file had downloaded, and she hit the little play triangle.

"Sorry, ma'am, looks like a bit of congestion up ahead. Do you want me to take another route?" the driver asked.

"Just use your judgement," Carrie replied, not bothered one way or the other.

"Very well, ma'am."

It was CCTV footage of Vauxhall tube station. Everywhere had been a lot quieter that day, but that was only to be expected after the prime minister's speech the previous evening. There were a mere handful of people on the platform, and Carrie's eyes honed in on Phillips straight away. He was standing at the far end, in deep conversation on a mobile phone, while waiting for the train to arrive that would take him the few stops to Victoria before changing to go to Westminster.

Carrie watched intently as Phillip's entire demeanour changed during the course of the conversation. She paused the footage and hit the speed dial on the phone before resuming the video.

"Yes, I'm watching it now. This is what we need to find out. Why did he decide to go by tube and not take the car? Who the hell was he talking to? Hang on a minute…"

Carrie paused as she continued to watch the action on the screen. Phillips sunk down onto a bench as if all hope had left him. He leaned forward, placing his elbows on his knees as he continued the conversation; then when it was finally over, he hung up but just held the phone in front of him for several seconds. Eventually, he placed it in his pocket and stood up again, just as the train was about to arrive. The glare of the lights got brighter as the shuttle came to the end of the tunnel. That was when it happened. Very deliberately, Phillips stepped straight off the platform. A split second later, the train entered the station and Phillips became nothing more than a dismembered collection of bones and tissue.

Carrie took a sharp breath. Even though she knew what had happened, seeing it was something else. Tears formed in her eyes once more, and she hunted in her pocket for a tissue to dab them away before she needed to reapply her makeup.

The driver pulled a small plastic packet from the glove compartment and handed it back to her. "There we go, ma'am."

She nodded appreciatively in thanks and then wiped her eyes carefully. "You still there?" she asked after she had finally gathered herself. "Okay, we need to find out what that conversation was about. I don't care whose feathers you have to ruffle, you get the number of the person he was talking to, and you find out what made the head of MI6 throw himself underneath a train when he was on his way to visit the prime minister of this country. Have you got all that? Right. I'll be there soon. Time is of the essence on this. No fuck-ups!"

*

"Thank you for taking my call, Prime Minister, I realise you must be very busy, but I wanted to handle this in person."

Despite having the office to himself, Andy took the phone off speaker and held the receiver up to his ear. "I'll always take a call from the commissioner of the Metropolitan Police, Sonya; what can I do for you?"

"Well, Sir, Edward Phillips—it turns out it wasn't an accident."

"Oh! So, what was it exactly?"

"It was suicide, Prime Minister."

Andy let out a nervous laugh. "What? There must be some mistake."

"I'm afraid not, sir. I've seen the footage myself. He deliberately stepped in front of a moving train."

"I don't really know what to say. He was on his way over to see me. Do we know why he would possibly do something like this?"

"The investigation is ongoing, sir, but I just thought you should know."

"Well … err … thank you, Sonya. Please keep me informed as to what you find out."

"Yes, Prime Minister."

No sooner had Andy ended the call than the phone rang again. "Carrie Marsh, line two for you," Mel said.

Andy hit the flashing line two light. "Carrie. I've just heard. Do we know anything at all?"

"No, Prime Minister. We're looking into it, sir. I'll let you know as soon as we find anything out."

"Okay, thank you."

"Oh, there is one other thing, sir."

"Yes?"

"Archer and Hamlyn seem to have acquired a vehicle, sir."

"Finally, some good news. Have we been able to establish contact with them?"

"Not yet, sir, but I'll keep you up to date."

"Okay. Thank you, Carrie. We'll speak soon."

Andy hung up the phone and hit the intercom button.

"Mel, get me Doug and Xander, please." He immediately released the speak button and pulled open the bottom drawer of his desk. He was about to reach for the bottle of Glengoyne when instead he closed the drawer and stood up. He went to the door, opened it and walked through the outer office, turning to Mel as he went. "Tell them to wait for me, I won't be long."

Andy walked through the halls with his bodyguards in tow like his life depended on it. He rushed up the stairs to the residence, leaving the two police at the front entrance. The children were with their nanny, playing in one of the bedrooms, but it was Trish that Andy needed to see. She was in the kitchen, slicing vegetables for dinner. Although they could have whatever they wanted made for them, Trish loved cooking, and it made her feel more normal. Andy took hold of the knife and placed it carefully down on the chopping board before turning Trish around to face him.

"Darling, what is it?" she asked, seeing the anxiety and bewilderment in his eyes.

"Edward Phillips killed himself on his way here."

She laughed, just like Andy had when he'd been told the same news. "Don't be silly, what is it?"

"I'm being deadly serious. I had a call from the commissioner and the new acting head of MI6. He threw himself under a train."

"Oh my God!" Trish let out a deep breath and guided her husband out of the kitchen and into the living room. They both sat down on the sofa, and Trish held his hand tightly.

"I needed to see you. All this going on, I just needed to see you. You and the kids are the most important things in the world to me. I spoke to Phillips's wife. She was distraught, that's when we thought it was an accident. What's this going to do to the poor woman? Why would he do something like that? What would possess him?"

Trish could see that Andy's mind was racing. "Come, sit back with me for a minute," she said, moving further onto the sofa. Andy followed her and the two of them remained there in silence for a little while, just holding each other.

"What could have driven him to do something like that?"

"I don't know, darling. Nobody ever knows what's going on inside somebody's head. It's a tragedy for his family, and it's a big loss for the country, but we're in the middle of the greatest crisis we've ever faced, and you can't let this unravel you. There'll be time to mourn properly later, but the country needs you to lead them now, more than ever. Let the police do their investigation. They might get to the bottom of it, they might not. Like I said, you never know what's inside somebody's head. But you have a lot more than just one life to think about."

Andy kissed her and sat up. "You're right. It just took me by surprise."

"Of course it did."

"And I needed to see you. Because seeing you always gives me the strength I need to get through anything."

Trish beamed. "I love you."

"I love you too."

"Okay, now get back to work," she said, giving him a lingering kiss on the lips.

"You have the most amazing effect on me. You always have."

"That's 'cause I'm the best wife in the world," she

said, smiling.

"How do you know that?"

"Because every night when you come to bed, you whisper it to me before kissing me on the back of the head."

"But you're asleep when I say it."

"No. I can't go to sleep until I hear it." She smiled, they kissed again, and Andy got up to leave.

When he walked back into his office, the anxiety was gone. Doug and Xander were waiting patiently for him. Andy sat down at his desk. "We've got a problem." He recounted everything he had been told by the police commissioner as Doug and Zander sat there with their mouths gradually opening wider and wider.

"Shit!" Xander said.

"This is bad for so many reasons," Doug added.

"The media will already have hold of this, I can guarantee it," Andy said.

"Yeah," replied Xander, standing up. "So, we need to do a press conference. Delaying tactics. I know exactly how they'll try to spin this. We need to get in there first." He took out his mobile phone and hit one of the speed dials. "Astrid, call a press conference regarding the death of Edward Phillips. I'll take it. Brief statement and then two minutes of questions. Make it A.S.A.P." Xander hung up the phone then immediately dialled another number. "Stephanie, it's Xander. We're holding a press conference regarding Phillips. You're going to get the first question; here's what I need you to ask, have you got a pen? Is it true that Edward Phillips was suffering from a terminal condition? Could this have had anything to do with his actions?"

A look of shock swept over Andy's face as he turned to look at Doug. Doug was watching Xander with a broad smile on his face. He nodded appreciatively at the quick thinking Xander had displayed.

"Read that back to me... Great, don't worry, Stephanie, I'm well aware of how this works. I've got something in my back pocket that's going to blow you away. You just have to give me a little while with it... Have I ever let you down before? Right, I'll see you soon." He hung up the phone and headed to the door. "Got work to do, catch you later."

Andy shook his head. "Dear God, you two are the spawn of the devil."

"Sometimes we need a little subterfuge, Andy. Doing it this way, the story will be hot for one news cycle. If we let them dig deeper, it leaves us open to a whole array of spin-off shit that will go on for days. *What secrets was he hiding? Phillips had met with the PM multiple times that day, then he takes his own life, why?* If we handle this in the right manner, we can put it to bed and start shaping the news the way we want it shaped."

Andy looked at him. "Let me have the office, will you? I need to phone Gaynor Phillips now and tell her that her husband committed suicide."

# 24

Carrie was on the phone to Gaynor Phillips when her second in command gently tapped on the door and put his head around the corner. She put a finger up to her mouth, implying that he needed to remain silent, before gesturing towards one of the two seats in front of her desk.

"That's very kind of you to say, Gaynor. I always regarded Edward as a dear friend as well as my mentor. I'll miss him. Like I say, as soon as I get any more news I'll be in touch, and in the meantime, if you need anything, anything at all, you have my number. Okay, Gaynor. Bye-bye." Carrie made sure the phone was securely in its cradle before looking toward her number two. "You'd better have some good news for me, Hawke," she said, sitting back in her chair and interlacing her fingers in front of her, almost as if she was praying.

Hawke's face twitched. "I'm afraid not."

Carrie let out a long sigh. "Go on."

"Whatever phone he was on, it wasn't his issued one."

"What?" She sat forward in the chair, unclasped her

hands and spread them on the desk with a thud. The glass of water next to her document trays shuddered, while her eyes bore holes into Hawke.

"Whoever he was talking to, whatever that conversation was about, it was not made from his MI6-issued phone," repeated Hawke nervously.

Carrie stood up. "Can this endless clusterfuck of a shitty day possibly get any worse?" She walked to the window and ran her fingers through her hair as she looked out over the Thames.

"What do you want me to do?"

"I want you to get that bloody phone."

"It's in a police evidence locker."

"We're MI bloody 6. This is national security we're talking about, just get that phone. Then find out who the hell he was talking to. I want to know everything," she snapped while she continued looking out of the window. She heard movement and saw the reflection of her office door open and close before she returned to her desk. "What the hell were you into, Edward?"

\*

The Two CV chugged along at a steady forty miles per hour. It was running flat out, and Mya knew she needed to find alternative transport as soon as possible; otherwise, it would take her the best part of five hours to get to the Channel. She reached into the back seat and managed to shuffle her hand through the flap of the bag, pulling out a box of breadsticks. She wedged it upright between her legs and opened it up, lifting the cellophane bag to her mouth and cutting the top open with her teeth.

Muppet's eyes were fixed firmly on her, watching every movement with great concentration. Most of the breadsticks were now in several pieces due to the bumpy ride they had endured once they left their safe shelf in the hotel kitchen. Mya pulled out a small handful of bits and placed them on the passenger seat in front of Muppet, who started choking them down without need for any prompting.

Mya reached back into the box and took out a couple of pieces for herself, which she shoved into her mouth greedily. They had seen little evidence of life since leaving Paris. The A-Thirteen did not provide the most spectacular views for a driver. It was typical of most freeways throughout Europe, but in the city, danger lurked on every corner; here it was vast openness, and if there was danger, she would see it from a mile away, rather than allowing it to leap out at her like a demonic jack-in-the-box.

She shovelled in another mouthful of broken breadsticks and reached around for the backpack to get a bottle of water, taking her eyes off the road for a second. She grabbed the water and, as she turned back around, applied the brake hard to negotiate a badly signed bend. At the speed the Two CV was going, it did not take long to slow, but as the open stretch of road in front of her came into view, her mouth dropped open releasing chunks of sludgy breadstick down her front.

"Oh fuck!"

*

Andy sat back with the phone still to his ear and swivelled his chair round to look out at the calming blue sky. It felt like he had been glued to the phone for most of the day, more so than usual.

"Okay, Elyse. We're not going to be held to ransom, they can either play ball or do it the hard way. I don't have a problem with them charging for their services, but they're not going to profiteer, especially from us. You go back to them and say this: 'It is essential that the distribution of food is not interrupted, as such an interruption would lead to public disquiet and, on a wider scale, this would affect our national security. Therefore, if they do not agree to continue said distribution at the previously agreed price, the government will have no option but to requisition all assets of the company at current market value. As such a requisition would render the distributor's workforce redundant, the said workforce including management and board members will be conscripted and subsequently redeployed to wherever is deemed suitable. You have until midnight tonight, and then the military will be taking over your depots as well as any plant and machinery currently in operation.' Now did you get all that, Elyse?" Andy turned the chair back around and took a mouthful of coffee as she read it back to him. "Excelle—"

The door burst open and Andy's seat shot forward, jerking the mug of coffee from his hand. Almost as if it was in slow motion, the hot, dark brown fluid spewed into the air as the mug itself plummeted to the floor. Andy looked towards the entrance. Taylor was standing there with a look of agonised horror on his face. The two bodyguards had hold of him, and Mel was behind them.

"Sir!" Taylor shouted.

"What the hell's going on?" Andy demanded, holding out his hand as hot coffee dripped from it onto the beige-and-red diamond-patterned carpet.

"Sorry, sir," Les said, "he barged through."

"Okay, it's okay," Andy replied. "I'll call you back, Elyse." He put the phone down and stood up, taking his handkerchief and dabbing the hot liquid away while heading towards Taylor. "What's the meaning of all this, Alistair?"

The two bodyguards kept a firm grip on Taylor as Andy approached. "Prime Minister, The *Indestructible*…"

Andy looked at his watch. "Our team isn't due to reach it for a while yet, what is it?"

"It's gone, sir."

There was a momentary pause. "Start making sense, man. What do you mean it's gone?"

"I need you to come to the cabinet briefing room, sir," Taylor said, gaining a little composure and realising he could not talk about matters of national security in such an open environment.

Andy stared at him a moment longer before going to collect his jacket. "It's alright, lads, let him go." The two bodyguards released their vice-like hold on the chief of defence staff, and all four of them headed out of the office. "Mel, you couldn't get that mess in there sorted for me, could you?"

Andy could not hear the exact words she used as he left the office, but he knew by the time he got back it would be as though the coffee had never been spilt. They walked down the corridor in silence; Andy looked towards Taylor and saw his face was still toned with anxiety. They reached the cabinet briefing room, and the rest of the senior military personnel had the same tortured look on their faces. Suddenly, a chill shivered down Andy's spine. These were men and women who had seen some of the most horrific sights anyone could possibly imagine. They had been and sent others to war. They carried the burden of command and the burden of life and death upon their shoulders every waking hour of each and every day. What the hell had just happened?

"Play it back," commanded Taylor. The lights dimmed as Andy took his chair at the end of the table and the military reconnaissance satellite footage replayed on the huge screen. It showed the HMS *Indestructible*, the five billion pound plus pride of the British fleet. Suddenly a series of intensely bright, almost white explosions all around the waterline of the ship made Andy's heart jump into his mouth. A secondary round of even bigger orange blasts occurred through the rest of the ship. The bridge was the first to vanish in a fireball and within a matter of a few minutes all that remained was a small amount of burning detritus. The surrounding water bubbled and waved and riled for a few moments longer, and a giant lake of black spread over the surface of the water.

Andy remained silent for a few more seconds

before standing up again and walking to the front of the room, still regarding the satellite images on the screen. He turned to the men and women around the table. "What the fuck just happened?" he demanded. He looked towards Taylor, who in turn looked towards one of the generals sitting at the table.

"General Walker has a lot of experience in this field, Prime Minister," Taylor said.

The general stood up and turned to the much younger man controlling the laptop. "Play it back, and when we reach the point of the first ignitions, pause it." He walked up to the screen, standing on the opposite side to Andy. The footage began again, and as the first explosions occurred, the images paused. The general pulled a pen from his pocket and pointed to the almost blinding white flurries. "These, Prime Minister, are thermite charges. Not small ones either. Thermite burns at two thousand degrees and these were planted strategically to ensure the ship sank as quickly as possible." The footage started rolling again, and the other huge blasts began to erupt all over the ship. "The other explosions, at my best guess, sir, were to destroy all navigational equipment, weaponry and as many personnel as possible before finally taking out the engines. These secondary explosions were an insurance policy, in my opinion, in case the thermite charges failed to work."

"But—" Andy broke off for a moment in an attempt to gather his thoughts. "So, this was done by somebody on board the ship with the deliberate intention of sinking it?"

"Yes, Prime Minister."

"Jesus!" Andy whispered, still flabbergasted. "So, what are everybody's thoughts on this?" He looked towards the general then towards Taylor and the rest of the experts assembled around the table.

It was Taylor who eventually broke the silence. "Sir, I think it's going to take us some time to piece this together. Given that there are no surviving witnesses. Given the impracticality of getting a team to the area to sift the wreckage in our present situation. Given that the communications on the ship were down for several hours before the explosions that sank her."

"So, you're saying we're clueless?" Andy glared at Taylor.

"No, Prime Minister. I'm saying it's going to take time."

Andy looked around the room. "Do we have anyone who's willing to go out on a limb and hypothesise as to what happened?"

"Sir," began General Walker, "Occam's Razor. The most obvious explanation is the likeliest."

"And that is?"

"We know there was an outbreak on board the ship. We don't know how severe that outbreak was. We know the ship diverted briefly before resuming its course for these shores. I believe there were three parties at work, resulting in these events, sir."

"Go on," Andy replied.

"I believe there were an indeterminate amount of reanimates still on board. I think there was a faction who wanted to get back home at all costs, and I think there were some who knew what it meant for the country if the *Indestructible* somehow made its way to these shores. Sir, I think what we've just seen is a display of heroism and patriotism of a truly historic nature."

"You're saying that you think someone blew up the ship to protect us?"

"I think that's exactly what happened, Prime Minister."

"Jesus."

\*

There was a knock on the door. It was Hawke. He walked over to Carrie's desk and placed an evidence bag containing a smashed and bloodied phone in front of her. "I'll get someone to look at the SIM card straight away, but it will be a miracle if we can get anything from the phone."

"Okay." She held the bag up in front of her, like a child holding up a goldfish won from a fair. "What the hell possessed him?"

"Hopefully, we'll be able to find out," replied Hawke as he took the bag back from her and headed out of the office, closing the door behind him.

Carrie leaned back for a moment, and slowly her eyes drifted from the computer screen. She stood up and walked to the window. She looked out over the Thames once more as a single boat chugged along the otherwise quiet river. "Why did you do this, Ed? And why today of all days?"

\*

Muppet continued to munch the breadsticks then lick away the remaining crumbs as Mya climbed out of the car and peered at the colossal pile-up a few hundred metres ahead. She saw moving figures and, even from so far back, she could tell by their behaviour that they were reanimates. She surveyed the surrounding area looking for options. The last turnoff had been several miles back, and there was no guarantee that she would not end up in the same position if she took another route.

She climbed onto the bonnet of the car, which dragged Muppet away from his crumb lapping. He tilted his head sideways as he watched her continue her ascent onto the roof. She looked beyond the wreckage to the other side. It was all clear. The crash had transcended the boundary of the central reservation and had ended up creating a blockage on both sides. Although few vehicles would have been heading towards Paris, Mya could tell the barrier had been smashed by another public coach. *What's with these coach drivers?* More cars had piled into the back, some had swerved to avoid collision and, in turn, been knocked on. It was like any other horrific pile-up, but any survivors would get picked off one by one by the horde of monsters sifting through the carnage like crows pecking at a carcass.

Mya looked to her right. Over the side of the crash barrier was a farmer's field. She jumped down from the top of the car and headed across to get a better view. There was no possible way to get the vehicle through, and even if she could, it would not be able to handle the rough terrain. She began heading back to the car and glanced towards the wreckage once more, but now there was something different. Some of the figures were suddenly getting bigger.

She had only just been able to make out what was going on, but somehow the reanimates had seen her on top of the car or heard the engine chugging. "Oh shit!" she said, sprinting back to the Two CV and jumping in. She slammed it in reverse and swung the wheel into a lock. As she brought the car around to a ninety-degree angle with the road, she looked through the side window and saw the creatures were becoming more defined by the second. She spun the wheel hard in the other direction and let her foot off the clutch. The car jerked then stalled, and that's when Mya's life flashed in front of her.

## 25

Andy had put in a call to Doug and Xander about the *Indestructible*, and was just heading through the outer office on his way to see Trish and the kids when the phone rang. "It's Carrie Marsh, Prime Minister," Mel said.

He let out a small sigh and retraced his steps. "Carrie, what have you got for me?" he asked as he picked up the phone.

"Our agents in France are in range, Prime Minister. I have an Apache chopper at the ready but with the no-fly order in place, we need your go-ahead."

"Hell, yes, you've got my go-ahead. Have we heard from them?"

"No, Prime Minister, but we're tracking their movement. I'm sending the authorisation across to you now. This will give me everything I need to get these guys into the air. Obviously, we're going to have to quarantine them when they all come back to us."

"The crew as well?"

"Absolutely. Can't take risks."

"Okay, so will they be heading up to Stornoway?"

"No, Prime Minister."

"I don't understand. I thought all returning personnel were heading there."

"The rescue mission for the *Indestructible*, Prime Minister; the military had made alternative arrangements. The HMS *Orion* is a landing ship that's in the middle of the Channel as we speak. It's surrounded by gunboats and is being surveilled by the most advanced equipment we have. The *Indestructible* team was going to go there for quarantine. It's fully kitted out to deal with around two hundred admittance, but given the covert nature of this operation, I think it would be suited to this operation rather than just sending it back to port, sir, don't you agree?"

"Yes." Andy loaded the document on his screen, typed in a key code, applied his electronic signature and hit submit.

"Thank you, sir, that gives me everything I need. I'll let you know when they're safe."

"Thank you, Carrie, and the second you get anything on the other matter—"

"The second I get anything, Prime Minister."

Andy hung up the phone and was about to head for the door again when the intercom beeped. Doug and Xander here for you, Prime Minister."

"Send them in," he said in an exasperated tone, slouching back down into his chair.

The door nearly hit the wall as it swung in. "Bastards," shouted Xander, throwing a copy of the *Evening Voice,* owned by one of the biggest newspaper publishers on Fleet Street, onto Andy's desk. Andy picked it up while Xander spat the word, "Bastards," for a second time.

Andy looked at the front cover. In big black, bold lettering, it said, "PANIC ON THE STREETS." The by-line read: "Governments around the world lost their grip as the contagion took hold. Are we next?" The main photo on the front page was an image of a pram being forced off a pavement into oncoming traffic.

"Don't tell me." Andy flicked to the main article on page five. It showed a series of grainy pictures, all featuring single-framed stills of some of the startling footage that was used in the video to try and win over the media. "They all signed fucking agreements!" Andy shouted as he stood up and threw the paper across the room, sending the individual pages drifting into the air like pieces of giant black-and-white confetti.

"I've already checked, their affiliates are running the same photos and virtually the same stories," Xander said, bubbling with rage.

"What time does this hit the streets?" Andy asked.

"The early editions are already out there," Xander replied.

Andy hit the intercom button. "Mel, get me the commissioner." He released the button and looked at Xander. "You and your people, make sure none of the stations pick this up. If they so much as hint at this story or grab a copy of the *Evening Voice* in their newspaper reviews, they'll be sorry." Xander left the room as quickly as he had entered.

"You tried, Andy. I thought you'd pulled it off. It's not your fault, but you always forget the one piece of advice that beyond all others would see you right in this life."

"And what's that, exactly, Doug?"

"People are cunts."

"I don't happen to subscribe to that ideology."

"I know. How's that working out for you?"

"The commissioner on line one, Prime Minister," shouted Mel through the door.

"Let me take this, Doug, and do me a favour; I want copies of all the signed confidentiality agreements from this afternoon's luncheon. It was watertight, wasn't it?"

"It was beyond watertight, Andy. But they obviously think in the middle of this crisis they can tie us up with freedom of the press shite and we won't have the time or the inclination to fight it, so it will all end up on a backburner, and by then it will be too late."

"Yeah, well, screw that, we're going to bury these fuckers. I won't be made a fool of. Oh, and check the phone records from Ashford's office. I wouldn't put a stunt like this beyond him for one second, and do you know anyone who can get his personal mobile records?"

Doug smiled. "That's my boy," he said, suddenly gaining purpose to his exit.

"Sonya, have you seen the *Evening Voice*?" Andy asked, picking up the phone. "Today's issue of the paper has not only breached a non-disclosure agreement but has by direct action caused a threat to national security. I want the place shut down, all records seized and a full investigation to take place. The owner and two members of the senior editorial staff were here this afternoon. They all signed agreements saying that, under penalty of prosecution, all matters discussed and all materials seen would remain confidential. I have the signed agreements on their way to me now. I want them arrested and held on domestic terrorism charges. Furthermore, any affiliates that have printed this story, regardless of the geographical location, I want their offices shut down too, so get ready to put a few calls in."

"Um … I can't just do this because you tell me, Prime Minister."

"Well, actually, I'm pretty sure you can, but I'm going to get you everything you need to make this all above board. Sonja, we can't have panic in the streets, that's what brought everyone else to their knees in a heartbeat. We can't let that happen here; do you understand me?"

"Yes, Prime Minister."

Andy hung up the phone and dialled a mobile number. "Doug, I want you to play point on this thing."

"Gladly."

"Have a word with the attorney general; make sure we've got all our ducks in a row. Get Richards whatever she needs to make sure this goes ahead, and keep me informed.

I want this to be fast, and I want it to be brutal, so none of the other bastards think they can get away with it."

"Yes, Prime Minister."

Andy hung up the phone. "Bastards!"

*

Mya lifted Muppet over the crash barrier and looked back one last time to see that the long line of reanimates was getting forever closer. She hopped over herself, leading the dog down the steep embankment before sprinting across the ploughed brown field. The two of them ran flat out for two hundred metres before Mya turned back to look at her pursuers. She had gained a slightly bigger lead, but she knew that was only temporary. The creatures did not have the dexterity required to hurdle the crash barrier and negotiate the steep incline, so, instead, they stumbled and rolled clumsily to the bottom of the embankment. As they gathered themselves at the bottom they lost vital seconds but would soon make the distance up as Mya became more physically exhausted. She needed the bag but toyed with the idea of ditching the L119A1 rifle. She decided not to make a rash decision and continued across the field.

The pair of them reached the border with the next field, which was walled with a thigh-high dry-stone wall. Muppet leapt straight over, as did Mya. She landed on the other side and cast a glance back. The procession of creatures joining the cross-country pursuit from the freeway had not abated, and a fast-moving line was heading towards her across the dry brown soil. Muppet and Mya continued to run; the happy-go-lucky dog was feeding off Mya's fear, and an altogether more serious look had adorned his face. By the time they reached the border with the next field, Mya was running on fumes. She had not eaten or slept properly, and now fatigue was beginning to affect her progress. She looked back again to see the creatures had begun to gain on them. She could not even estimate the number that were now in pursuit.

"C'mon boy." She set off a little slower this time, mindlessly heading in the same direction; then she saw something. It looked like a farmhouse, about a third of a mile away at her eleven o'clock position. There were a few tall trees helping line the border with the adjoining field, so she had not seen it further back, but now she switched direction and with this new small modicum of hope powering her strides, she began to feel a little less tired. *Maybe somebody there can help us. Maybe they have a vehicle.*

Despite seeing a lack of people on the streets of Paris, she knew they were there. The odd twitching curtain told her terrified Parisians were hiding from the outside world, hoping it was not as bad as it seemed and that tomorrow they would wake up and it would all have been just a horrifying dream. Out here, though, there were fewer people, and surely that meant a greater chance for survival.

Muppet squeezed through the hedgerow into the next field, and Mya followed, snagging her rifle on a thick branch and wasting valuable seconds freeing it. But then her goal was in sight. The house was bordered by trees, making an L shape, while the front of it sat overlooking miles of open land. As she got closer, though, she saw the white paint was not so white. Drain pipes and guttering had become loose and were hanging from the roof and walls. The two of them entered the yard, and Mya's heart sank. Nobody had lived in this place for years. There was no help. There was no refuge. The full pain and weariness of running flat out for so long hit her like a cannonball. This was the end of the road.

\*

Andy sat at his desk, desperately wanting to go see his family but knowing he had way too much to do. He had a country to lead, and right at this very moment, it felt like everything was teetering on the brink.

He looked at the front cover again as it adorned the *Evening Voice*'s website. *This could be it. This could be the defining moment when it all turns to hell.*

"My wifey sense was tingling."

Andy looked up and saw Trish standing in the doorway. He smiled and stood up, rushing across to meet her as she flung her arms around him. "God you're a tonic for tired eyes."

"I met Doug a few minutes ago, he told me what had happened."

Andy pulled back from her, and the smile drifted away from his face. "I was an idiot. I thought I could appeal to their better nature. I thought I could rouse their sense of patriotism and doing the right thing."

"Your motives were good. They always are. You had to try it this way."

"Yeah, the road to Hell is paved with good motives or something like that."

Trish laughed. "Right, sit down with me," she said, going back to close the office door before taking his hand and walking across to the large couch that Andy only ever used when dealing with dignitaries. He slumped into one corner, and Trish squeezed next to him, throwing her arm around his shoulder and kissing him. "Out of all the people there, how many let you down?"

"We don't know yet. We haven't seen tomorrow's editions."

"But think about it, Andy, if someone else was going to do this, and *The Voice* got the drop on them, it would be plastered all over their websites before the papers were anywhere near ready for print. And that's not to mention the TV channels. They'd all hit back with a bigger, more sensationalist story, so at the moment, we're just looking at one newspaper."

"I suppose."

"Suppose nothing, you know I'm right. So, what

have you done in response?"

"We're shutting them down for the sake of national security and charging the three who were here under the terrorism act."

Trish let out another small laugh. "Okay, so you're handling it. You're sending out a message. The others will see what happens and all fall in line. Trust me. I know people."

"I told you, you should be in this job and not me."

"Ha! No thanks. Weren't you listening? I know people. Why the hell would I want to deal with them more than I have to?"

Andy smiled a sad smile before kissing Trish on the lips. "I was on my way to see you when this latest disaster hit."

"Oh. Why exactly?"

He looked her in the eyes. With her, he did not have to be the leader of the country. He did not have to be anything but himself. Tears began to run down his face, but Trish quickly wiped them away with her thumb. "Andy, darling, what is it?"

"I lost the *Indestructible*."

"What do you mean?"

"I mean I lost every man and woman on board. Sixteen hundred servicemen and women. People who were prepared to put their lives on the line for their country. I lost them."

"How? What happened?" Trish asked, pulling back.

"Someone sunk the ship."

"What?"

"We don't know the details. We don't know who, or why or—"

"Oh God, Andy," she said, throwing her arms back around him. "Oh, darling, I'm so sorry."

Andy allowed himself to melt into her warm embrace. This was just what he needed. "I guess I'm going to be working through the night, or at least until the early hours, but I want to have dinner with you and the kids."

"Don't be silly, you don't have to."

"No. I want to. I need to."

"Okay. I understand." Trish caressed the side of his face and leaned in to kiss him once more before standing up. "I love you. I'm so proud of you. Whatever happens, that will never change."

She turned to leave but paused as she opened the door. "You can't control everything, Andy. You couldn't know the *Indestructible* was going to be sabotaged. You couldn't have stopped the death of those men and women. The only thing you can control is how you react, and that's why I know the country couldn't be in safer hands." She closed the door behind her, and Andy just sat for a moment as her words lingered in his ears.

He got up and walked across to the door; popping his head around the corner, he asked Mel to join him before heading back to his desk. Mel came in, shutting the door firmly behind her. She sat down in one of the chairs opposite Andy. "I need your help."

"Anything," replied Mel without hesitation, "you know that."

Andy nodded. "I do. I need you to speak to Will for me, find out the protocol for what happens next. Whenever we've lost servicemen and women before, I've telephoned the families. I can't do that for sixteen hundred people. We're in unchartered territory here. I need you to find out what needs to be done and get the ball rolling."

"I think you know, don't you? You just can't bring yourself to ask me."

Andy looked down at his hands. "You know me too well."

Mel smiled and scooted closer, reaching over the desk and putting her hand over his. "You want to make the calls, but you can't. You want to send each of those families a personal letter, but you can't, and failing a personal letter, you'd want to sign every last one of the letters that are going to be reeling out of that printer downstairs, but you can't."

He looked up towards her. "They deserve better."

"Yes, they do. But they died in service of their country, and right now, your country needs you more than anything."

Andy let out a long sigh. "You're right. I know you're right, Mel, but I hate it. I hate that I can't pay them the respect they deserve."

"Save the rest of the men and women of this country, Andy. That will be paying them the ultimate respect." She let go of his hand and stood up. "I'll get on to this straight away." She exited the office, leaving Andy alone with his thoughts once more.

\*

"Well?" asked Carrie as Hawke walked back into the office.

"We've got something."

Carrie's eyes widened. "Don't leave me in suspense. What?"

"The last number he called."

"And?"

"It was an ex-operative."

"What are you talking about?"

"The person he called before throwing himself from the platform was ex MI6."

Carrie sat back in her chair as her mind whirred into action. "Who?"

"Laura Scarrow."

"She was leaving here just as I was starting. What the hell did they talk about?"

"We'll find out soon enough. I've got a car heading to her place now. I'll let you know as soon as they arrive back."

"Okay, thanks. Good work, Hawke."

"Thank you, ma'am," he replied before exiting the

office.

*What the hell were you doing talking to an ex-operative on a private phone? I really hope you weren't tied up in any dodgy crap, Ed.*

\*

"Thanks for calling me back, Alistair. Listen, we're obviously going to need to do a press conference with regards to the *Indestructible*. We can limit the information we give out by explaining it's a national security matter, ongoing investigation, multiple agencies, yadayadayada, but I don't want this to be the first time the families are finding out about it. Where are we with informing next of kin?"

"It's in hand, Prime Minister. We have procedures in place for such an eventuality, so it's not an issue," Taylor replied.

"I'm not sure whether to be impressed or mortified that we have procedures in place for something on this scale. Okay, thank you." Andy hung up the phone and dialled another number straight away. "Xander, is it ready? Okay, I'm on my way, Taylor said it was in hand."

Andy got up and walked to the door. "Okay, Mel, I'm heading down to the press briefing room."

"Yes, Prime Minister."

The two bodyguards followed him down the hallway. "I think this is the worst thing I've ever had to do."

"If I may say, sir, you couldn't possibly have done any more. You were mounting a rescue attempt. What happened couldn't have been predicted, sir," Les said sympathetically.

"You heard what happened?"

"It's difficult not to overhear sometimes, sir."

"I suppose it is."

"My point is, Prime Minister, any other man would have slept easy taking the advice of the chiefs, and the way our system is set up, sir, that would have been the right thing to do, and you could have had a clear conscience. But you went that extra mile. You gave them a chance they wouldn't have had otherwise."

"Didn't really work out, did it? But I appreciate your words, Les. I really do."

Xander rushed up to meet them in the hallway and gave Andy the speech. "It's just being put on the teleprompter now."

Andy stopped and read through it in the middle of the hall. He nodded occasionally then looked up towards Xander. "You wrote this?"

Xander nodded. "I know we joke around sometimes, but at the core, we share the same values, Andy. Those people were heroes. Anyone who puts on a uniform to serve their country is a hero."

Andy stuck out his hand, and the two of them shook. "It's perfect. I couldn't have asked for better. Thank you, Xander."

Les pushed the door open, and Andy walked through. Immediately, a volley of questions began to bounce off the walls. Andy heard the word *Indestructible* a number of times. Had it been a leak? Or had it been trickled through from a heartbroken relative? Sixteen hundred families, it was impossible to keep a lid on something this big.

Andy climbed onto the podium and the autocue began to roll.

"My fellow citizens, it has been less than twenty-four hours since I addressed you last. I brought you news of the planetary tragedy that was underway in the form of the reanimating virus. I told you of measures that we were putting in place to make sure the same fate did not befall our shores and our citizens. Although I can confirm that we have had not one instance of an outbreak, I do nonetheless come to you with grave news; news that I am still struggling to come to terms with myself." Andy paused, and suddenly he was overcome with emotion. He managed to hold off tears, but for the time being, he was unable to carry on. He reached to the small shelf built into the podium and picked up a glass of water, taking a drink and replacing it before breaking through the tense silence once again.

"I told you last night that we were recalling all military personnel serving overseas to these shores. Well, earlier today, a tragic incident befell the sixteen hundred plus men and women on the pride of our naval fleet, the HMS *Indestructible*..." He paused again and looked down at the podium before looking back up to the autocue.

"Sixteen hundred brave souls who wanted to do nothing but protect their countrymen and serve their country. Sixteen hundred brave souls who worked tirelessly to keep us safe. Sixteen hundred brave souls who have now lost their own lives in pursuit of those ideals. This is, without a doubt, the worst day of my premiership. It is a tragedy I will carry around with me forever, and to the families of those sixteen hundred, I can only say this: We are forever in your debt. I am forever in your debt. Today, I feel your pain. Today, I feel your loss. Our country mourns our fallen heroes. I mourn our fallen heroes."

He paused, gave a brief nod, and stepped down from the podium. Xander stepped up to take questions, but the shouting voices were all calling to be heard by the prime minister. Even after he left the room, the shouts continued until he was down the corridor and out of earshot.

# 26

The hellish growls of the reanimates drifted on the breeze as Mya stood in the farmyard weighing her options. She glanced behind her. It would not be long before the first creatures were upon them. "C'mon boy," she said between laboured breaths. The pair of them ran behind the house, immediately seeing a stable, which appeared to be in a better state of repair. There were two stable doors, one bolted shut, one half open. Mya popped her head inside and despite the dinginess of the interior she could see it was empty. A narrow, high, crud-covered window allowed enough daylight through to give the occupants some light when both doors were closed, so she quickly opened the bottom half of the door for Muppet to run through, slid down the outer bolt, and pulled the door to, using the small thumb lever on the handle to lift the latch and place it back down into the groove on the outside of the door.

Mya quickly unshouldered her rifle and removed the carrying strap, which she threaded through the handle and tied around the oak support beam that stood next to the entrance. She pulled on it hard to test its strength just as the first creature smashed into the door with a shuddering bang. Mya jumped back as the sheer force and loudness took her by surprise. Muppet began to bark frantically. It was the first time Mya had seen him truly startled since they had met up. She swung the bag off her shoulder and unclipped the strap from that too, heading to the other entrance as more bodies began to batter against the oaken slats of the first door. The noise was like a hundred out of tune timpani drums playing a symphony for the dead. The slats continued to move in the door frames and what appeared at first like sturdy barriers between the interior of the barn and the outside world suddenly looked much less secure.

The growling accompaniment added to Muppet's heightened level of hysteria as no matter how much Mya tried to calm him, he would not stop barking. Eventually, she sat down beside him realising there was nothing more she could do. There was no escape from this foul-smelling tomb, and all either of them could do now was wait for the end.

*

"She's here," Hawke said, popping his head through Carrie's door.

Carrie jumped to her feet and followed him out. They disappeared down a short corridor and into a small interrogation room where two armed agents stood. The red lights were already on both cameras signifying that they were running as she and Hawke took seats on the opposite side of the table. There was half a glass of water in front of Laura Scarrow, and it was evident that she had been crying.

She was an attractive woman in her mid-fifties, but the trailing mascara and bloodshot eyes told Hawke and Carrie that the world had just come crashing down on her.

"Thank you for coming in voluntarily," Carrie said.

Laura didn't answer for a moment, and when she

did, it was in little more than a whisper. "It's okay."

"What was your relationship with Edward Phillips?" Carrie asked, having no time for small talk or putting her interviewee at ease.

"He was my boss, and when I left MI6, we became friends. At least, I thought we did," she said weakly.

"And when was the last time you spoke to him?"

Laura began to sob again. It took her a few moments to bring herself under control before she finally answered. "This afternoon."

"And what did you talk about?" Laura burst out crying again. "You do realise how serious this is? You do understand what's happened?"

"I understand. I understand better than anyone," she rasped, bringing her head up to look Carrie straight in the eyes. Tears were flowing down her face, and as she spoke a thick strand of saliva dripped onto her chin. She wiped it away with the back of her hand and brought her eyes back down to the table.

"So, what was your conversation about?"

Laura took another drink of water, grabbed a wadded-up handkerchief from her sleeve, then wiped her eyes and blew her nose before continuing. "He knew I was short of cash, and he offered me a job."

Carrie and Hawke threw a concerned glance towards each other before turning their attention back to their interviewee. "What kind of job?"

"He wanted me to follow someone and take pictures. He said he thought there was a mole at MI6 and he didn't know who to trust."

"A mole? Follow who? What pictures?"

Laura took another drink. "He was a banker. A man by the name of Diamond. He said he couldn't give me all the details, but Diamond was a person of interest, and it was essential to find out who he met with."

"Okay," Carrie said, getting more confused by the minute. The word mole still echoed in her ears. *Some first day on the job.*

"I didn't realise. You've got to understand, I didn't realise until this afternoon."

"What are you talking about?"

"The photos. I thought I was doing something good."

"You need to rewind. What photos?"

"They took my phone off me," Laura said, nodding towards the small red plastic box sitting on a table in the corner of the room.

"Yeah, so what? That's standard procedure."

"If you bring it here, I can show you."

"Show me what?"

"It's easier if you just see it."

Carrie's chair squeaked as she stood. She walked across to the box, picking up the phone and transporting it back across to the table. "Have we swabbed this?" she asked, looking back at the two agents by the door.

"Yes, ma'am," one of them replied.

A short, sharp laugh left Laura's mouth. "I might be a gullible idiot, but I'm not a murderer, and if I was, I wouldn't want to blow myself up too."

Carrie passed the phone across to her, and Laura unlocked it. She swiped the screen until a gallery of photos appeared and then slid it back across the table. "Nice photos," Hawke said. "You should sell these to *Playboy*," he said with a smirk on his face.

Carrie did not break into a smile. In fact, her heart broke a little. "Gaynor."

Hawke looked across towards her. "What?"

"That's right," Laura said sadly.

"I never knew her. He never had a picture on his desk, he barely ever spoke about her. I just thought I was taking photos of Diamond's bit on the side. I had no idea I was taking snaps of Ed's wife or I would never have got involved."

Carrie closed her eyes. "Oh God."

"When he spoke to me today, he told me everything. He apologised for misleading me and coming up with the story about the mole and who Diamond really was. He said he'd always valued me as a friend and told me that he'd sent payment directly to my bank account. And that was it, he just hung up." She burst out crying again.

Carrie began to reach across the table to place a comforting hand over Laura's, but she stopped herself. "We may need to ask you further questions at a later date."

Laura wiped the tears from her eyes as she stood up. "Well, it's not like I can jet off to the Bahamas now, is it?"

"Thank you again for coming in," Carrie said, rising from her chair and leaving Hawke to finish up. She took the long walk back to her office and closed the door. *What a sad end to a remarkable life.*

*

"Okay. I want this to be the briefest of briefs," Andy said as Xander sat down.

"You got somebody due?"

"No, but before I spend what is likely to be the rest of the night in this office, I want to enjoy a quick dinner with my family. I just need a little bit of normality, Xander."

"I understand. I'll make it quick. Okay. The *Evening Voice* is officially out of action until further notice."

"What does further notice mean?"

"It basically means forever. All their affiliates, and I mean every last one, removed the story and recalled all the early editions. A few might have got out there, but when they heard what happened to the Three Stooges, they couldn't have been more obliging. It's rattled absolutely everyone. All the national dailies have sent their front pages across. They're all leading with the *Indestructible*, and they're all dealing with it in a very respectful and patriotic way."

"I didn't see the press conference after the speech.

Did you get many questions?"

"Yeah, I got asked what happened, which is only natural, and I told them all available resources are being put into finding out exactly what happened, but at this stage, we don't know, and it would be disrespectful to the brave men and women who lost their lives, as well as painful for their families, to start playing guessing games. That pretty much shut down the questions. I got a couple about Phillips, but they were fairly straightforward to dispatch too." Xander smiled. "I'm going to be around most of the night too, so I dare say we'll catch up later." He got up and headed to the door.

"Xander!"

He turned from the entrance, "Yeah?"

"Thank you. Thank you for everything. You're a great press secretary but an even better friend."

Xander smiled. "Doug and I will always have your back, Andy," he said before heading through the door.

*

Mya's eyes darted around the dim interior of the barn. The window was not much bigger than a shoebox and way too high to get to. Suddenly, there was a sledgehammer thump against the door to her left and the diagonal plank of oak that held the individual slats together buckled.

The volume and rapidity of Muppet's barking became almost as deafening as the growls and thuds from outside as he ran across and stood in front of the crumbling wood. Another flurry of hammer blows was delivered, and the wooden strut caved further. Mya ran to the door and pushed with all her might against the centre of the damaged plank in the hope that she could strengthen it enough to stop the top half of the barn door from caving in. If it had been just one beast, she might have stood a chance, but the relentless battering from multiple creatures meant the integrity of the strut was literally disintegrating right before her eyes.

She stepped back and ran across to pick up her rifle and bag. The middle vertical panel and the one next to it suddenly caved, and for all Muppet's bravery, even he ran into the far corner of the barn.

Mya looked at the second door and, although it was shuddering in its frame as the demonic ghouls on the other side continued to pound with their hands and bodies, it was, for the time being, holding. She went across to the compromised entrance, placed her back almost against the far wall opposite it, and carefully laid the bag down beside her. She did not have enough rounds of ammunition for every monster out there, but she was going to take as many of them down as she could. She brought the scope of the rifle up to her eye, ready.

A creature's arm thrust into the barn, finally dislodging two central panels. It reached into the stale murk, and even in the diminishing light, a glacial shudder ran down Mya's spine as she looked into its eyes. She angled the gun down for a second in horrified awe as she regarded the unbridled malevolence on the beast's face. It was all for her. She had seen these creatures had little in the way of reasoning skills, but that look was pure evil, and evil required intent. Another panel gave way and then another as the integrity of the top half of the barn door fragmented further. More grasping fingers raped the brief sanctuary Mya had found, and now, as the final scene of the final act began to play out, Mya cast aside all thoughts but one.

She began to fire, and the more she fired the more she wanted to fire because in the enclosure of the small barn the reports deafened her to Muppet's terrified barks, it deafened her to the creatures' inhuman growls and gurgles, it deafened her to everything but the job at hand.

Foreheads and noses caved in, demolished by Mya's bullets, as one by one, creatures flopped and collapsed. The upper bodies of the first two beasts fell forwards, their bottom halves wedged between the door and the throng of creatures behind desperate to sink their teeth into Mya's flesh.

With each monster she slayed a new one took its place, but she remained focussed, she remained in control. Even when the bottom half of the door began to crumple as well, and she took out her Glock as the bullets ran dry in her rifle, she kept firing. This was her last hurrah, and she was going to go out singing louder than anyone.

## 27

Andy was walking down the corridor, a small smile finally bleeding onto his face at the prospect of having dinner with his family, when he saw Carrie Marsh heading towards him.

"Prime Minister, am I able to have a word, sir?"

The smile left Andy's face in an instant. He knew if she had come to see him in person, it was not going to be a single word, and in all likelihood, it would not be good news either. "Let's go back to the office."

Carrie followed Andy and the two bodyguards down the corridor; just she and Andy walked into his office, and he closed the door firmly behind him.

"What's this about, Carrie?"

She let out a deep sigh and just sat there, regarding the prime minister. "Sir, may I speak freely?"

"I'd prefer it," Andy said, gesturing for her to take the seat opposite.

"Ed Phillips was a great man and a hero. I wouldn't be where I am today without him and whatever happened to him mentally shouldn't take away from the fact that he was a loyal and faithful servant to this country."

"You've lost me, Carrie. What are you talking about?"

"Prime Minister, Edward Phillips took his own life because he found out his wife was having an affair."

"What? Gaynor? No, that's nonsense. How did you come up with that?"

"It's true, sir. I interviewed a former MI6 operative who remained in contact with Ed. She was the one who unwittingly took the photos of Gaynor and her lover. I think with the events of the last couple of days, Ed just lost hope. I think he decided he had nothing left to live for. Even with everything that's going on, I suppose people still have their lives, still have their own demons to fend off."

Andy reached into the bottom drawer of his desk and removed the bottle of whisky and two glasses. He poured healthy measures into each and slid one across the table to his guest. "Maybe I was too hard on him. Maybe I was putting him under too much pressure. Maybe I was a contributing factor in all of this."

"Prime Minister, this is nothing to do with you or me or anyone but Gaynor and Ed. He lived for her. He was devoted to her, and I think losing her with everything else that's going on was the final straw. For some people, family is everything; it's why they get up in the morning, it's what drives them to do all they do." She took a drink from her glass.

Andy let out a sad sigh. "I suppose I can relate. If I lost Trish and the kids, I can't imagine what I'd do." They sat in silence for a moment, taking the odd sip. "Do you have anyone, Carrie?"

"I've got a cat, sir. Most of the time he's completely indifferent towards me; occasionally he bites and scratches me and once in a blue moon he shows me some genuine affection. To date, it's the most positive relationship I've been able to develop with a member of the opposite sex."

Andy laughed and took another drink. "Have we

heard any more from our people in France?"

"We've dispatched the Apache, but no word as yet. I do have a little more information about the hard drive though."

Andy swivelled his chair round to face her. "And?"

"When the firewalls went down, and we started wading through the oceans of data from Russia, we found out about this hard drive. They had a French double agent who had identified the position of the laptop that had been stolen from the Russians a year previously. That in and of itself wasn't of interest to us, but the fact that this reference came under the heading Konets Sveta threw up a red flag straight away. Basically, it means Doomsday in Russian, and it's a term we have heard repeatedly in relation to the outbreak."

"So, there could be information on there that can help us combat this thing?"

"There could be, sir. On the other hand, it might be a recipe for a cocktail of the same name, but we did a risk assessment and thought it would be worth acquiring."

"Well, let's hope for everybody's sake that's the case." They each raised their glasses and finished off their drinks.

"Thank you, sir. I'll be sure to give you an update the moment I have any more information regarding our two operatives."

"Thank you, Carrie. I can see now why Edward wanted you as his deputy."

"Thank you, sir," she replied nodding before leaving the office.

Andy sat there a moment longer digesting the information about Phillips; then he almost sprang to his feet and walked out of the office, turning to Mel on the way. "I'm going to have dinner with my family. If you need me, you can get me there," he said, turning towards her as he carried on walking.

"Yes, Prime Minister."

\*

Mya dropped the empty Glock, and it fell by the side of the used-up magazines that lay at her feet. She grabbed Seb's Browning from the bag, and as soon as she picked it up, she thought it felt light. She fired five rounds, and that was it; she was out. The light had got gradually worse as the relentless attack had gone on, and now, with the bottom half of the barn door badly buckled and the last of the ammunition used up, it would only be a short amount of time before it was all over.

She ran to the side wall and pulled an ancient-looking pitchfork from a hook. What had made the situation worse as the bodies had piled up outside was that some of the creatures had managed to stumble over the door and into the barn. Each time, Mya had put them down quickly, but now she would have to engage hand to hand, and these things were fast. As she approached, another beast climbed the rotting steps built by the bodies of its dead brethren and tripped, falling over the threshold in a clumsy heap. It immediately jumped to its feet; at the same time, yet another creature, excited by how close Mya was, desperately reached towards her, and another, and another. Suddenly, Mya realised she could hear again. She could hear Muppet's terrified barks; she could hear the constant dirge of the growling beasts. She could hear the breaking wood as the bottom part of the door finally began to give, and she could hear the top half of the other door burst open as the bolt shattered. *I'm finished. I'm finished.* A single tear rolled down her face, and she thought about that little florists shop in Chelsea once more.

And then she could hear something else. A familiar chu-chu-chu-chu-chu—and the sound of a loud motor. It was a helicopter, an Apache—she knew the sound of those whooshing blades, oh so well. She thrust the pitchfork through the skull of the beast as it sprung from its crouch towards her. It fell in a useless heap and as another sound, the sound of heavy machine gun fire, began to ring its death knell for the creatures outside, Mya pulled the pitchfork free and turned towards the creatures barging their way through the bottom half of the barn door as it crumbled.

She shoved the fork hard, taking the top clean off the head of one of them, causing her to overshoot. Another grabbed her tightly by the arm, while yet another reached for her face. She saw bloody explosions in the corner of her vision as still more reanimates got carved into pieces by the Apache's machine gun fire, but it was all in vain. She was in the grasp of the beasts now. She tried to free herself from the grip of the first while desperately pulling her face back from the lunging hand of the second, and that's when the third stumbled over the remains of the broken door and pounced.

She did her best to struggle free as the third beast leapt towards her, and that's when she caught another blur out of the corner of her eye. Muppet launched into the air, wrapping his teeth around the bicep of the creature who had once been a hotel concierge but was now trying to sink his teeth into Mya. The dog bit down hard, not able to tear through the hotel uniform but managing to send an involuntary spasm through the musculocutaneous nerve, causing the creature's fingers to spread wide and subsequently lose its grip on Mya. Muppet tried to remain attached, but the creature shook him off, violently, and the dog went somersaulting into a corner, letting out a small yelp before he gathered himself once more.

It gave Mya all the respite she needed, though, as she brought the pitchfork up with her now free arm. The two centre prongs thrust up through the chin of the creature hurtling towards her, and in a heartbeat, its grey eyes closed forever as she took the beast's weight. In one movement, she angled the fork down and the hideous monster fell to the ground before Mya spun around swinging the old hay shoveller by the lower part of its handle like a baseball bat. The back side of the metal fork and shaft battered two more creatures, one of them a hulking figure, in the head, dazing them for a second, before she drove the fork through the air once more and pierced the concierge through his grey eyes with the two centre tines. Mya felt the sludgy resistance of the brain as she plunged her weapon in. The beast collapsed with a satisfying sound as its head cracked like a coconut on the ground.

The reanimates outside continued to be decimated by the hail of bullets. Mya had not seen the Apache, but she could tell it was parallel to the barn. Of course it was; they would not risk cutting her up with friendly fire. It was then that she saw holes appear in the far wall as stray bullets began to cut through.

"Oh Jesus, fuck!" she screamed as more bullets danced off the ground in her direction. The two creatures she had knocked off balance with the fork had found a firm footing once more and were heading back towards her, but there were no more reaching arms as the red explosions outside diminished in number. She swung the fork one more time, battering them. One staggered and the bigger one fell into the far wall. Mya shot her head around; the spray of errant bullets was still coming. She whacked the staggering creature again, and this time it went down.

She got ready to leap to the side, but then the sound of gunfire stopped. She glanced back; two dozen round peepholes had appeared in the far wall, but no more were being created. She looked to the door. No further creatures were trying to gain entry. This was it. It was these two. She thrust the fork into the head of one like she was spearing a fish; it fell still straight away while the other regained its footing and leapt towards her. Mya pulled at the handle to dislodge the fork, but the wooden shaft was all that came out. She glanced down, and the still figure had the metal prongs lodged firmly in its skull.

She looked back at the wooden handle with the slightly rotten end. *"Oh shit!"* she screamed as she was hammered off balance by the reanimate who in life was probably a rugby prop forward or even an offensive lineman. As she hit the ground, she rolled instinctively, and the body of the huge beast banged down beside her like a felled oak. Although winded, Mya jumped to her feet once more. The shaft of the fork lay underneath the huge creature as it scrambled on the ground.

Mya unleashed a powerful kick, her toe smashing into the side of the beast's temple, and it let out a rumbling growl that sent a tremble running through her. It began to lumber off its belly once more, making a clumsy grab for her as it did. She sidestepped its arm and, taking advantage of the clumsiness of the ghoulish monster, swept down and slid out the wooden handle of the fork, bringing it up again in one circular movement before unleashing a flurry of vicious blows to the back of its head.

The first two smashes merely stunned it and it paused in its ascent to its feet with one knee still on the ground, but then the third, fourth and fifth blows put it back face down on the floor. It continued to struggle for a while, but then, as the back of its skull caved, exposing the beast's brain and eviscerated nerve ends where the broken bone had shredded the soft tissue, all movement stopped. Mya kept going though. She kept raising the fork handle, somehow fascinated by the lack of spraying blood as the congealed ooze slowly globbed onto the floor and clung to the bottom end of the shaft like the thickest of strawberry jams.

Just then, she glimpsed further movement and spun around, ready to attack. She brought the wooden shaft of the fork up but dropped it to the ground with a clatter as she saw two special ops soldiers standing there, rifles at the ready.

"Are you Mya Hamlyn?" asked one of them. Mya did not reply. The sweat poured down her brow as her lungs desperately sucked in the evening air. "Are you Mya Hamlyn?"

"Yes. Yes, I'm Mya."

"Where's Archer?"

"He didn't make it."

The soldier touched his ear. "This is Wardlaw. We've got Hamlyn. Archer didn't make it. Repeat, we've got Hamlyn, Archer didn't make it."

Mya stood there for a moment, surveying the horrifying landscape of shredded bodies. She looked across into the corner and saw Muppet, who was watching everything, clearly traumatised by the events. She got down on her knees and put out her arms. "Come here, boy. Come here," she said, and hesitantly the dog began to limp across to her. He whined a little as she stroked him. "It's alright, baby, I'll get you seen to when we get back," she said, climbing to her feet and going to collect her bag.

"We can't take a dog with us," said the soldier.

"This dog saved my life. I'm not going anywhere without him, and let's face it, you're not going anywhere without me, are you?"

The soldier let out a tired sigh. "Come on then," he said.

Mya handed the other soldier the bag, and she carefully picked Muppet up, carrying him over and through the mountain of bodies. The dog's body tensed as they approached the waiting helicopter, but as they climbed on board and he sprawled over Mya's lap, he began to relax again.

"You were bloody lucky to get out of there alive," said one of the soldiers.

"Tell me about it."

The Apache took off rising higher and higher into the air. Mya took one last look at the battleground in the twilight and then closed her eyes. It was over.

\*

Trish had needed to delay dinner another ninety minutes since her husband's arrival. He had received call after call, and as much as he wanted to just spend some time with his family, he could not neglect his duties. Now, though, Andy was sitting at the head of the table; his two daughters, on either side, were in competition to blurt out everything that had happened to them that day at school. Trish was in the process of serving and just for a few moments he was able to live in a different reality. A reality that did not involve the world going to hell; a reality that did not involve him making life-or-death decisions that would affect an entire nation. The subdued lighting over the table lit his entire world and everything in the shadows was not his concern for now.

A happy smile swept across his face as he looked towards his two daughters. He could not recount a single word either had said, but just seeing them was enough of a tonic. Trish took her seat opposite him, and the same loving smile lit her face too.

"Shall we tuck in?" she said..

"Smells amazing," Andy replied, about to pick up his, but then the fantasy came to an end as the mobile phone on the table in front of him began to ring. His shoulders slumped as he reached for it.

"Carrie. Go ahead," he said, rising and walking into the kitchen.

"I'm afraid Archer didn't make it, Prime Minister. We have Mya Hamlyn and the laptop."

Andy let out another heavy sigh. "How did he…? What happened?"

"It was a lousy piece of luck, sir. There was a gas explosion. Caused the vehicle they were in to crash."

"Jesus!"

"I know, sir. Archer had been in more life-or-death situations than I can count, and it was something like that that got him."

"Will you send me his next of kin details?"

"Yes, sir."

"But Hamlyn? She's alright?"

"She had a close shave, sir, but she made it."

Andy let out a breath. "That's something, I suppose."

"Yes, Prime Minister."

"And the laptop? I suppose it's too early to say whether we can glean anything from it or not."

There was a pause on the other end of the line. "Let me just say, sir, if I'd have been in the same position. I'd have made the same call."

"What do you mean?"

"Our analysts will trawl through every line on there, but after a very brief initial examination, it does not provide us with any intelligence we do not already possess."

"You're saying Archer died for nothing?"

"We had to know, sir."

"So, what did it contain?"

"Excerpts from a diary that we were already in possession of thanks to Archer. The names of scientists who worked on the project. Forecasts and projections of the spread if this thing ever got out."

"And why did the French have this?"

"It's complicated, sir."

"Go on."

"One of the scientists working on the project was French."

"Carrie, let me get this right. You're telling me a French scientist helped create this thing?"

"We're not sure who created it, sir. And technically, he became a Russian citizen back in the late eighties, but the laptop was acquired from him."

"No wonder the French wanted to keep all this under wraps. But why would it be hidden at the Élysée Palace?"

"The head of the DGSE was convinced that the Russians had infiltrated the organisation. If they found out about the laptop, it would compromise French assets working within the Russian security agencies. So this was temporarily stashed until they could clean house. I mean who's going to break into the Élysée Palace, sir?"

Andy let out a long sigh. "Nothing's ever simple with spies, is it? Even with all this going on, we're still playing our games."

"I'm sorry I don't have any better news for you."

"Don't worry. I'm getting used to it now. Is there anything else, Carrie?"

"Not for the time being, sir, no."

There was a long pause on the line. "I still can't believe this thing is man-made. I can't believe people would want to create something like this."

"Sir, nobody has clean hands on this one. Despite the ban on biological weapons, practically every developed nation has had clandestine programmes at one time or another."

There was another pause. "I suppose we reap what we sow."

"Yes, Prime Minister."

"You will let me know if anything useful is found on that hard drive, won't you?"

"I will."

"Thank you for the update, Carrie, I dare say we'll speak soon."

"Yes, sir. Thank you, Prime Minister."

Andy hung up the phone, put it in his pocket and headed back out to the dining area. The children remained buoyant, but Trish had a look of apprehension on her face as he sat back down. "Everything okay?" she asked.

He looked towards his children, and the tension and worry left him once more. "For the next few minutes anyway."

"I thought you might have to head back down."

"Wild horses won't drag me away right now. I've been looking forward to this all day."

"Me too," Trish replied.

The two children began their meals, but Andy and

Trish just gazed towards each other for a little while. She mouthed, "I love you." He mouthed it back. Warmth enveloped the two of them for a moment, and they smiled, that smile that just belonged to them and no one else.

Whatever heartache lay ahead, and there would be heartache by the tonne, as long as they had each other, they could keep fighting. As long as they had each other, they had hope. A single truth echoed in both their minds at the same time. There was nothing more important than family.

The End

# A NOTE FROM THE AUTHOR

I really hope you enjoyed this book and would be very grateful if you took a minute to leave a review on Amazon and Goodreads.

If you would like to stay informed about what I'm doing, including current writing projects, and all the latest news and release information; these are the places to go:

Join the fan club on Facebook
https://www.facebook.com/groups/127693634504226

Like the Christopher Artinian author page
https://www.facebook.com/safehaventrilogy/

Buy exclusive and signed books and merchandise, subscribe to the newsletter and follow the blog:
https://www.christopherartinian.com/

Follow me on Twitter
https://twitter.com/Christo71635959

Follow me on Youtube:
https://www.youtube.com/channel/UCfJymx31Vvztt
B_Q-x5otYg

Follow me on Amazon
https://amzn.to/2I1llU6

Follow me on Goodreads
https://bit.ly/2P7iDzX

Other books by Christopher Artinian:

Safe Haven: Rise of the RAMs
Safe Haven: Realm of the Raiders
Safe Haven: Reap of the Righteous
Safe Haven: Ice
Safe Haven: Vengeance
Safe Haven: Is This the End of Everything?
Safe Haven: Neverland (Part 1)
Before Safe Haven: Lucy
Before Safe Haven: Alex
Before Safe Haven: Mike
Before Safe Haven: Jules
The End of Everything: Book 1
The End of Everything: Book 2
The End of Everything: Book 3

The End of Everything: Book 4
The End of Everything: Book 5
The End of Everything: Book 6
The End of Everything: Book 7
The End of Everything: Book 8
The End of Everything: Book 9
Relentless
Relentless 2
Relentless 3

Anthologies featuring short stories by Christopher Artinian

Undead Worlds: A Reanimated Writers Anthology
Featuring: Before Safe Haven: Losing the Battle by Christopher Artinian
Tales from Zombie Road: The Long-Haul Anthology
Featuring: Condemned by Christopher Artinian
Treasured Chests: A Zombie Anthology for Breast Cancer Care
Featuring: Last Light by Christopher Artinian
Trick or Treat Thrillers (Best Paranormal 2018)
Featuring: The Akkadian Vessel.

# CHRISTOPHER ARTINIAN

Christopher Artinian was born and raised in Leeds, West Yorkshire. Wanting to escape life in a big city and concentrate more on working to live than living to work, he and his family moved to the Outer Hebrides in the north-west of Scotland in 2004, where he now works as a full-time author.

Chris is a huge music fan, a cinephile, an avid reader and a supporter of Yorkshire county cricket club. When he's not sat in front of his laptop living out his next post-apocalyptic/dystopian/horror adventure, he will be passionately immersed in one of his other interests.

Printed in Great Britain
by Amazon